# WHEN I WAS TEN

Also by Fiona Cummins

*Rattle*
*The Collector*
*The Neighbour*

# WHEN I WAS TEN

## FIONA CUMMINS

MACMILLAN

First published in paperback 2020 by Macmillan

This edition first published 2021 by Macmillan
an imprint of Pan Macmillan
The Smithson, 6 Briset Street, London ECIM NR
*EU representative:* Macmillan Publishers Ireland Limited,
Mallard Lodge, Lansdowne Village, Dublin 4
Associated companies throughout the world
www.panmacmillan.com

ISBN 978-1-5098-7696-9

1 3 5 7 9 8 6 4 2

A CIP catalogue record for this book is available from the British Library.

Typeset in Scala by Palimpsest Book Production Ltd, Falkirk, Stirlingshire
Printed and bound by CPI Group (UK) Ltd, Croydon, CRO 4YY

Visit **www.panmacmillan.com** to read more about all our books
and to buy them. You will also find features, author interviews and
news of any author events, and you can sign up for e-newsletters
so that you're always first to hear about our new releases.

For Isaac and Alice, always

*But for God's sake, I was a kid; what else could I do but lie?*

> – Mary Bell in *Cries Unheard* by Gitta Sereny

*Tell Tale Tit, your tongue shall be slit; and all the dogs in town shall have a little bit.*

> – Nursery rhyme, nineteenth century

# PROLOGUE

## Sunday, 20 April 1997

The girl is twelve and she is running.

Her feet pound the grass, powered by the twin engines of grief and fear. She does not stop until she reaches the summit of Saltbox Hill.

Below her, the village huddles under the cloak of an impending storm. She bends at the waist, panting and crying, and it is hard to breathe. Across the bruised horizon, she glimpses Hilltop House and her nausea ripens into a darkness she dare not think about.

There are cars, so many cars with blue and white livery and flashing lights, and they snake along the stretch of road between the stuccoed mansion and her own smaller home.

*The grown-ups are dead.*

The sky trembles with thunder. The girl's body vibrates with it too. She glances upwards as a lightning arc blanches the clouds. Sporadic drops of rain hit her arms, as if they can't be bothered, and then harder and faster until she is soaked through.

She starts running again, seeking shelter from the down-pour.

An oak tree crowns the hill and it's there the girl heads, damp seeping into her trainers, deep cuts of sorrow inflaming her heart. In this baptism of rain, she thinks: *The sky is grieving too.*

The air is sharp with ozone but it is not enough to rid her of the old-penny scent of blood, or the sweet-rot sickliness of the makeshift bedroom downstairs.

*The grown-ups are dead.*

Her mother.

Mrs Carter.

Dr Carter.

*Deader than disco*, her father would say, in that *deadpan* tone of his, and an appalled laugh spills from her.

It is her birthday tomorrow but there will be no celebration. Cards, yes, but of condolence, the first pushed through the letter box at lunchtime. No cake with pink icing, but still-warm lasagnes left on the porch, condensation collecting on their tinfoil lids. She swipes the back of her hand across her eyes and runs harder.

The girl is almost at the tree, spring thickening its leaves, branches spread in welcome. Their faces blink on and off in her memory like the rotating lights of a merry-go-round. *Mother. Mrs Carter. Dr Carter.* To her twelve-year-old self, their deaths are entwined like brambles, choking everything.

She has told a lie. A big one.

There is no way back from it now.

She pauses to catch her breath, bent in half, hands on knees. Across the valley, two private ambulances pull out of Hilltop House. She watches their slow progress through the village but they are too far away to be anything more than grey smudges on the skyline.

The water sheets off her shoulders, trickles down her neck. Her hair hangs in clumps around her face. She is a handful of footsteps from the tree when the sky lights up again.

The girl lifts her head and watches the shape of lightning against violet clouds. She waits for it to happen again. She is still waiting when a crack opens up above her and a bright bolt strikes the right upper quadrant of her back.

The lightning moves at one-third the speed of light. It haloes her. It scorches the silver necklace at her throat, flashes across her torso, the current scrambling the electrical impulses of her heart. It exits through the soles of her feet, leaving two coin-shaped holes and singe marks on her trainers.

The girl is thrown to the grass, her body smoking, the grumble of thunder in the air.

# PART ONE

*WHO?*

# 1

**Thursday, 13 December 2018**

In eleven minutes and fourteen seconds, Catherine Allen, who only wants to be ordinary, will be dead.

She doesn't know it yet. Her face is pressed into the clean sheet she smoothed across their bed that morning, darkness wrapped around her like an old friend. Mouth slightly open. Deep and even breaths.

The snow began to fall at midnight and hasn't stopped. Four hours later, it covers the square of their front garden, the roof of their boxy cottage and the street outside. A thickness that suffocates the sounds of the night until it is too late to run.

Even then, she can't be sure what disturbs her. A minute ago, she was asleep, a reprieve from the turmoil of the last few days. Now here she is, jerked into wakefulness like a fish on a hook, eyes wide in the still of their bedroom, the thunder of adrenalin in her veins.

*Honor?*

She listens to the blackness, for the cries of her twelve-year-old daughter. Honor's night terrors, a recent affliction, have been known to wake up the rest of the family, but tonight she is quiet.

The tip of Catherine's nose is cold. The heating went off hours ago and the air tastes of ice. She pulls the duvet over her head. Immediate warmth. The sound of her heartbeat in her ears.

*Intruders?*

She strains to hear beneath the quickening of her own breath. Some nights, she is convinced of footsteps tracking across the kitchen floor or the whisper of voices in the hallway, but there is never anyone there.

Edward rolls over, dragging the duvet with him. His snoring fills up all the silent spaces, and she nudges him with her foot. He stops snoring and starts grinding his teeth.

She despises that sound, the grating of enamel against itself. She touches his jaw, trying to hold it still. Edward only grinds his teeth when something is on his mind. He's been doing it a lot lately.

But she's hardly seen him this week, and when their lives have collided over a late dinner or half an hour's television, she hasn't liked to ask why he's been keeping her at arm's length.

She knows it isn't a woman, at least not in *that* way; even though the years have deepened his boyish good looks into the kind of crumpled attractiveness that makes the school mothers look twice, Edward's always had strident views on fidelity. But he is short-tempered and secretive with his phone, shutting down the screen whenever she surprises him, staring at her with an expression she cannot place.

Last Thursday night, he lied to her. *I've been playing*

*squash, love. With Mark from work.* But one of the fathers from football saw him getting off the train from London when he was supposed to be on the court.

On her bedside table, the clock clicks forward another minute. Each tiny hair on her arm rises until her skin is stippled with goosebumps.

*4.07 a.m.*

Even now, that combination of digits has the power to root her in place.

Twenty-one years ago, in another bedroom and another life, a different clock stopped forever at precisely the same time, a web of hairline cracks across its face.

Catherine never speaks about that night. The past is put away now. It will not define her. She tries her best not to think about it, but every now and then it shoves its way in, ugly and unwelcome. The devil's clock, her mother called it, those hollow hours before dawn when the darkness is full of horrors and sleep will not come.

Her memories unfold like a macabre chain of paper dolls.

The bodies of her parents. A black pool spreading across the carpet. The moon's reflection in the handle of the scissor blade buried in her father's neck. Her mother's limp hand hanging over the bed, pastel-pink varnish on her nails.

Her older sister, pyjamas soaked with blood, blonde hair like a halo, being led away by police.

How she had loved her then.

Catherine closes her eyes and calls up Honor's face, all braces and apple-red cheeks. Laughing and dancing, making up songs. Warm hands. Wholesome and happy. A talisman to protect them all.

A car door slams outside.

Edward stirs again. Catherine half rises from their bed. In this pretty village on the anonymous edges of an Essex market town, most inhabitants are asleep by ten o'clock.

As she crosses the bedroom to the window, arms wrapped around herself to keep out the cold, a blue light begins to pulse against her floral wallpaper, a neon wash that keeps time with her heartbeat.

With trembling fingers, she nudges the curtains apart, instinct warning her to be discreet.

On the road outside, there is a battalion of parked cars. A knot of figures in hats and gloves are gathered by her gate, their breath coming in smoky gasps. Television cameras. Lights. A babble of voices.

The urgent carousel of a police car's beacon.

Catherine covers her mouth with her hand. She knows what this means and has prayed every night for more than twelve years – since that first, faint line on her pregnancy test – that it would not come to this. But the events of the last few days prove she's been stupid to think otherwise.

She pulls on her jeans and a jumper and grabs the packed rucksack she keeps hidden in her wardrobe. Stumbles across the landing into Honor's bedroom. The night light is on and she glimpses herself in her daughter's mirror. Mousy hair, brown eyes, not overweight exactly, but a comfortable body. An ordinary thirty-one-year-old woman.

Forgettable.

The girl mumbles something unintelligible. A tear trickles down Catherine's cheek. She presses her palm against her daughter's face and feels something inside her break.

'Wake up, Honor. We have to go now, sweetheart.'

Her daughter kicks out a restless foot and turns towards the wall. Catherine shakes her again, more forcibly this time. When Honor doesn't react, she tugs at the duvet. 'It's time to leave. Come on, love. Get up.'

Mussed-up hair and screwed-up eyes. One pyjama trouser halfway up her leg. A yawn, and through that, a mumble. 'What's happening, Mum?'

Someone bangs on the front door.

Time slows. Catherine is aware of each catch of her breath and drum strike of her heart. Edward is awake now too. She can hear him, moving about in their bedroom. Every part of her longs to freeze this moment, to protect her girl from *Before* and *After*, and preserve the life she has made for herself and her family. The life she never expected to have.

But while she possesses a great many talents, she is not yet able to stop time.

In one minute and twenty-six seconds, Catherine Allen will be dead.

# 2

Three days earlier —
Monday, 10 December 2018

Catherine had never understood that song. She *liked* Mondays. To her, Mondays meant a new week, and every new week pulled her further from her past.

This Monday had begun in the way they usually did. Catherine had said goodbye to Edward, who was wearing a shirt she had ironed and carrying a leather satchel the right side of stylish. She watched him walk down the narrow lane towards the bus stop that would take him to the station. At the bend in the road, before he disappeared behind the conifers, he would always stop and wave. He had done this for the last twelve years, since Honor was born. But on this particular Monday morning he did not break his stride, but walked on, head bowed into the knifing wind.

Catherine lingered on the doorstep in case he changed his mind, but after a couple of minutes, she realized he wasn't coming back. The sting of it surprised her. Even so, she boiled milk for porridge and pasted on a smile for her daughter, whose hair was still damp from the shower, resisting the urge to nag her to dry it before she walked the short distance to school in the winter chill.

Honor was quiet that Monday morning, mauve shadows beneath her eyes, rolling blueberries around her spoon but not eating them. Her mobile was on the table and the girl checked it obsessively. Once upon a time, she would have devoured her breakfast, chattering non-stop about the day ahead. Not now. She was changing, hardening, on the cusp of adolescence.

'Looking forward to the Christmas holidays?' Catherine smeared redcurrant jam on a croissant, eyes firmly on her plate. Honor did not enjoy scrutiny. It made her clam up.

She sensed rather than saw her daughter's shrug.

'I suppose so.' The ghost of a grin, a flash of her old self. 'No homework.'

Honor put down her spoon, leaned against the back of her chair and yawned for what felt like a long time. Catherine risked a glance. Her daughter had covered her mouth, but through the gaps between her fingers, her teeth were full of metal. It gave her the appearance of a snarling animal.

'Tired, love?' This was a sensitive subject, but the words were out of Catherine's mouth before she could bite them back.

Another shrug, and a flick of her hair, but when Honor's eyes met her mother's, Catherine saw shame in them. 'Did it happen again?'

''Fraid so, but I'm sure you'll grow out of it soon.' A concerted attempt at jollity. 'We can make another appointment with the doc—'

In a burst of petulance, Honor shoved her hands against the edge of the table, cutting short her mother. Catherine's coffee cup wobbled, but she buttoned down the urge to shout. Her daughter didn't mean it. At twelve, embarrassment was a powerful driver of behaviour. As God was her witness, Catherine knew all about that.

She stood up and put an arm around Honor's shoulder. 'Is there something on your mind, love? You can talk to me about anything, you know. I promise I won't get cross. The doctor said stress or worry can trigger—'

'I'm fine.' Her rebuttal was clipped and impatient. She shook off her mother's concern and left the kitchen, breakfast uneaten.

Not for the first time, Catherine wondered if lying about her daughter's nocturnal disturbances might make for a quieter life. But while Honor's friends were still inviting her for sleepovers and Catherine was persuading her to decline, the girl deserved the facts.

Although she had lied about so many things, Catherine refused to airbrush the truth about what happened to Honor during the night. Protecting her daughter was her primary motivation. She'd been doing it since she was born.

Despite her claims to the contrary, Catherine knew Honor would rather die than risk exposing herself to ridicule by the alpha girls in her class, who were the head-tilting, shiny ponytailed, insincere types. Her mother didn't blame her. Catherine had extensive experience of her own with girls like that.

Mostly, it began with the scratching. Honor would claw at her arms, dragging her nails down her skin, marking it with chalky tramlines that reddened into welts.

Catherine, a light sleeper, would catch the creak of Honor's bed as her scratching intensified and she thrashed around, throwing out her arms and kicking against her covers.

Sometimes, Honor would scream, a primordial expression of fear that was dragged from a secret place inside her, a sound that belonged in the past, to long-dead ancestors clad in animal pelts, cornered by their nightmares while hunting in the dark.

Sometimes, she would whisper.

This whispering frightened Catherine more than the screaming. She would slip from her own bed and stumble down the hallway to her daughter's room, unease crawling across the nape of her neck. She knew what she would find when she opened Honor's door. The girl pressed into her pillows, blonde hair spread around her shoulders, eyes fixed on a distant corner of the wall.

While her mumbling was incoherent, her daughter's body language was not. Arms stiffened into sticks, the cords of her neck pronounced above her collar bone, panic carved into the planes of her body.

Catherine would smooth back her daughter's fringe and settle her back into bed, waiting until the shadows left her and she softened into sleep.

In the morning, Honor would have no memory of it, but the sight of her daughter's distress would linger with Catherine through the daylight hours, the winter sun too weak to banish her sense of dread.

The front door slammed, shaking a picture of the Allen family that hung on the wall. Honor had left for school without saying goodbye.

Catherine hurried into the hallway, a dirty porridge bowl in each hand, even though it was too late. 'Have a good day, love,' she said softly.

With husband and daughter gone, the house settled into morning quietude.

As soon as the breakfast dishes were cleared away, Catherine switched on her computer and logged on to her share-dealing platform, checking the performance of her stocks and shares.

She was later than usual, unlike those early-bird suits in the City, who exchanged family life for the pursuit of money. Although she had never been a trader in the salaried sense of the word, she had taught herself, dabbling in small sums of money at first, making a profit here and there.

Nothing had surprised her more than discovering she had a gift for it, an instinct for the markets that allowed her to support herself and contribute to the family finances. Getting a job which involved keeping her past a secret had always seemed like scaling an unconquered mountain. Thank God she didn't have to.

She pecked at the keys, relishing the pockets of drama played out through the rise and fall in share prices, the buying and selling, the mistakes and triumphs. About half past ten, chilled from sitting still at the kitchen table, she stopped work to go outside and fill up the basket from the log store.

It was snowing, the first of the season. The flakes settled on her eyelashes and her hair, and on the cashmere wrap she had draped around her shoulders. She drew in lungfuls of cold air and its sharpness filled her up. From her garden, which overlooked Coggsbridge's narrow main street, she could see the fluorescent lights of the butcher's, a stick figure carrying a shopping bag, head bowed, and a bobble-hatted toddler, face raised in wonder to the sky.

When Honor was born, a sun rising over the dark valley of Catherine's teenage years, moving to this village, which reminded her so much of her childhood home, had allowed her to start again.

Back inside, she set the basket next to the wood burner, logs damp with melting snow. A spider ran across the bark and she recoiled, dropping the hearth brush. Mostly, she did not mind the silence, but in that moment, the house felt lonely. On impulse, she reached for the remote control on the coffee table and switched on the television.

A magazine-style show was broadcasting, the presenters full of sunshine smiles. She wondered what it felt like to be on the inside, burnished with the gleam of success and belonging. A famous chef was talking about home-made mince pies and cooking for family. Bright studio lights. Puffs of icing sugar. Laughter. In contrast, the sitting room had darkened in the shadow of snow clouds, the faces in the photographs on the mantelpiece blurring into grey.

Catherine opened the door to the wood burner and built a lattice of kindling over the grate. She unwrapped a fire-lighter and tucked it between the sticks, the kerosene fumes making her cough. She was concentrating on what she was doing, only half an ear on the television.

The tempo of the programme changed to the strains of the ITV morning news bulletin. Catherine fumbled with the matches and dragged one across the box's striking surface. It flared into life. As she leaned forward to throw it into the stove, the newscaster began to read the headlines.

Catherine's back was to the screen, and, at first, the words didn't penetrate. But as the man's voice echoed around the room, she froze, mid-breath, an animal caught in a hunter's cross hairs.

The delivery of each sentence was crisp and precise and

dispassionate. Catherine did not move, *could* not. But inside, her body betrayed her. Blood charged through her veins, flushing her face and filling her ears with a roaring sound that drowned out the television. She felt her heart crashing in her chest, a sensation of light-headedness. Her mouth was dry. The chill from the room crept under her skin and into the marrow of her bones.

Her life – the ordinary, dull, *precious* life she had fought so hard to build – tilted sideways.

But still Catherine could not move, not even when the match she was holding burned down to its nub, blistering the skin of her thumb.

# 3

My name is Brinley Booth. When I was twelve, I was struck by lightning.

Aunt Peg insists it was God's doing, that he fired a thunderbolt at me for telling a lie. I thought it was because I'd been stupid enough to stand under the oak tree at the top of Saltbox Hill, but she's said it so many times over the years I'm almost convinced she's right.

Mind you, Aunt Peg blames God for everything. For allowing my useless lump of a father to run off with Maureen Connolly. For giving Mum a tumour that ate up her insides. For making my thighs rub together when I walk. How can God be responsible for how many biscuits I eat? Everyone worries about me being fat. Except me. I worry about running out of Ginger Nuts.

Being struck by lightning doesn't smell like roast pork cooking, before you ask. And everyone does. Instead, I steamed like a pudding in a pot, electricity vaporizing the rain on my skin, and the sweat on my nearly teenaged body. My ears filled with ringing bells, my body engulfed in a halo of white. Mum's necklace was so hot it burned my neck, although I can't remember much more than that. I do know it felt like being thumped on the back.

Ah, yes, my back.

Always a talking point. Because the lightning gave me a gift. A scar in the shape of a tree, pale branches spreading up my spine and across my shoulder blades, fern-like fronds curling around my neck. The delicate fractal patterns of a Lichtenberg figure, otherwise known as a lightning tree. Google it, if you don't believe me.

It happened a day before my thirteenth birthday. Lucky for some, you might say. I'd survived, hadn't I? The newspapers called me a 'walking miracle'. If only they'd known the truth. I'd *wanted* to die, just like my mother.

The bolt – a direct strike – discharged millions of volts into my body, bursting dozens of blood vessels and stopping my heart. Death was much closer than I'd realized before. For months, I checked the weather forecast twice a day and ran up Saltbox Hill whenever it rained. But the odds of a second strike were one in nine million.

It never happened again.

For many victims, the lightning tree disappears within hours. Not me. With my colouring, the branches left a permanent imprint on my skin, covering a third of my back. But as the years rolled on and my scars faded, so did the memories. Now weeks can pass and I barely give it a second thought.

Except today. Something happened this morning that brought back that moment on Saltbox Hill when the sky cleaved apart, like my childhood. As I dip fat chips into the runny egg yolks Aunt Peg has cooked – I go home for lunch every Monday, deadlines permitting – I mull it over, a tremor in my fingers.

# WHEN I WAS TEN

I was in the newsroom, writing up a story for tomorrow's paper about a woman who saw the face of Elvis in her potato. Yes, I know. But this was penance for a previous indiscretion that almost cost me my job.

Technically, it wasn't my fault. A freelancer overheard me talking about my off-the-record conversation with a famous actor's publicist, who insisted his client would rather 'eat his wig' than appear in a film with his ex-wife.

And it was definitely not my fault that same freelancer sold the details of my private conversation to a rival newspaper, who used it in their diary column.

The publicist shouted at me for five minutes and is now refusing to speak to anyone at our paper. That *is* my fault, apparently, and the potato-face story is my punishment.

Not that I expect anything more. Colin, the news editor, has never warmed to me. He's that type. His eyes glaze over when I speak. Every time I suggest an idea, he sucks his teeth and says, 'No, Brinley. That won't work for our readers.' I can't decide if it's because I'm younger than him, overweight or a woman. Probably all three.

Anyway, I was in the office, and had just typed this Pulitzer Prize-winning line:

An Elvis fan has made a spud-tacular discovery during her weekly shop.

My desk is midway down the newsroom and tucked out of sight of Colin. This might sound like a boring and irrelevant detail, but it's not. Because my desk is next to a television.

Sky News runs on a permanent loop with the sound

turned down, so I don't hear it at first. But when I take a break to relieve the tedium of potato-based puns and buy a coffee from the canteen, a headline catches my eye.

**HILLTOP HOUSE MURDERS**

I stand completely still. The words blur. I blink and refocus. A ticker is running along the bottom of the screen and I follow its progress.

EXCLUSIVE: DO CHILDREN WHO KILL DESERVE OUR FORGIVENESS? SHANNON CARTER GIVES FIRST TV INTERVIEW TO MARK 21ST ANNIVERSARY OF 'ANGEL OF DEATH' MURDERS

A woman's face fills the screen.

My blood pressure drops. A swoop of dizziness loosens my knees and pricks at my skin, and I can't breathe. I can't do anything except watch the way her mouth moves and the fluttering of her hands in her lap.

'Budge out of the way,' says Lawrie Hudson, the chief reporter, coming up behind me. 'Boss wants an exclusive on this.' He reaches for the remote control and turns up the volume.

It's been twenty-one years since I've seen Shannon Carter. Seven thousand, nine hundred and five days since she was led by the police from Hilltop House in blood-stiffened pyjamas, a rusty streak across her cheekbone, white-blonde hair matted with clots.

An angel touched by death.

Dr Richard Carter and his wife, Pamela. Asleep in their

bedroom. Stabbed fourteen times with a pair of scissors in a frenzied and brutal attack by their daughter.

Their bedroom had white curtains and white wallpaper. It had wardrobes with sliding glass doors and artex swirls across the ceiling. A sheepskin rug and a lava lamp.

I had played hide-and-seek in that bedroom. I had teetered around in Mrs Carter's too-big high heels and fur coat when I was ten. I had sat at the dressing table, patting powder on my face and spraying perfume on my wrists.

I knew that bedroom – *that house* – as well as my own. Because I had lived next door to them since Shannon was born, and their killer was my friend.

*You're probably going to ignore this. Don't worry, I understand. Please don't feel bad. After all, I'm just a stranger on the internet. My mother always told me not to talk to strangers. I expect yours is the same.*

*Perhaps it will make things easier if I tell you a little about myself. Then we won't be strangers anymore. My favourite flowers are daffodils, my favourite season, spring. Music, the smell of rain on warm tarmac, the buzz of the city, the peace of the countryside, I love them all.*

*You don't have to reply, of course. You probably won't. But I've got the oddest feeling this could be the beginning of something important for us both.*

# 4

Catherine ran her blistered thumb under the cold tap, but already the skin was puckering and filling with fluid.

A fragment of memory pierced her. Her mother, leaning against their kitchen sink, the sound of water drumming against stainless steel. Christmas Day, 1996. The last Christmas.

Giggly on her third peach schnapps and lemonade, Pamela Carter had been taking the turkey out of the oven when she lost her balance in her new fluffy mules, tipping scalding fat over her forearm.

Catherine's older sister Shannon had screamed, alerting their father. Richard, in shirt and tie, had sworn at the sight of his Christmas dinner on the kitchen floor. Even though he was a doctor, he had, as punishment, refused to dress the wound. The blister had been yellow and oozy and left a scar.

Catherine pressed down on her own blister to dispel the image of her mother. Permed hair and lipstick. Foundation that left orange streaks across her neck. Circles of blusher that reminded her of a clown.

She did not want to think about Pamela or Richard or

Shannon. Why on earth had her sister agreed to be interviewed by those documentary makers? Had she not considered the effect on Catherine of any of this?

It was an unspoken pact, but both sisters had always shied away from the limelight, the heat of media scrutiny. Deliberately dragging their tragedy back into the headlines was self-flagellation of the worst kind.

Once upon a time, she had loved Shannon with everything she had. Catherine had been the calm, capable one while Shannon, although eighteen months older, was fragile and sensitive, the more childlike of the two.

It was Catherine who'd stood up to their father when he'd forced Shannon to eat her dinner from a dog bowl, receiving a slap across the face for insubordination.

When they had scratched one of Dr Carter's records by accidentally dragging the stylus across the vinyl, it was Catherine who'd scrubbed the bathroom tiles with her toothbrush, shouldering her sister's share of the punishment as well as her own while Shannon had wept in the corner.

When Shannon had crept into her sister's bed for comfort, it was Catherine who had rubbed her back, wiped away her tears and dreamed up grandiose plans for their escape.

She hadn't seen Shannon since the last day of the court hearing, a bitterly cold afternoon in December 1997. Catherine had been wearing her school uniform, and couldn't remember much about that time except the constant fidgeting and the look of remorse on her older sister's face when the guilty verdict was returned.

Her memories of family life before the murders had become faded, like a blanket that had been washed over and over again until the colour had disappeared and the edges were frayed, no scrap of comfort left in its thin folds. She had her own family now. That was enough.

Catherine turned off the tap. Her thumb stung, a physical pain rather than low-level anxiety, her constant companion. She welcomed the distraction.

From the kitchen window, she could see her back garden. The snow had covered the grass and the roof of the summerhouse, and was falling steadily. If it carried on at this rate, there would be a couple of inches by lunchtime. She wondered if they would close Honor's school. It didn't take much these days.

The telephone in the hallway began to ring. A brusque sound, it startled her. Nobody used the landline these days except cold callers. She had meant to cancel it but had never got round to it.

'Hello?'

'Mrs Allen?'

'Yes, that's me.'

'I'm calling from the office at Sweetwood.'

She recognized the voice. How strange that a moment ago she was thinking of Honor's school, and here was one of the receptionists, Mrs Samuels, on the other end of the line.

'Is Honor unwell today, Mrs Allen?'

Even though she knew the answer, Catherine paused, as if the break in time might alter the implication of that question.

'No, she's – I mean, she was fine at breakfast.'

'It's just that she hasn't registered this morning and we wanted to confirm the reason for her absence.'

Catherine's stomach performed a slow-motion roll. At once, a series of scenarios began to play out in her mind, each more devastating than the last. Truancy. A hit and run. Abduction by a stranger in a car. With her family history, catastrophizing was second nature.

'She left home at her usual time.' Catherine's fingers tightened around the receiver. 'She's never missed school before. Something must have happened.'

'Perhaps she had an appointment she didn't tell you about.'

'She's twelve,' said Catherine. 'She doesn't have appointments I don't know about.'

But a fissure of doubt opened up.

'Well, you might want to give her a call on her mobile,' said Mrs Samuels briskly. 'The forecast is for more snow. Mr Lexden is thinking about sending pupils home at lunchtime. I'd hate her to turn up when everyone else has left, especially in this weather. Please do let us know if you track her down.'

The nerve above Catherine's lip began to twitch. It did that when she was stressed. She pressed the tip of her finger to it until the spasm stopped and tried to formulate a plan.

She checked her mobile to see if Honor had texted or tried to call, but there was nothing except a junk email about final ordering dates for Christmas hampers.

When she tried her daughter's phone, it went straight to voicemail.

The kitchen was colder now, shadows pushing out the light. The snow was like torn feathers falling from the sky. Catherine hesitated, and lifted her car keys from the hook.

She slipped on her leather gloves and wrapped a scarf around her neck.

Then she stepped outside into the white world.

The streets of Coggsbridge were almost empty, most of the early-morning shoppers seeking shelter from the weather. With its timber-framed houses and old bridge crossing the River Blackwater, the village looked Christmas-card quaint in the snow.

Catherine drove carefully along the route that Honor took to school. The thought of getting stuck terrified her, but not as much as not knowing what had happened to her daughter.

Snowflakes settled on the windscreen, the wipers a beat too slow to fully clear them. Honor had been born on a twilight December afternoon so cold the hoar frost had lasted all day. This morning's air had the same taste of winter about it.

As Catherine scanned the streets for a slight figure in a mulberry-coloured coat, she told herself Honor would be fine. Perhaps she had been held up for an unexpected reason and missed registration, slipping past the receptionists and straight into class. She was probably in one of the science labs or the art studio, unaware of everyone's concern.

Her eyes flicked from the road to her phone on the passenger seat, but it remained silent. 'Come on, Honor. Where are you?' Her muttering sounded too loud in the car.

By now, the snow was falling so thickly it had blanketed the asphalt, the trees and the tiled roofs of the houses. It had the odd effect of muffling the sound of the engine.

At the school, the playground and fields were empty. Catherine checked her watch. Less than an hour until lunchtime. Everywhere was colourless, the sky and the air filled with relentless frozen eddies.

She drove on, through the back roads this time, the fields blank and accusing. A pheasant ran across the whitened earth and burst upwards, startled by an unseen enemy. Its gold and green plumage and distinctive red wattle reminded her of festive wrappings. But there was no splash of mulberry, no discarded school bag or slender figure trudging through the snow.

Twenty minutes later, when there was still no sign of her daughter and her tyres were beginning to stick, Catherine turned the car around and headed home.

The house was freezing, and so Catherine relit the fire and boiled the kettle for tea. She would give it until two o'clock and then she would call the police.

She wondered how long it would take them to discover the brutal truth about her family history and if they would agree to keep it from her husband and daughter.

Catherine cradled her mug and watched the flames lick the glass of the log burner. Having a daughter had always been a risk. A son might have been different. Provided some distance. But in Honor, she glimpsed the shadows of her own childhood, the parts of herself – and her older sister – she despised. She found herself wondering if an instinct to kill was hereditary, woven into one's DNA, like eye colour or height.

A petal from the poinsettia plant on the coffee table fell, landing on the glass like a splash of blood. She breathed deeply. *One. Two. Three. Four.* Counting, her old strategy.

Once – and only once – had she come close to telling Edward everything. Honor had been no older than a month or two. Catherine had been so young herself, nineteen and exhausted, wrung out by a colicky baby who never seemed to sleep. Edward had taken the day off work, sent his wife of three months to bed and taken over, changing nappies and organizing bottles.

At twenty-seven, he had matured into a thoughtful young man. She had seen a different side to her new husband, his face lit with love for them both. How glorious it had been to hand over the responsibility of their daughter for a few hours. How grateful to him she had felt. Having Honor had deepened their relationship in ways that had surprised her. So tempting, then, to imagine the relief of unburdening the horrors of her past onto his shoulders.

When she had woken up, the house was silent. She had gone downstairs and Edward was dozing on the sofa, Honor nestled into his chest.

She had watched him sleep, peace settled into the lines of his face, and she knew then that she would never tell him about the murder of her parents. It would do nothing to lighten her load. All it would mean is that he would carry it too – and its weight was heavy. Too heavy. The pressure might break her precious new family of three, and she couldn't risk that.

As far as Edward and Honor were concerned, her parents and sister had died in a house fire. All photographs, all belongings, had burned with them. No culprit was ever found. She had told the lie so many times she almost believed it herself. Her husband accepted – with reluctance – that she did not wish to talk about it.

Twelve years ago, in that giddy flush of new love, when they were still unwrapping each other's truths, he had peppered her with questions, probing her tragedy with gentle but insistent fingers: in the corner of the sticky-floored basement club where they'd danced with each other that first night, eyes catching like silk on roughened wood; over the guitar riffs of a band they'd both loved, sipping pints, bodies pressed up close against the bar; amongst tangled sheets in a suite he'd booked for her nineteenth birthday, her first stay in a hotel and the night their daughter was conceived.

But his concerned interest had the opposite effect. Catherine, finding her way in the world as an adult, shut down and refused to talk about it, preferring to lose herself in the visceral pleasures of sex instead of confronting the brutalities of her personal history. This baffled Edward, who had risen rapidly to become the chief executive of an environmental charity and was used to persuading others to behave as he wished, albeit in a charming way. But because he was also a sensitive man, he had learned, over time, not to push her. For that, she was grateful. The past was a distant place, peopled by strangers, and she no longer visited it.

A log shifted in the burner and the creaking sound of fire brought her back to herself. She put her mug of cold tea on the table.

Less than a week, that was all. The documentary would be screened on Thursday night. A day or two of newspaper headlines. And then the Hilltop House murders would slip back into the shadows and she could breathe again. Edward and Honor need never find out.

A jingle of metal, as familiar as home, followed by the click of a key turning in the front door broke apart the silence. Catherine leaped from her chair but forced herself to walk, not run, down the hallway.

A mulberry-coloured coat. Shiny blonde hair. The thump of a school bag against polished wood. Tiny puddles of melting snowflakes.

'Hi, Mum.'

'Where have you been?' Catherine spoke with a quiet control, but there was steel in her words.

Honor's laugh was louder than usual. 'At school. Where else?' She turned her back on her mother, hanging her damp coat on the hook. 'I mean, I was a bit late, but who can blame me when it's double maths?' She laughed again and unwound her scarf. 'They've sent us home. Mr Lexden says the snow's getting too bad and it's a health and safety issue.'

A fork in the road.

Catherine could confront her daughter. Explain about the phone call from the school office and unleash the full force of her temper. Or she could let it go for now. Savour the peace. Give Honor the benefit of the doubt while maintaining a watchful eye over her.

'Can I have a cup of tea, Mum? I'm freezing.'

And just like that, the moment passed. Catherine surprised herself by letting it.

Later, when Catherine was preparing dinner, she sent Honor into the garden to break the ice on the bird bath. As she peeled potatoes, her gaze landed on her daughter's phone. She had always impressed upon Honor the price of ownership was allowing Catherine to check it at any time.

She washed her hands and dried them on a tea towel. The phone felt warm and she wondered what secrets it held. Before she could find out, Honor was opening the back door into the kitchen, smelling of cold, her cheeks pink. Catherine slid the phone back onto the worktop. *Benefit of the doubt.*

'It's still snowing and I slipped on the steps,' said Honor, rubbing her hip. A crust of ice decorated her gloves and the back of her coat.

'Give them to me,' said Catherine. 'I'll pop them in the airing cupboard to dry.' She was rewarded with a smile and a fierce hug. She hugged her daughter back, breathing in the smell of her apple shampoo, enjoying their closeness, and decided she'd been too suspicious. Punctuality had never been Honor's strong point. She'd been late to school, that was all.

As she stood on the upstairs landing, she heard Honor go into the sitting room and switch on the television. She pictured her daughter curled on the sofa, a blanket across her knees.

The sky was darkening, light bleeding from the day. Out of the window, she watched a street lamp come on, a water-fall of snow captured in its muted colours. The rich smell of casserole filled the house and Christmas was on its way. Catherine was struck by a pang of contentment, despite the morning's events.

She laid her daughter's gloves across the boiler and found a hanger for her coat. She slipped a hand into its pocket, seeking out other damp belongings that might need drying. Her fingers closed around a scrap of paper.

She scanned it. Closed her eyes. Read it again.

A bus ticket to Halstead, a town about nine miles away. Bought at 8.47 a.m. that morning. A child's return.

*Thank you for your message. I didn't expect you to reply so quickly (or at all) but I'm so glad you did. You asked what prompted me to get in touch. Your name, I think. It's been such a long time since I've heard it – so pretty, but unusual, wouldn't you say? – and it reminded me of another time in my life. A dark and painful time, if I'm being honest.*

*Chinese food and puppies! What's not to love? How wonderful to learn your favourite Shakespeare play is Much Ado About Nothing. Excellent taste – it's one of my favourites too. Full of secrets and hoaxes, the ultimate sleight of hand. Do you think everyone has secrets? I do. There's a delicious thrill in holding close a scrap of knowledge that no one else shares, a power to it. I'd forgotten about it until now but when we were younger, we had a secret code, a method of communicating that only we knew about.*

*Never underestimate the importance of holding back a little something for yourself. The currency of secrets is more valuable than anything else, even money.*

# 5

It takes eight minutes to get from Aunt Peg's flat to Canary Wharf on the Docklands Light Railway, but longer in the snow.

By the time I get back to the office, I'm so late I walk the long way around and slip in past the digital team instead of the news desk. Erdman, the new foreign correspondent, raises a hand and calls out a greeting, but I frown at him, and he lets it drop. Too late, though. Colin has spotted me. He strides across the newsroom floor, twirling a biro like he's Billy the Kid.

'Brinley Booth, where the fuck have you been? That wasn't a lunch break, it was a piss-take.' He points the biro at me and pretends to shoot.

'I was meeting a contact.' I nod towards the large windows overlooking the Isle of Dogs, which frame the falling snow. 'It took longer than I thought.' The lie comes easily but I don't feel bad. Colin is an obnoxious bully.

'Well, I hope you got a bloody good story.'

'Of course.' I smile, full of sweetness and deceit and Aunt Peg's egg and chips. 'I just need to make a few calls.' And then, the clincher. 'You'll love it, Colin. It's a biggie. Fingers crossed I can stand it up.'

He grunts, pacified for now. I'll need to come up with something decent, though. It's been a while since I've had an exclusive worthy of the front page and Colin won't let this drop. He's got the memory of an elephant.

'Get back to work, then,' he says, making a shooing gesture. 'And give Lawrie a hand when you've finished, will you?'

Lawrie is on the telephone when I slide into my seat, but he raises an eyebrow at me and fakes a yawn, so I know it's not important.

Someone has stuck a Post-it note to my computer screen. A scribbled name and number. I don't know who it is. It's either a) a complaint b) a story so dull it will never see the light of day, or c) an elderly reader who just wants to chat. The best tip-offs from the public usually come through the news desk, handed out, like sweets, to favoured reporters. I remove my notepad from my bag and place it on the desk.

Lawrie puts down the receiver and tugs at his fringe. 'That's five minutes of my life I'm never going to get back.'

'Waste of time?'

He doesn't answer, distracted by the ping of an incoming email. 'Is everything OK?' I pose the question, not because I don't know the answer, but because I can see it isn't, I like Lawrie and Colin has told me to help.

'The editor wants to splash on the Hilltop House murders tomorrow' – my breath catches in my throat at the mention of this spectre from my childhood – 'and I need a top line.'

*A top line.* Stupid phrase, isn't it? But it's exactly what it says on the tin. The killer angle. The exclusive. The opening sentence of the story that will persuade readers to buy our newspaper above all others, especially our tabloid rivals.

I imagine the shock on Lawrie's face when I tell him that I lived next door to the Carter family; that arterial blood is bright red and venous blood is darkly rich, like wine; that Shannon Carter – the tearful star of this headline-making documentary – wasn't wearing any shoes when the police led her away and she left bloody footprints on the pavement. That a killer isn't always who you think she is.

But instead I grimace and express my solidarity. 'Nightmare.'

Lawrie runs his hand through his hair again. It sticks up and makes him seem younger than he is. I wonder if this is what he looks like when he wakes up in the morning and then I push the thought away with both hands. As if *that's* going to happen.

Embarrassing as it is to admit – I'm thirty-three years old, for God's sake – I've never spent the night with a man. Quick and perfunctory sex, yes. Actual long-term relation-ship, no. It's not that I don't want to meet someone. But I don't like showing my scars, inside and out. I prefer the dark corners of alleyways or a stranger's car, where I can keep my shirt on and the pain of my past to myself. Anyway, Lawrie has a girlfriend and she's beautiful, and that is the end of that.

'Have you asked the ITV press office for some exclusive footage?' It's an obvious avenue, but perhaps, amid the hectic pace of the news day, it hasn't occurred to him.

'Done that. They've refused.' He sucks on his pen. 'Apparently, they want to keep the story running all week, so they're releasing fresh extracts of the interview every day, to whet the public's appetite. They're going after the biggest slice of audience share when it's screened on Thursday night.'

'What about the family?'

Lawrie shrugs. 'Not much left. I've been trying to find a cousin or an aunt, but no joy so far.'

'Shannon Carter?'

'They'll have tied her in to an exclusive deal.'

'Her sister?'

Lawrie gives me a look. 'No one knows where she is. And she's never spoken to the media. Not a single interview. Mind you, that would be one hell of an exclusive.' He takes a cigarette paper from his jacket, fills it with tobacco, rolls it, sniffs it and slides it behind his ear. Then he picks up the phone again.

I busy myself by typing *Shannon Carter* and *Carter sisters* into the library system and calling up all the news stories they've been mentioned in since our computerized archive began twenty-two years ago.

Lawrie looks exhausted. I'd like to help him. It's my job, after all. To find stories and put them in the paper. But I can't bring myself to mention it. Colin would force me to write a feature brimming with tabloid clichés about living next door to a House of Horrors. I can see it now.

Headline: **MY FRIEND, THE KILLER**. Subhead: *From schoolgirl to slaughterer.*

It's well past six o'clock by the time I've finished going through the cuttings, searching for ideas for follow-ups.

Lawrie is still sitting at his desk, his forehead furrowed in concentration, his fingers flying over the keyboard. He's been granted a reprieve, for today, at least.

A graduate trainee sent out to knock doors in the Carters' home village in Kent has turned up a distant relative and persuaded him to say a few words. This relative has provided a collect photograph – a never-before-seen image of Dr and Mrs Carter taken by his mother at a restaurant a few days before they were murdered. It's not going to set the world on fire, but the trainee was savvy enough to get the only copy, so it's an exclusive, and enough for the front-page story that Lawrie's been tasked with pulling together.

When I'm sure that Lawrie doesn't need any more help, I say goodnight. His head is down and he doesn't answer, but I don't blame him. When I'm on a tight deadline, the outside world is a muffled echo and all I can hear are the words in my head.

The DLR platform is full of smartly dressed bankers, laden down with bags of Christmas gifts from the shiny shops of Canary Wharf. They gleam with the patina of money and success. I look down at my scuffed trainers and make a mental note to buy some new shoes.

A thin layer of snow is covering the pavement when I walk from Poplar station to Aunt Peg's flat, past pinched-together terraces and estates with broken windows. Two teenagers laugh and bump my shoulder as they walk by, their faces lost inside the cavern of their hoods.

On the stairwell, there's the neck of a glass bottle. A screaming argument from somewhere in the tower block echoes down the concrete corridor. The estate's signature perfume of piss fills my nostrils.

'Only me, Aunt Peg,' I shout over the television as I let myself in.

Technically, she's my great-aunt, my late grandmother's sister. But when my mother died and I could not stand to be near my father, she was the only family to offer me a place to live. At a time when the foundations of my life were shifting beneath my feet, she provided a bedrock of stability. Now she's eighty-four and needs a bit of extra help, and with the cost of London living, I haven't quite got around to moving out yet. As far as I'm concerned, Aunt Peg is my family now.

From my bedroom window, I watch the triangle of Canary Wharf blink in the distance and wonder, not for the first time, how I can make my mark at the newspaper.

As the trains grind through the snow and the city is pinpricked with thousands of lights, a voice in my head whispers to me. The answer, it says, lies in the shoebox stuffed at the bottom of my cupboard. The faded photographs of the Carter family. Three or four pencil drawings. A few handwritten letters forwarded from the secure children's home in the weeks and months after the trial.

This collection of memorabilia from one of the country's most shocking murders in living memory would bring me to any editor's attention. Multiple front-page exclusives. Syndicated around the world.

But there's a reason I'm reluctant to reveal my connection to the Carter family, and it's not just because I don't want my photograph in a national newspaper. The truth is, I know more about these killings than the police ever did. Many years ago, I boxed up that knowledge, packed it away and labelled it DO NOT OPEN. But it's haunted me ever since, colouring everything with a shade named guilt.

If I write the defining story of my career – and it *will* define me, I'm certain of that – it will open a Pandora's box.

The trouble is, once the lid's off, there'll be no going back.

# 6

It was completely dark outside.

Catherine put a spoonful of sweetcorn on Honor's plate and a dollop of mash. She had dished up Edward's dinner first, but he hadn't waited for either of them and was shovelling forkfuls into his mouth. When she caught his eye, he mumbled something about being hungry and poured her a glass of sparkling water as a peace offering. She served herself last. The beef's red wine sauce was too thin and it bled into the potato, turning it a watery pink.

She put down her knife and fork, appetite gone.

What she had begun to call the Bus Ticket Issue filled up all the worry-space in her head. Based on the evidence, it would appear her twelve-year-old daughter had not been to school that morning.

Uncomfortable questions jostled for attention. Where had she been? With whom? What was so urgent it couldn't wait until the weekend? And why was she being so secretive?

Truancy was a rite of passage for some, Catherine understood that. But Honor was still young – *too* young – and had lied with convincing ease.

Much as she hated to admit it, her daughter was pulling

away from her and she needed to handle this situation with care. Not to alienate her, never that, but to encourage her to open up and confide her truths, as she'd done so willingly in the past. If she raised the mystery of the bus ticket now, over dinner, Edward would want to analyse and discuss it, as he had done when she had first told him about the fire and her family. Given the elastic-thin state of his patience at the moment, he would probably shout, but Catherine knew that approach wouldn't work with their daughter. Honor would storm off and clam up.

Perhaps she should sleep on it. If the school was closed again tomorrow, they'd have a proper chance to talk it through while Edward was in London. Yes, that was the best course of action. Feeling better, she took a sip of water and tried out a tentative smile on her husband.

'How was your day, love?'

He grunted and speared a mushroom. 'Same old.'

Catherine waited for him to continue, but it was clear his contribution to the dinner-table conversation was over. Edward was an excellent mimic. He often made them laugh with stories of office politics and the petty bureaucracies of government regulators. But he'd barely said a word since getting home. She wondered if something had happened at work.

Outside, the snow was still falling. It gave the night a textured feel, like the air was rippling. They ate in silence until Honor poked at her casserole and said, 'I'm full, Mum.'

'But you've hardly touched your dinner.'

The girl shrugged. 'I don't want any more.'

'Honor, you need to eat—'

'Don't fuss. If she says she's had enough, leave her be.'

Edward's voice was knife-sharp, cutting through their exchange. Catherine bit back a retort, unused to being snapped at, but not wanting to escalate the tension. Honor stared at her plate.

Her husband pushed back his chair and its legs scraped across the tiled floor. An ugly sound, abrasive, and a marked change from his default setting of laid-back good humour. 'I've finished too. I'll do the washing-up later.'

'What's up with Dad?' Honor whispered as soon as he'd left the kitchen, leaning into her mother, a conspiratorial intimacy between them.

'Work, I expect,' said Catherine, gathering up knives and forks. 'He's probably had a bad day.'

But she didn't believe that. In all the years she had known him, Edward rarely left his dinner. Even if he was unwell, he always managed to eat *something*, dry crackers or a piece of toast. In the early years of their relationship, he would sometimes order two main courses in a restaurant, a sheepish grin on his face, not an ounce of fat on him. But tonight he'd left half his meal on his plate.

In the sitting room, Edward was sprawled across the sofa, remote control in hand. Honor sat next to him and Catherine took the armchair by the wood burner.

When Honor was little, they'd always left the washing-up until she was in bed, wanting to spend every spare moment with their daughter, grinning daftly at each other, drunk on love. That habit had stuck. An hour or two of television had now replaced warm milk and bedtime stories, but Catherine had always loved this part of the day. The three of them together in one place. Family time.

Edward cycled through the channels, a habit that irritated Catherine, who was trying to read her book. Honor was fiddling with her mobile phone, hair shielding her face. Eventually, Edward settled on Sky News.

The newscaster's voice moved smoothly between news items. *Brexit. The weather. London's seventh gang-related stabbing in a week.* Catherine felt a burning in her chest. Acid. She needed a drink of water. A change of scene. She half rose from her chair.

And then, a face as recognizable as her own.

The woman had silver streaks in her hair, even though she was only thirty-three. The blue eyes of her childhood were now dish-rag grey. She looked tired, the facts of her brutal history evidenced in dulled skin that seemed too loose for her skull. A raw patch of eczema blazed on her jaw.

Shannon Carter.

Her sister.

Catherine gripped the arm of her chair to stop her softening knees from giving way completely. Tiny black dots blinked on and off in her vision. Distant screams and the scent of blood, rusted wire and the butcher's counter played on a loop in her memory.

But she could not tear her gaze away.

The television camera was focused on Shannon Carter's face. Her eyes seemed to stare down the lens and into Catherine's. It was a pre-recorded interview filmed in a hotel suite somewhere in London, and, as she spoke, Catherine noticed her lipstick had bled into the feathery cracks above her mouth. Her voice had deepened over the years, the flat vowels knocked into shape. She still had a horseshoe-shaped mole on her cheek.

'There is something that has bothered me for a long time,' said Shannon, her hands folded in her lap.

'Can you explain to the viewers what that is?' The interviewer. Male. Sympathetic. Off camera.

'My sister. I never got a proper chance to say goodbye to her. To say sorry. For everything that happened. For what I did.' Her gaze dropped away. An incisor indented her bottom lip. 'I've been able to build a new life for myself. I hope she has too. We *both* lost our parents that night, and I think everyone forgets that.'

'If you knew your sister was watching this right now, what would you say to her?'

Shannon lifted her head and spoke directly into the camera. 'I'm so sorry. I hope you can forgive me. I would love to see you again. I want to know how you are, and what your life is like now. To let you know I still love you and—'

Shannon's face disappeared and was replaced by a scene in a kitchen. Raised voices. Muted colours. From the glare of studio lights to the depressing environs of Albert Square. Edward had flipped channels again and landed on a soap opera.

Catherine's legs were trembling. She leaned back into the armchair to gather herself. Edward was no longer lolling on the sofa, but sitting up straighter, an expression of puzzlement on his face. Honor looked up from her mobile phone with mild interest.

'Can you imagine,' she said, 'what it would be like to have a sister who stabbed your parents to death?'

'Might be a bit awkward at Christmas.' Edward chuckled to himself, his earlier bemusement vanishing into mirth. He switched channels again.

Catherine's tongue was so dry it had stuck to the roof of her mouth. Her legs had stopped shaking, but she felt scooped out inside, as if someone had forced a hand into her chest and pulled out her heart.

On autopilot, she released an obligatory huff of laughter at Edward's weak joke and stared at the television, but had no sense of what she was watching. Catherine's gaze went beyond the screen and to the blood-spattered walls of her childhood.

*Can you imagine what it would be like to have a sister who stabbed your parents to death?*

Honor's tone had been laced with incredulity, fascination even. And something thicker and darker. Repulsion.

As far as Honor and Edward were concerned, the fire that killed her family had been caused by a faulty tumble dryer. Catherine had escaped their tragic fate because she'd been staying the night with a friend. Simple lies. Easier to remember.

Hearing Honor's distaste at the murders – even at twelve, the curl of her lip made her look as though she'd trodden in something unpleasant – confirmed Catherine's instinct: she'd been right to shield her husband and daughter from the bloodied truth of her past.

She'd do almost anything to keep it that way.

The cottage was sleeping, the draught of winter blowing through the gaps in its windows with determined breath. The blizzard had stopped. A pause in the darkness.

The street outside was deserted apart from a fox that picked her way across the frozen front gardens, stopping only to sniff the air. Parked cars were covered with a layer of ice. Nimbostratus clouds gathered overhead, laden with snow that would begin to fall again in an hour or so.

The village slumbered on in the way that country villages do.

Honor was lying in bed, one arm flung behind her head, the other wrapped around a cuddly giraffe. A strip of moonlight seeped through the curtains, pooling silver on the carpet. Her face was a pale blur against the night.

She murmured and moved beneath her duvet, restless. Her breathing sharpened. A cloud covered the moon and the bedroom was steeped in shadows. The walls looked black in the thick of the night and seemed to undulate in the darkness, as if they were leaking history – or something more distasteful – through the brickwork. The air was cold.

Honor sat up in bed.

She screamed.

The noise was so sudden it broke open the night-time stillness of the house. It was the scream of a thousand terrors. The sound of fear made real. It was tarry with shame and sorrow and loss, of unexplained secrets, crouching in the darkness.

For Catherine, who was asleep in a room across the landing, it was enough to wake her. Her eyes opened, the thunder of blood in her ears. The house was silent for now, but her body was tensed. She knew what her wakefulness meant and she waited for its reason to reveal itself.

Honor screamed again.

Catherine threw off her duvet and ran to her daughter's bedroom. She did not stop to pull on her dressing gown or push her feet into slippers, and the chill stung her skin. But she barely noticed, intent on chasing the shadows that stalked her child's sleep.

At first, she couldn't see her. But the cloud cleared the moon, and by its gleam, she found her, cowering by the bookcase. Her daughter's eyes were fixed on the wall.

'Sweetheart,' she said, reaching for her. 'You're dreaming.'

Honor did not acknowledge her mother. She was looking at something that Catherine could not see.

Catherine bit her lip. The GP had warned them that the sudden onset of Honor's night terrors could be down to the stress or worry of starting secondary school. He'd advised them not to interact or try to wake her, unless she was in danger of hurting herself. 'It's likely she won't recognize you and will become more agitated,' he'd explained. But maternal instinct kicked in. She wanted to rescue Honor from the darkest reaches of herself.

Honor began to whisper. Catherine shook her gently. Spoke her name. But the whispering continued, like an incantation. She sat on the carpet next to her daughter to wait it out.

Honor's sentences were indistinct, rolling from one to the other, a slurry of vowels and consonants. Every now and then, Catherine recognized a word, but the meaning was lost inside the confusion of sounds. She shivered, her pyjamas scant protection against the freezing temperature.

Her daughter's back was pressed against the spines of her books, as if disappearing into the pages of child-hood comfort might save her from her nightmares, and her arms were outstretched, a shield to ward off the unseen. The girl flinched, knocking *Aesop's Fables* from the shelf, tipping over a potted cactus and breaking one of the Murano glass fish she'd lovingly collected since her father had brought her first one back from a work trip to Italy.

The thud of the falling book seemed to have an effect on Honor. Her murmurings slowed into song and Catherine picked out the rhythm of a long-forgotten favourite. The hairs on her arm lifted in response. Honor's voice was the scratch of teeth against glass.

'*Ladybird, ladybird, fly away home,*
*Your house is on fire, your children will burn,*
*All but one, that lies under a stone,*
*Fly thee home, ladybird, 'ere she be gone.*'

The girl smiled vacantly at her mother and silence stretched between them, thin as ice.

Somewhere in the cottage, a toilet flushed. Edward was awake. And as quickly as it started, Honor relaxed into herself again. Dimples and apple-cheeks. Blinking. Sleepy-eyed.

She allowed Catherine to guide her back into bed and tuck the covers around her. She reached for her giraffe, and she was twelve again. Within seconds, her eyes were closed and she was breathing evenly. Catherine's precious girl. Her mother kissed her forehead and stroked her fringe. For a minute, she watched her sleep.

Through a gap in the curtains, the moon was high and bright. Catherine held back the fabric and looked into the garden below. Ice crystals glinted in the wash of light. The world was still again. A winter tableau.

Catherine gathered up the pieces of broken glass and put them on the windowsill, out of harm's way. She used her fingers to sweep dirt from the fallen cactus into her palm.

*Ladybird, ladybird, fly away home. Your house is on fire, your children will burn.*

As the doctor had said, these night terrors could be a manifestation of anxiety, of hidden concerns or stresses, the subconscious flexing its muscles. But terrifying as it was to witness her daughter in the grip of an attack, they were a recent affliction, most likely caused by surging hormones or friendship worries. Honor didn't mean anything by it. She *couldn't* know the truth about Catherine's past. She was asleep and had no sense of what she was saying.

On the carpet, the book of fables lay open, its pages spread out like a fan. She had bought it for Honor on her eighth birthday, when her daughter was still pleading for bedtime stories.

She picked it up, feeling the heft of it in her hands, the moon spotlighting the printed ink. 'The Boy Who Cried Wolf'. Another of Honor's childhood favourites.

She read a sentence or two, the opening lines as comforting as a warm blanket, and it calmed her.

These night-time episodes left Catherine feeling bruised and worn-down, emotion sucked from her until she was paper-dry inside. The events of earlier that day – Honor's truancy, Edward's snappiness and the shocking and unexpected reappearance of her sister – had heightened that feeling. She yawned. Time for bed. Tomorrow was a new day.

She closed the book, but not before she had read the last line, the moral of the story. The words made her heart thump with guilt and shame.

'*For none believes the liar, even when they speak the truth.*'

*You like the idea of a secret code? Well, I'll let you into a secret if you promise not to tell. Beatrice is not my real name. Names, I've discovered, can be a burden. I expect you can guess why I chose it as my avatar, knowing our shared love of a certain Shakespeare play.*

*Like you, I live down south. It's a simple existence. It took me many years to find my place in the world and preserving it has become the purpose of my life. I would fight with everything I have to protect it.*

*I don't have much family – it's a long and complicated story for another time – but I've learned to accept it, although it still breaks my heart. Even when life is full in other ways, it is possible to be lonely. Empty days and hollow nights. Plays tricks on you, the silence.*

*You said you felt lonely sometimes. What about your family? Are you close?*

# 7

'There was so much blood. That's what I remember most. I know it sounds strange, but I was only twelve. I had no idea a body could hold all that.' Shannon Carter's voice cracks. A silence electrifies the newsroom. 'It was warm and smelled of pennies.'

Three or four journalists are clustered around the television, including Lawrie, who is scribbling notes on his pad. For once, I slip in unnoticed. I'm not very good at being on time. Late, I believe those pedantic types call it. I prefer to think of it as running behind schedule.

Lawrie catches my eye and jerks his head towards the screen. I dump my bag on my desk, switch on my computer and join him, morning coffee in hand.

The ITV press office has released another exclusive extract from Thursday's forthcoming interview. To give credit where it's due, they're playing a blinder. The Hilltop House murders have been part of the national news fabric for years, horrifying and fascinating us in equal measure. Dr and Mrs

Carter's extended family have never spoken about the killings. Apart from the trial and the endless newspaper stories discussing what drives a child to kill, the coverage was thin, lacking in facts, mostly gossip and speculation. But this is a genuine scoop. Shannon Carter's first interview – and she is mesmerizing.

'That's tomorrow's story sorted,' I say to Lawrie, who is chewing the end of his biro. He's split the plastic covering and the thin tube inside. His tongue is black from leaking ink.

'I wish.' He swipes a hand across his mouth, glum. 'It's great stuff, yes, but they've put it out too early. You know what Colin's like. He'll be bored of it by this afternoon. He'll want our own exclusive.'

The male interviewer – one of ITV's most high-profile news presenters – is talking now. He's all over-whitened teeth and expensive made-to-measure suit, but he's asking the question that everyone wants an answer to, so I forgive him his trespasses.

'Your parents were viciously murdered, stabbed in cold blood, twenty-one years ago. What's changed? Why have you decided to speak about it now?'

'Money,' calls out one of the feature writers – Lucy Rosewell, I think – and everybody laughs.

But Shannon Carter can't hear the derision in the newsroom. She's locked behind a glass screen. She lifts her shoulders, slides her eyes away from the camera. 'I need to accept some responsibility for what happened. I have so many regrets.' She takes a deep breath. 'Obviously, this has coloured my whole life and, as I get older, I want to try and put it behind me. But most importantly, I want to reach out to my sister. She's out there somewhere. It won't be easy, I know, but I'd like us to connect again. *That's* my reason for agreeing to this interview.'

The television cuts to scenes from outside Canterbury Crown Court. December 1997. A small figure is hidden under a blanket. Tried as an adult because, according to the judge, the nature of her crime was so serious her right to anonymity should be waived. Cameras flash and strobe. A metal barrier is holding back the press, who collectively strain against it. Shouted questions. Running photographers. A prison van that pulls away. The picture is grainy, before the days of high definition. When I swallow, it feels like something is stuck in my throat.

The news item finishes and my colleagues drift away to get on with the day's stories.

Lucy Rosewell is writing a feature about children who kill. Their histories are well documented, stitched into the nation's psyche, but these horrors are too familiar now for me to feel much.

This disconnect concerns me. When it's your job to write about the brutality of the human race, it's easy to become numbed to it. That, or exhilarated by the prospect of a 'good' story. I can't decide which is worse.

Colin is walking through the office, so I pick up the phone and pretend I'm talking to someone.

'Conference?' Colin's tone is bullish. This is a worrying sign. He rests his foot on Lawrie's desk, legs splayed apart, trousers straining against his groin. A display of masculinity and power. In his mind, at least. 'What have you got for me?'

Morning conference starts at 11.30 a.m. The heads of each

department – including news, showbiz, sport and features – outline the day's best stories to the editor. Ritual humiliation is not uncommon.

Lawrie opens his mouth, but before he has a chance to speak, Colin cuts in. 'We should be out on this, digging up something decent. Have you got an address for Shannon Carter yet?'

'That new trainee, Matt, is on the case, but there's been no sign of her since Saturday,' says Lawrie. 'Classic buy-up technique. ITV will have her squirrelled away in a cottage or hotel somewhere.'

Colin nods. 'Try and track down a mobile number for her. We might be able to get to her that way, catch her unawares.' He rubs a hand across a couple of days' worth of stubble. 'What about the sister?'

Lawrie stares at Colin as if he's an idiot. He *is* an idiot.

Colin puffs out his chest. 'I don't give a fuck if she's difficult to find, sunshine. That's your job.'

I can't pretend I'm on the telephone for much longer so I place the receiver into the cradle, and try to look busy. It doesn't work.

'That goes for you too, Brinley. Give Lawrie a hand. The editor wants to splash on this again tomorrow. And we don't want our arses kicked by the opposition, do we?'

I consider replying with my own set of rhetorical questions – *Why are you always such a dick? Did you go on a special training course to become one? Have you ever heard of deodorant?* – but I'm not convinced Colin will see the funny side.

'Right, send me a list-line for conference based on the snippets of the interview released this morning,' says Colin, 'but I'll need something new by the end of the day.'

As if we need reminding.

Colin heads over to the show business desk. I can hear him shouting at the TV editor for failing to get any exclusive Shannon Carter quotes from the ITV press office, but she's tougher than me, and tells him to fuck off and let her get on with her job.

'What do you need me to do?' I don't want to tread on Lawrie's toes. I've only been at this paper for a few months and there's politics at play, a hierarchy. Still, this is my chance to stop rewriting press releases and agency copy, and get involved in a breaking news story. To make my mark.

'Let's head to Hilltop House. The Carter family will be long gone, but there might be people in the street who lived there during the murders and remember them.'

My heart sinks.

Lawrie is putting his notebook, laptop and dictaphone into his satchel. 'Where is it again? Gloucestershire?'

'Kent,' I say.

'I'll just clear it with Colin, and then we'll get going.'

'I don't mind staying here and pulling things together.' I try to hide the hope in my voice.

Lawrie shakes his head. 'No, it's better if there's two of us. We can split up and cover more ground.'

It's been twenty-one years since my mother died and I moved to Aunt Peg's flat in east London, but the street of my childhood is still vivid in my memory. The Carter house was beautiful. Double-fronted and full of character, riding the crest of a hill, a patchwork of fields spread out beneath it. At Christmas, lights twinkled through the windows like a Victorian greetings card, a wreath of holly on the door.

Our house was much smaller, the poor relation. Cracked

paintwork and weeds. A tumble of overgrown trees. But I always thought we were the lucky ones because we had the privilege of looking through the glass into their lives.

When Lawrie returns, I hand him a piece of paper – Hilltop House's full address – and he smiles at my efficiency, impressed by what he considers to be my excellent research skills.

As my car is outside Aunt Peg's flat – it's too expensive to park in Canary Wharf – we agree to go our separate ways and meet down in Kent as soon as possible. 'Don't dawdle,' says Lawrie. 'We need to hit the ground running.'

The station platform is empty. A vicious wind nips at my exposed face. The sky is throwing down hail and it sounds like uncooked rice being shaken up in a plastic bottle. Inside the warmth of the DLR train, I press cool hands to my cheeks, hoping to quell the churn of nausea.

At home, I add extra underwear and my toothbrush to the overnight bag that's a permanent fixture in the boot of my car, and grab the shoebox of memorabilia, just in case.

When I left the village two decades ago in the back of Aunt Peg's dented hatchback, watching until Saltbox Hill and the river had faded from view, I swore I would never go back to that place of darkness. Too full of memories. Too much history. Too many buried secrets.

But I was lying to myself. Just like I've lied about everything else.

*You want me to call you Hero? What a wonderful idea – our very own secret code! And Beatrice and Hero were cousins. Wouldn't it be strange if we were related? I mean, that's partly what prompted me to send you a message in the first place. Looking at your picture was like staring into a mirror of the past.*

*Isn't it a coincidence that neither of us has much family? I'm so sorry to hear about the tragic losses you have experienced. I have also experienced loss in the most devastating of circumstances. It seems we have a lot in common.*

# 8

Catherine folded the sheet into an untidy rectangle, struck by the smell of fabric conditioner, of home. She shook it out again and refolded it until the edges formed a knife-sharp line. Old habits died hard. Fold once, twice and then again, and smooth out the cotton. The comfort of routine. It had sustained her during the darkest days.

She placed the clean laundry in a drawer. Some women found cooking, cleaning, washing and ironing – the four pillars of domestic life – too prosaic for their tastes. Several mothers from the school paid other women to change beds and press shirts while they drank coffee and spent their mornings at the gym. But Catherine embraced the mundanity. She let herself fall into it. She had spent too much time dreaming of being ordinary to ever become bored.

Fresh snow had fallen in their Essex village overnight. The school remained closed and the trains into London were suspended until further notice. Edward had taken himself off to the study to work. The door was closed and every now and then, when she walked past, she heard him murmuring into the telephone.

It struck her that she had no idea how he spent his days, or with whom.

Her husband had barely spoken to her in the last few hours. In bed, in the navy darkness of early morning, she had moved towards him and placed an arm around his waist, but he hadn't turned to her like he usually did. His body had tensed, as if he was considering something, and hope had taken flight inside her, but then he had rolled away and headed into the shower.

In the tangle of duvet, her cheeks had flushed. Humiliation, her oldest friend. She placed a hand on the sheet. Still warm. The irony did not escape her when he had been so cold.

It hadn't always been that way. Up until a couple of weeks ago, they'd had sex on a regular basis, and spent a handful of evenings a month at gigs or restaurants in the surrounding towns. On the Wednesday before last, he'd booked a babysitter and left work early to surprise her. She remembered it quite clearly because she'd been on the telephone to Eliza when he'd appeared in their bedroom, carrying half a dozen bird of paradise flowers, and made her jump. He'd thrust them at her and, across their orange beak-like petals, had given her a funny sort of smile. She'd hung up quickly and kissed him hello.

For the rest of the evening, he'd been very quiet and she'd assumed there were problems at work. But his mood hadn't lifted, and while she had caught glimpses of his natural affability during his interactions with Honor, he had remained subdued. A tiny part of her wondered if he had lost his job but was pretending to go to the office every day. She had heard stories about men who did things like that.

In the kitchen, she chopped onions, carrots and celery for a soup she was making for lunch. Nutritious and hearty food. Another way to show love for her family. She could hear Honor moving around upstairs, and she imagined her daughter in slippers and dressing gown, frowsy-haired and heavy-eyed.

Honor was too old to build a snowman, but perhaps they could go sledging together and have a snowball fight. Hot chocolate by the wood burner. Biscuits fresh from the oven, spiced with ginger and cinnamon. Watch a film, bundled under blankets.

A perfect kind of day.

She did not allow herself to dwell on the truth that reality rarely lived up to the fantasies of her imagination. Or that distractions were temporary. For a while, at least, she could pretend that Honor was still her sweet-faced girl and Shannon Carter nothing more than a smudged-out face from the past.

The heating was on but the air vibrated with cold. The snow on the trees was thick and ice-blue in the morning light. The village would hunker down today, trying to stay warm, wrapped in silence. That's why Catherine looked up, surprised, at the low thrum of an engine.

The car was inching up the lane. Given the weather, it was not a surprise to see the driver navigating with such care, but the vehicle – a blue Nissan Micra – was moving *too* slowly.

Catherine stood at the sink and watched as it drew level with her kitchen window.

Two figures were in the front seat and she didn't recognize either of them. The man at the wheel had flecks of grey in his beard and a bump on the bridge of his nose. His companion, a much younger man, leaned forward in the passenger seat and peered around him, straight at her. Wide, easy-to-smile mouth. A sweep of fringe. He said something to the driver and both men looked away, as if they were deliberately trying not to be noticed.

The engine revved once and the car swung away. This time, it moved too quickly and the wheels skidded on a patch of ice. Catherine pulled in a sharp breath but let it go when she saw the driver had regained control, and then the car was gone.

Peace settled over the street again. Somewhere in the distance, a chaffinch sang, the notes pure and loud in the frozen landscape. The episode had taken less than ninety seconds. If the car's tyres hadn't left parallel grooves in the snow as confirmation, it might never have happened at all.

# 9

The Justice Secretary slammed the door of the black Jaguar XJ and grunted his thanks to the driver. He was running late, and in a foul temper. He didn't want to do the interview – it was the job of his subordinate, the Prisons Minister, who'd rushed off to Liverpool because of a family bereavement – and he'd been strong-armed into it by the Number 10 press office.

'Prisoners are entitled to rehabilitation blah-blah-blah,' said Romily Dawson, a senior member of the communications team. 'It'll only be five minutes or so. You can do it with your eyes closed.' She'd crossed her arms, lips pursed. 'And it's good for your profile. Might tilt the tide of public opinion back in your favour.'

He'd raised his eyes skywards at the blatant manipulation, but a part of him knew she was right. His proposed hard-line reforms of the Prison Service had been met with a howl of outrage by those *Guardian*-reading purveyors of political correctness and, by Christ, they were legion, although not in his constituency, thankfully. Well, they would dance to a different tune if one of their daughters was raped and murdered. The world was changing and he didn't like it.

But he understood the need for moderation, or at least, the illusion of it.

The saloon pulled away from the icy kerb. For a moment, he envied the driver his freedom. Half an hour with a cup of tea and yesterday's *Evening Standard*. But he had a job to do today. An important one. *He* was important.

Geoffrey Heathcote, Member of Parliament, Secretary of State for Justice and Lord Chancellor, brushed a speck of lint from his suit and pushed open the doors of the BBC's Wogan House.

The interview had gone jolly well. The host of Radio 2's lunchtime news programme had allowed him to explain his point of view and chastised that lefty lunatic Carmina Amcott for her interruptions more than once. God knows which hole in the ground she'd crawled out of. Bloody rent-a-gob. At least he'd been articulate and well informed.

'Of course offenders, particularly juvenile ones, should be allowed an opportunity for rehabilitation,' he'd said. 'But we can't deny we're seeing increasing numbers of young people committing violent crimes. Take knife attacks. It's like a disease. We can't just ignore it. *That's* why we're introducing tougher sanctions within the prison system. Discipline and deterrents are important. We have to make sure young offenders don't *want* to find themselves back in our institutions, that they don't get too comfortable. Our role is to rehabilitate them so they can return to society as decent human—'

'But surely, Mr Heathcote, treating them as adults is not the answer,' she had shot back. 'Some of them are still children. Solitary confinement, inability to deal adequately with mental health issues, drug abuse, violence, neglect, loneliness, the list goes on. Don't you think the Prison Service should be tackling its inherent problems first? Or move towards a system of community-based care, tailored to the individual, so they can remain with their families or support networks like church or school?'

'But that's exactly what we are doing, Ms Amcott,' he'd said, smooth as a knife through butter. 'We want to steer the young people of this country on the right course. Everybody needs a second chance and that's what rehabilitation is. Repeat offenders are becoming a drain on the taxpayer. But we need to ensure the prospect of prison is a deterrent itself.'

He permitted himself a self-satisfied smile. Carmina Amcott had left the studio as soon as they had gone off-air. She was in a hurry, she'd insisted to the producer, but he suspected she hadn't enjoyed being bested on live radio in front of seven million listeners. As for him, he was happy to linger for a couple of minutes. He could relax now it was over.

The presenter – a decent chap he'd known since their days at Eton – put on 'Chain Gang' by Sam Cooke, took off his headphones and sipped his coffee.

'Bravo, Geoffrey. You came across as measured and reasonable.'

Heathcote grinned. 'Thanks for having me on the show. I rather enjoyed it.'

'Getting a bit of flak at the moment?'

The politician took a cloth from his pocket and polished his glasses. 'I'm used to it. Part of the job.'

'Tell me about it. Doesn't mean we have to like it, though.'

The show's producer directed the presenter towards the flurry of texts and emails that had begun to pour in during the music. The broadcaster scanned some of them.

'Lots of messages praising your stance.' He rubbed his eyes. 'And a few on the Carter case.' He winked at the producer. 'Maybe we should do an item on that. Fancy another go in the hot seat, Geoffrey?' He grinned at the MP to show he was joking and fiddled with a couple of switches on the broadcasting desk.

Heathcote hesitated. Like so many of his political colleagues, he was a bit of a peacock, tempted to show off his insider knowledge. But even he knew better than to share the information that had come his way a couple of hours ago. Because of the attention the Carter case was attracting, he'd been informed – confidentially, of course – that the notorious Angel of Death had been rehoused within his constituency, although not her precise location. It had come as a shock. While it was not unusual, as a Member of Parliament, to represent convicted criminals released from prison – they were entitled to the same rights as his other constituents and were allowed to vote, once they had served their sentence and re-registered – rarely were they as high-profile, and he had strong feelings on this particular case.

'It's a complex situation,' he eventually said.

'Do children who kill come under your rehabilitation programme?'

The MP shrugged. 'She's out of prison, isn't she? Living her life.'

'But does she deserve that? A chance at a decent life after what she did?'

Heathcote's stomach rumbled. He had forfeited breakfast for an early run, planning to grab something later, but then he'd been called into a meeting about recruitment issues within the judiciary. His thoughts strayed to lunch – Langan's, perhaps, or The Wolseley – and his ministerial hat slipped. He was chatting with an old friend and, still reeling from the information he'd received that morning, he forgot where he was and all the reasons he was supposed to keep his prejudices in check.

'Bring back the death penalty, I say. If a child is that evil, what are they going to be like as an adult? To tell you the truth,' he lowered his voice, as if confiding a secret, 'I don't think even years of rehabilitation could alter that innate instinct to kill.' He leaned back in the chair, satisfied at having a private outlet for an issue that had been bothering him since he became aware of ITV's *Angel of Death* documentary and now felt even more of a political – and personal – hot potato, enjoying the chance to posture and opine in intelligent company.

Through the glass, the studio manager was standing up and slicing one hand above the other in a vehement cutting motion.

The presenter put his headphones back on and listened.

His face paled. He glanced at the minister and pressed a finger to his lips. Then he pointed to the microphone on the desk in front of where Geoffrey Heathcote, Cabinet minister and high-profile member of Her Majesty's government, was seated.

A tiny light was on. His microphone was live and broadcasting to the nation.

# 10

The village is how I remember it, but different.

The Hope and Anchor stands on the green, as it always did. But now the faded sign that used to creak in the wind is freshly painted. Clean windows and glossy brickwork. Chalkboards promising expensive charcuterie and craft beers. A curl of smoke rises from the chimney and dissolves into the cold air.

I walked these streets as a child. I played on the green and spent my pocket money in the village shop. Picked apples from Mrs Guthrie's orchard and fed the horses who lived on the farm. Easter egg hunts and harvest festivals. Carol-singing on frosty days. A safe place to grow up. We rode our bikes everywhere, the Carter sisters and I. Until the murders, and then I stopped being a child and became a liar.

Saltbox Hill looms in the distance, the branches of the lone tree on its crest clutching at the sky. I wonder if scorch marks still scar the trunk. I wonder if lightning has ever struck there again.

Lawrie is already outside Hilltop House when I pull up. He's huddled with three or four rival reporters, comparing notes, exchanging information. It's a delicate dance. Don't give away too much, just enough to stay in the game when it counts.

My hands are shaking so I grip the steering wheel until they've steadied. Hilltop House may have a different name now but I can see through its windows and into the shadows of its past. It whispers and teases me. The sound of music. Laughing with the Carter sisters. Mrs Carter's lemon-scented candles. The heavy heat of hiding under the duvet with Shannon.

A bar of chocolate is on the passenger seat. I break off the first strip. Six squares. It sticks to my teeth and tongue. Rinse and repeat until half the bar is gone.

*Get out of the car, Brinley.*

I force myself to look at the house next door. *My house.* Once Mum had passed away, I couldn't bear to live there, the sense of loss pressing up against me, pinning me down until I could no longer breathe, the fresh, clean air of my childhood polluted by lies. In the space of six months, everything changed. My father became a stranger to me. My mother was dead. The girls next door were gone. And so was I.

Time has clouded the glass of my memories. It's been twenty-one years and I cannot summon the rise and fall of her voice, the pressure of her hand on mine. I remember her wedding ring, the scent of her perfume, the material parts that made her my mother. But the physical side – the softness of her body, the lilt of her laugh – are lost some-where down the years, faded from overuse, misshapen from being taken out and pored over.

My family home, on the other hand, hasn't changed at all.

Lawrie is walking towards me. I make myself open the car door, and offer him the bar of chocolate. It buys enough time to salve the burn of tears at the back of my throat.

'You made it.' He breaks off a couple of squares, but isn't smiling. Anxiety tugs at me.

'What's up?'

'The *Daily Mail* is on to something,' he says.

'How do you know?'

'They've come mob-handed, but only two of them are here. Which begs the question: where are the rest of them?'

He breaks off another piece of chocolate without asking. I like that about him. 'Fuck's sake,' he says, pushing it into his mouth. 'I bet they've got a brilliant lead elsewhere and they're chasing it up.'

'So how do you want to play this?' I wouldn't usually defer in this way, but Lawrie is the chief reporter. This is his circus. For now, anyway.

He checks his watch. 'I'm going to head to the school. See if I can talk to a receptionist or the headteacher, try and dig out some old photographs. They'll probably give me short shrift, but at least I'll be there when the school day ends and can chat to some of the parents.' The wind knifes at us both and he buttons up his coat. 'Why don't you try the houses up and down this road? See what they can tell us about the Carters. Knock at Hilltop. Find out what it's like to live at the scene of a brutal double murder.'

With that, he's gone.

I want to tell him I was a pupil at the school he is talking about. That I know what it's like to crawl through the broken glass of a shattered community. That walking up the path to Hilltop House is like walking in the blood-soaked footsteps of a ghost.

I *will* tell him.

But there are other demons to face first. Aunt Peg's voice fills my head, the mantra of my jumbled-up childhood. *Courage and caution, Brinley Ada Booth.* It's what she told me at my mother's funeral, a scarred shadow of the girl I was. It's what she told me when she drove me to her flat, and on my first day at a new school, and when I struggled to make friends, and when my father and Shannon stopped writing to me and I cried myself to sleep for weeks.

It's what she'd tell me now, standing at the garden gate of the place I used to call home.

The paintwork is the same colour, a pale blue wash. The door is black and a plastic holly wreath is tied to the brass knocker with a red ribbon. For a moment, my heart stutters, uncertain. On the first day of December, my mother used to hang an identical one. But she is earth and dust. I saw what death did to her, the waxy sheen to her skin, the open hinge of her mouth, a glimpse of tongue.

The bell's tone follows the same rise and fall as our old bell. It *is* our old bell, I realize. A part of me thinks about turning back, but it's too late because a shadow fills the glass, and I touch the notepad in my pocket to remind myself why I'm here, and the door opens.

A woman is standing there. Late fifties. Greying curly hair and an oversized checked shirt. I don't recognize her, but it's clear from her expression she knows who I am.

'Malcolm,' she says, throwing a glance behind her. She repeats it, threading his name with urgency. '*Malcolm.*'

'My name's Brinley Booth and I'm from the *Daily*—'

'I know who you are.' The woman glances down the hallway again, and it's clear she's uncomfortable, willing Malcolm to appear. One hand rests on the door, as if she's planning to shut it in my face.

This is the part of the job I hate most. I paste on a friendly, approachable smile and plunge on with my spiel. 'I'm writing a piece on the Hilltop House murd—'

'Malcolm!' She barks out the name again, and it snags on my memories, like cloth on barbed wire. I don't know why it didn't occur to me before, standing here in the bitter December cold, or during all the years that have passed, but now it's as clear as the scar on my back.

'You're Maureen, aren't you?'

She doesn't answer because a man has appeared next to her. He's white-haired, with a face that looks like a crumpled-up paper bag. He smells of Brylcreem. There's a nick on his jaw, crusted and dark, and I know it's because he uses an old-fashioned horsehair shaving brush, foam and a cut-throat razor.

'Hello, Dad,' I say.

*Thank you for your kindness. I don't talk about it much – the memories are too painful – but perhaps we can share our stories when we know each other a little better. I don't have many friends. Friends can make you vulnerable. But I like talking to you, Hero.*

*And how about you? Who are the most important people in your life? What you said about the lack of family resonated with me. It's a certain type of loneliness, isn't it? Let's face it, blood ties are stronger, they bind us together in ways that friendship can't. What about your mother? Are you close?*

# 11

'Why don't we have any photographs of Granny and Grandpa?'

Catherine was rolling out gingerbread dough at the kitchen island and Honor was sitting opposite her, watching. There was no escape. She willed herself to appear calm and breathed through her nose to fight the nausea that overwhelmed her whenever her daughter asked difficult questions.

'They were destroyed in the fire.' She handed Honor the pastry cutter and busied herself with shaking currants from the bag. 'Don't forget to press down hard.'

'Doesn't anyone else in your family have pictures of them?'

'Goodness, I don't remember. It was so long ago.'

'Why don't you ask them?' Honor placed the first gingerbread man on the baking tray. 'Or I could ask them for you, if you like.' She wrinkled her nose, as if puzzling something out. 'Mum, why don't we have any contact with your family?'

Catherine cut out another biscuit and peeled the dough from the floury work surface.

'Life can be complicated, sweetheart.'

'Could I see them? If I wanted to, I mean.'

Catherine did not know how to answer that question. The hole she had dug for herself was so deep she could never climb out of it without being buried under its collapsing walls.

She was rescued – temporarily, at least – by the ringing of her mobile. *Eliza* flashed up on the screen. It didn't surprise her. They didn't speak as often these days, but her timing, as always, was impeccable. She must have seen the documentary trailers.

'I was just calling to see how you are.' The voice at the end of the line was warm and unexpectedly welcome.

'I'm fine.'

'Sure?'

'I think so.'

Honor was pushing currant eyes into rolled-out dough and singing Christmas songs, and she angled herself away from her daughter, pressing the receiver closer to her ear so she could hear what was being suggested.

'Shall we meet for a coffee sometime this week? It would be good to catch up.'

A salty wash of tears filled her eyes. Eliza Sheen was one of only a handful of people who knew the truth about her horrific past. She had been a part of Catherine's life for so long now, since it had happened, and she had never judged, not even when Catherine had judged herself.

They agreed a date and time, and talked for a couple of minutes about the weather and the madness of Christmas before ringing off. Banal, but comforting.

When she turned around, Honor was cutting out more shapes, absorbed in her task. Secondary school had rubbed the softness from her, and in the last few months, she had shed the tender skin of childhood to reveal the hardened shell of adolescence. Rudeness. Mood swings and acne. A loss of interest in Guides and piano. Slicking on lip gloss and pouting into the camera. Periods and bras, Snapchat and secrets.

But every now and then, Catherine glimpsed the eight-year-old who had drawn and coloured careful pictures of elephants, or the ten-year-old who still held her hand, or the generous heart of the twelve-year-old who was raising money for a girl on her football team diagnosed with pancreato-blastoma, a rare childhood cancer.

Honor was using a small paring knife to carve holly leaves and bells with the leftover dough, and something about the sight of the blade glinting in the kitchen light, moving between small fingers, made Catherine's knees loosen.

She steadied herself against the worktop and tried not to think of her sister, but Honor's blonde hair, the intelligence in her eyes, even the graceful way that she walked, was a living reminder.

The room filled with the scent of heat and spices.

When the biscuits had cooled, Honor decorated three of them with their initials. H for Honor. D for Dad. M for Mum. Such careful lettering. Beautiful. A trio of gingerbread figures lined up in a row, their hands touching like paper dolls.

Her own little family. All Catherine had ever wanted.

But later, when she went to make a cup of tea and put them on a plate, she couldn't help but notice her own biscuit had cracked in two, an uneven fracture through its heart.

# 12

The Right Honourable Geoffrey Heathcote could feel his mobile phone vibrating in his pocket. He slid it out and swore under his breath. Eighteen missed calls, several from lobby journalists.

He sank lower into the back seat of his ministerial car and closed his eyes.

As soon as he'd realized the microphone was live, the Justice Secretary knew it was bad. But he would have to wait a few days to find out exactly how bad. If it was a quiet news day, he was in the shit.

A part of him wondered whether his old school friend had done it on purpose, as a way of boosting ratings for his radio show. Now he actually thought about it, they had never been that close. In fact, Heathcote vaguely remembered taking a swing at him during the traditional initiation into their House during the broadcaster's first week at Eton. But even if it had been deliberate, the damage was done. This was every politician's worst nightmare: throwaway comments made when he'd believed himself off-air, exposing him as a liar and a hypocrite.

In the front seat, John, the driver, discreetly turned off the radio.

'Where to, Mr Heathcote?'

'Westminster.' There was no point in burying his head in the sand. He would have to ride it out. Perhaps he could pass it off as a tasteless joke. Romily Dawson would have to handle it. It was her fault he'd agreed to the fucking interview in the first place.

He called his wife and warned her to expect a bumpy twenty-four hours. Heathcote was not some wet-behind-the-ears politics graduate. He understood he was at the mercy of the news agenda, that events could escalate beyond his control or defuse, like smoke. Breaking stories were like jigsaw puzzles. If all the pieces slotted into place, the resulting bigger picture led to widespread coverage. If there were gaps that couldn't be filled, the same stories were quickly forgotten. All he had to do now was hold steady, keep quiet and not make things worse. With a bit of luck, the whole mess would blow over by tomorrow night.

# 13

'Christ alive, Brinley, what the hell happened to you?'

He looks me up and down as if I'm nothing but the sum of my body, as if I haven't sweetened the bitterness of his absence in the only way I know how, drowning in secret wrappers and too much sugar. As if he hadn't buggered off two decades ago when I needed him most.

'Still the same old Dad,' I say.

He has the grace to look sheepish.

There are so many questions I want to ask him, like why are they living in our house when I thought he'd sold it years ago and moved to Spain, and where is the rest of my mother's jewellery, and why hasn't he been in touch?

But I don't say any of it. Because I look at the arms I'd remembered as muscular and strong, and see that they are withered. I notice the way his mouth turns downwards, and the reek of discontent, and realize I don't feel a thing. All I can think of is Aunt Peg, stroking my hair as I cried for my mother, helping me with my homework and cooking stew and dumplings from scratch.

'So what brings you home after all this time?' he says, lounging against the door frame, his arm bent at the elbow and resting above his head. Maureen has slipped away and it's just him and me.

'This isn't home, Dad. It's a place I used to live.'

'Still as tetchy as ever, I see. Some things never change.'

Less than a minute to slip into the familiar groove of our relationship, rusty from disuse but still well worn. I turn to leave, exhausted by the emotion of seeing him again, but he calls out before I reach the end of the garden path.

'Actually, I *am* interested, Brin. Seriously. Why have you come back?'

Part of me wants to keep going, to put as much distance between us as possible, but curiosity is pulling at my strings too, and so I turn and walk back to him.

'I'm a journalist now. On a story.'

He jerks his head in the direction of Hilltop House. 'Next door?'

'One and the same.'

'I remember that little bitch. I never trusted her. I liked the other one, though. Quiet, mind. Wouldn't say boo to a goose.'

'Do you remember much about that night?'

'Your mother was dying, I remember that.'

He looks a bit misty-eyed so I nip that in the bud. 'Yes, while you were getting your end away with Maureen Connolly.'

But he doesn't rise to it. And I suppose I'm glad they're still together and he didn't throw away his marriage for nothing.

'She couldn't get comfortable so the nurse gave her morphine. Eventually, she fell asleep. She looked just like she did when I met her.' His face relaxes, as if he's stepped back into the memory and he's buying her that first gin and tonic at the Hope and Anchor. 'I sat by her bed all night. We knew the end was coming.' He sighs, soft with sadness. 'About six in the morning, I heard the sound of the sirens. It wasn't light yet, but they were so close. When I saw how many ambulances there were, I knew something terrible had happened.'

What my father does not say is that he was drunk and careless, and by early afternoon, when the bodies of Dr and Mrs Carter were brought out of Hilltop House, my mother had been dead for several hours too.

'And then what?'

His eyes are glassy from peering down the long tunnel of shared history. 'I saw them bring out that little girl. The blood on her pyjamas. She was crying, but when she saw me looking out of the window, she smiled at me.' He shakes his head, disbelieving. 'She *smiled*.'

I take out my notebook and pen, but when I start to write, my father interrupts, and says, with his customary bluntness, 'What are you doing? Don't write it down, for God's sake. I don't want to be in the newspaper.'

Sighing, I slip the pad into my pocket. This is not an infrequent occurrence. Some people are happy to be photographed and quoted, a flirtation with fame, an injection to the ego. For others, it's a terrifying prospect, committing one's name to the starkness of newsprint, running the gauntlet of spiteful below-the-line comments from online readers.

It's cold on the doorstep. A light snow is falling, landing on my coat and scarf. The idea of driving home to London in this weather fills me with dread. My father lifts his eyes to the pale grey skies. There's a gruffness in his voice.

'Look, why don't you come in for a minute?'

I'm not sure how I feel about his invitation, but then he says, 'I've got something that belongs to you,' and the decision is made.

Being inside the house is like walking hand in hand with my past.

The carpet is the same ugly swirl of colour. The mahogany telephone table still stands in the hallway, next to a matching stool with claw feet. Even the smell hasn't changed.

Homesickness, intense and sudden, squeezes my heart. As the years have passed, the hole left by my mother's death has closed up. Not completely. Never that. But it's no longer the raw, bloody mess it once was. Standing here, in the home we shared together, the wound splits open again. An urge to hear my mother's voice; to feel the press of her hand on my shoulder; to dance and sing and laugh together overwhelms me, but she's not here, and it's as if I'm realizing it for the first time. A pain in my chest burns like a lightning strike.

'Make sure you take your shoes off,' my father says.

Maureen brings tea and a tentative smile, but she doesn't stay, hovering in the sitting room for a minute, then disappearing when my father jerks his head at her. 'Hop it, Mo. There's a love.'

He heaps three sugars into his tea and does the same for me, even though I stopped taking sugar years ago, which is ironic when you think about it.

'I'll be back in a minute. Stay there.'

*Where else am I going to go?* But in the interests of keeping the peace, I stop myself from saying it out loud.

When he comes back, he's carrying a box of oddments. Old photographs, school reports, diaries, ticket stubs, handwritten letters. He thrusts them at me. 'I thought you might like these.'

Childhood treasures. Familiar still, even though it's years since I've seen them. I glimpse a ticket to *Cinderella* at the Albany Theatre. My mother took me when I was eight or nine. A postcard I bought during a holiday in Cornwall. The uneven rectangle of my grandmother's death notice, cut out from the newspaper. But I make myself stop. If I wait until I get back to Aunt Peg's, I can pore over these forgotten gifts one at a time, savouring the memories.

We drink our tea. We don't talk, but then we never did. I don't need to look at my watch to know it's time to leave.

'Is it all right – I mean, can I use the toilet?'

'Upstairs,' he says.

I remember, but I don't say so. Memories nudge me with their sharp elbows, and I need to get out now, to breathe the clean air of my future, not the stale odour of my past.

The carpet on the upstairs landing is cream and thick. I don't recognize it. Wedding pictures of Maureen and my father line the walls, but there's none of me or my mother. A bedroom door is ajar and I glimpse a flowery bedspread and silk cushions.

The door to my old bedroom is shut.

A telephone – the landline – rings. 'Can you get that, love? I'm making pastry and my hands are dirty,' calls Maureen from the kitchen, and I hear my father shuffle into the hall to answer it, the rumble of his voice.

From the top of the stairs. I can see the rounded ends

of his slippers. He's sitting down. My sense of curiosity – a blessing and a curse – starts to smoulder, and before I can change my mind, I push open the door to my childhood.

Except it's not my bedroom anymore. This doesn't come as a surprise. Aunt Peg always said he let me down quicker than a puncture.

There's a sofa, and a potted plant and desk with a computer. A waste paper basket. A lamp. My bedroom is now an office and there's not a single trace of me. I suppose I should feel sad, but I don't. My father is not a part of my life, and it's clear I'm no longer a part of his. All those years wondering whether he missed me, and the answer is here in a few paper clips and some box files.

The only thing that hasn't changed is the door embedded in the opposite wall.

We used to play in there, the Carter sisters and I. It was larger than a cupboard, but not as big as an extra room. My winter clothes were stored there, and the family suitcases. We called it our den.

Our hiding place.

A light sweat stipples my forehead. I hold myself still and listen. My father is still talking, and without thinking, I cross the room in three strides. I remember how the door sticks, and the need to brace one hand against the wall while tugging gently to soften its opening grunt.

I step inside.

I'm back to being twelve. The smell of moth balls and hand-stitched lavender bags. Unpainted walls. Off-cuts of old carpet on the floor. Unlit and musty, it hasn't changed at all. Except now I have to stoop and the room feels much smaller.

The ghosts of the past come out to say hello. Three little girls, playing Murder in the Dark.

Barely aware of what I'm doing, I feel my way along the plaster to an alcove with its dusty shelves, tucked behind a half-partition wall. I run my hand along the top shelf. In my damaged skin, I can feel it, that itch of memory. My fingers close around a slim notebook that has been lying undisturbed for twenty-one years. I put it in my pocket.

My father is still on the telephone when I make my way downstairs.

The street is frozen into stillness. No dog walkers or children or cats on the prowl. It's too cold even for that. A brief goodbye to my father and I doubt I'll ever see him again. I hesitate, unsure where to try next. But then I see Lawrie barrelling down the road towards me. His cheeks are pink and he's talking to someone on the phone.

'Come on, mate. You owe me.'

A pause.

'A name. Just a name. I'll do the rest.' Silence. 'No one will know it's come from you.'

Another pause.

'A grand. Can't go any higher than that.' He nods. 'Cash. I'll keep it off the system. Don't want to find ourselves in court.' He laughs and winks at me, then puts his finger to his lips. His contact is talking, and Lawrie's gone quiet, chewing his thumbnail. Then he's nodding again. 'As quick as you can, mate. It's urgent.'

He hangs up, grinning at me. 'The shit's hit the fan. Geoffrey Heathcote dropped a bollock on Radio 2. The editor hates Heathcote's guts so tomorrow's splash is sorted. But he wants us to stay here tonight, see what else we can turn up on the Carter sisters.'

I take a deep breath. It's time.

'I might be able to help you with that.'

# 14

Edward was ignoring her.

At first, she thought she was imagining it. But when she knocked on the study door and carried through his coffee and one of Honor's biscuits, she caught him shutting down the news website he'd been reading on his computer and pretending to be on the telephone. He would not meet her eyes.

She placed the mug on a coaster. Their wedding album had been removed from its drawer and lay open on a photograph of the two of them at their engagement party, as if someone had been poring over it. The knot in her stomach tightened. She looked so young. Vulnerable, even. Her hair was much lighter and she was too thin. Her resemblance to Shannon was striking. It gave her a jolt to remember herself like that.

Had Edward been looking at those pictures? Or Honor, perhaps. And if so, why? With the Hilltop House murders back in the news, it felt too uncomfortably close to home to be coincidence. Was it possible her husband had overheard her telephone conversation with Eliza, her only real connection to the past? But surely he would have spoken up if he'd had the slightest inkling who she was.

Either way, her likeness to her older sister upset her,

even if it hadn't survived into their thirties. When the snow had cleared and she was alone, she would get rid of that photograph. *All* the wedding photographs, if necessary. She smoothed out the tissue paper, shut the album carefully and left without a word.

The rest of the afternoon crawled by. Honor had shut herself away in her bedroom. 'Homework, Mum.' Edward had not come out of the study. Catherine sat alone in the sitting room, watching the sky darken and the snow fall, butterflies brushing their wings against her insides. Unsettled. That was the word. As if her life was a pool of water and its surface had been disturbed.

As a general rule, she didn't watch television during the day, but this was not an ordinary day. The snow lay thickly across the garden. Winter was everywhere, the air taut with it. She could taste it when she opened the back door to throw crumbs to the birds, and smell it in the woodsmoke, and feel it in the tiled floor of their north-facing kitchen. And she was in need of distraction.

An auction of antiques and collectibles. A teatime quiz show. The opening beats of the BBC's *News at Six*.

Her hand hovered over the remote control. She should change the channel. But a masochistic need compelled her to watch on.

The slaughter of her parents had graduated into the lead news item of the day.

A man who seemed familiar was walking briskly along the pavement of a smart London street, a look of concentrated nonchalance on his face. He held a briefcase in one hand and snowflakes were settling on the shoulders of his double-breasted woollen overcoat.

Camera crews and journalists surged towards him in a fluid pack, shouting questions, demanding answers.

'Mr Heathcote, do you really believe the Angel of Death should have been hanged?'

'What do you say to accusations of hypocrisy, Lord Chancellor?'

'Are you planning to resign, Justice Secretary?'

The man – she recognized him now as the government minister in charge of prisons – turned to face the media scrum gathered at his garden gate. He spoke with a plum in his mouth. 'I have nothing to say at the present time. If that changes, you'll be the first to know.' A pause. 'Probably before I do.' The journalists laughed.

The VT cut away to a colour photograph Catherine had never seen before, pulling a gasp from her. Her fingers flew to her lips.

Catherine and her sister, Shannon, swinging on a hammock in the garden at Hilltop House. Six and eight years old. Blonde-haired, blue-eyed moppets.

Someone with intimate access to the family must have given it to a BBC journalist, although she could not remember who had taken the picture or why they would have done such a thing. The betrayal made her skin crawl.

A thrum of anger at her sister. Why on earth was she giving interviews, putting their tragedy back into the public domain? Once she had loved Shannon so much she would have died for her. But the past had no place in the present. Catherine's life had moved on.

She switched off the television, blood singing in her veins. Her hands were shaking and she was grateful for the dark veil of evening that shrouded the room. She breathed in through her nose and repeated to herself the advice her counsellor had given her. *Small steps, Catherine. One foot in front of the other.*

When the heat in her cheeks had cooled and she had regained control of her emotions, Catherine shut the door and walked quietly upstairs.

In the bathroom, she glanced at herself in the mirror. She looked old. A beaten-down mess. Untidy eyebrows. Patchy dry skin. Broken fingernails. Strands of blonde-grey pushing up through her roots. Her hair needed dyeing again.

She set to work with her tweezers. Moisturized her skin. Filed and shaped her nails. Ran warm water over her hair, working in the brown dye until she was back to her best self again.

Then she pasted on a smile and went downstairs to try and mend her family.

# 15

The pub restaurant is empty except for the handful of photographers and journalists sitting at the table, drinking wine.

And vodka and beer and whisky and rum.

The reporter from the *Sun* swallows his last forkful of steak, pushes his empty plate away from him and downs the rest of his pint. He's using a cocktail stick to free a fibre of meat from the gap between his teeth, and then he checks his watch and says, 'First editions will be dropping soon.'

From the smirk on his face, it's obvious he has a great story. We'll know soon enough. If we've missed something we shouldn't have, the night editor will call us when tomorrow's newspapers land at around 10.30 p.m. My stomach twists into a knot.

The Hope and Anchor is surprisingly upmarket these days. Warm sandstone, flickering candles and fresh holly and ivy garlands strung across the fireplace. Lawrie insisted on rooms for us both – and our photographer, Garth – because it's where the rest of the Fleet Street pack is staying. Alliances are formed, not by pounding pavements and 5 a.m.

doorsteps, but over a drink and a war story or two. Between us, we've filled every room.

But the luxurious carpets, expensive dinners and super-king-size beds come at a price – the pressure for an exclusive angle is intense.

As I swallow the dregs of my bottle of beer, I spot faces from *The Times* and the *Daily Telegraph*. A man from the *Daily Express* is smoking a cigarette outside.

The Press Association journalist is talking about going clubbing in the next town. She's young and drunk, and keeps putting her hand on Lawrie's leg. I want to tell her to fuck off, but she's oblivious, flicking her long hair over her shoulder and laughing too loudly.

'Do you want some coke?' she says.

'I don't like fizzy drinks,' I say, deadpan.

She nudges Lawrie and grins. He doesn't grin back. 'Brinley, you're so sweet,' she says. Patronizing cow. I despise being called sweet. Not much of a cocaine fan either.

Lawrie's mobile is ringing. Our eyes meet. 'Shit,' he says.

He gets up from the table and huddles in the corner, away from the pack. The conversation is short and to the point. When he comes back, he shows me an image on the screen of his phone.

The reporter from the *Sun* – I think his name is Russell Parker – leans over my shoulder, admiring his front-page exclusive, a satisfied grin on his face. If I remember correctly, his nickname's The Undertaker because he always wears black and often shows up at murder scenes.

'Looks good, doesn't it?'

'You kept that to yourself,' says Lawrie, shoulders squared, clearly annoyed.

Russell punches him lightly on the shoulder. 'All's fair in love and newspapers. You know the drill. Anyway, in the interests of transparency, it came from a tip-off to the news desk. I only followed it up.'

Even I can tell he's lying, not wanting to lose ground with the rest of the press pack, who might decide to cut him loose for failing to give the rest of us a heads-up.

'Sorry if I've landed you in the shit, mate.' Russell pats Lawrie on the back, conciliatory. 'Won't happen again.'

No, it won't. Because journalists can only get away with stitching up their colleagues once. No one will trust him now.

Even so, the story in the *Sun* is a good one. They've tracked down Pamela Carter's elderly mother. An exclusive interview and never-before-published photographs of the family. The headline is in bold and reads, **I'D HANG HER TOO**, a reference to the Justice Secretary's faux pas. I start to read the story. Second paragraph:

> She might be my granddaughter but she deserves to die for what she did.

Strong, emotive words, propelling the national conversation onwards. It makes our splash calling for Heathcote's resignation seem weak and out of date.

I make my way to the bar for another round of drinks, wondering if Maureen Connolly still works here, but there's no sign of her. It's more crowded now, women in sparkly dresses and overstuffed men in suits, a rowdy sales team spilling out of their Christmas get-together.

One of them – a younger man, all slicked-back hair and

attitude – stumbles drunkenly into my shoulder, knocking me off balance and making me drop my purse.

'Be careful,' I say.

'Someone pushed me,' he says, leaning against the bar. His eyes are unfocused but he looks me up and down, and a sneer distorts his face. 'I wouldn't touch you by *choice*.'

Although I'm used to the disdain of strangers, especially men, each word is a barb, scratching the thin membrane of my confidence. My instinct is to hide away, to shield myself from his aggressive posturing, but instead I say, 'That's not necessary.'

And then he's in my face, pushing his breath into mine. 'Yes. It is. Fat bitch.'

Before I have a chance to react, Lawrie and the *Daily Telegraph* reporter are by my side, warning him to back off. The man puffs out his chest, as if he's considering taking them both on, but then raises his palms in submission and walks off. I flick two fingers at his retreating back.

I order our drinks and Lawrie carries them back to the table. It's just the two of us now. The other reporters are deep in conversation. One or two have slipped off to bed, ready for tomorrow's early start.

Lawrie hands me my beer and sits down next to me. 'We have to tell Colin about your connection to the Carter sisters.'

'What? No, we can't.' My words are a hiss. 'I told you that in confidence.'

'Come on, Brin.' He leans into me, a gentle nudge. 'You must see what an amazing story it is. It would do wonders for your profile. Name in lights, and all that.'

How can I explain that I don't want a profile? I've never

been the sort of journalist who hankers after fame. I like people and their stories. Nothing more, nothing less.

Lawrie's eyes are brown and flecked with gold. His leg is touching mine. It's distracting. 'We're in the shit,' he says. 'We haven't got anything else.'

There it is. In a nutshell.

'I'll think about it,' I say.


In my hotel room, I unpack my overnight bag, change into my pyjamas and sit on the edge of the bed.

Only then do I allow myself to examine the notebook I'd retrieved from the bedroom of my childhood home.

It's been twenty-one years since I've seen it. Twenty-one years since Shannon Carter pressed it upon me during that confusing, bloodstained night. *Be careful, Brin. Put it in a place no one will find it.*

And no one did. The journal is bound in cheap gold-coloured cloth. A peeling strawberry sticker clings to the outside, tacky with old glue. Clumps of dust line the papery groove that runs between its fabric covers. On the back is a smudged handprint, a rusty stain. Stored in a cool, dry room and out of direct sunlight, time has hardly left its mark.

This is evidence. I broke the law. Perverted the course of justice. Lied and lied again. Even though I was twelve, I understood what I was doing was wrong. That knowledge has haunted me ever since, casting its long shadow across my life.

In the quiet of the hotel room, there's a rising fug of mustiness and something oddly sweet. I lift the notebook to my nose and catch the faintest strawberry scent from the sticker. Even after all these years, its perfume has endured.

I open it.

And I'm back there, back to being a girl on the brink of adolescence. Back to scribbling song lyrics and secret messages and love notes to boys we mooned over but never spoke to. Back to witnessing things no twelve-year-old should.

Scrawled inside the cover in untidy handwriting are these words: *This book belongs to S. Carter.* Through the corridor of years, the past reaches out and touches me.

I turn to the first page.

It's a child's pencil drawing, surprisingly accomplished. The graphite has smudged, but the knife still curves. Its blade, shaded into steel, is crowned with drops of blood, coloured in with red felt-tip pen. A single line is written beneath it.

*Tonight I'm going to kill my mother and father.*

# 16

## Wednesday, 12 December 2018

On his penultimate day in government, Geoffrey Heathcote ate two boiled eggs and a kipper, more of a Last Breakfast than a Last Supper.

He wore his favourite tie – blue with yellow spots – and kissed his wife on the cheek. She was peering through a slat in the shutters of their multi-million-pound Mayfair residence. 'They're still out there.'

'It's tomorrow's fish and chip paper,' he said, with a dismissive wave of his hand. 'It will all be forgotten by next week.'

His wife was hopeful. Barbara Heathcote enjoyed the status that came with being a Cabinet minister's wife. She wasn't ready to relinquish it yet. 'Don't let them pressure you into resigning,' she said. 'We all make mistakes. You can ride this out.'

He kissed his wife on the forehead. 'I can,' he said. 'I will.'

By lunchtime, his confidence was beginning to falter. His slip-up had been dissected on ITV's *Good Morning Britain*,

LBC, BBC Radio 4, *Loose Women* and in the offices of *Private Eye*.

It was on the front page of most of the tabloids and all of the broadsheets. A cartoonist had sketched him in a noose with the caption *Heathcote commits political suicide*. Poor taste, perhaps, but the artwork was trending on social media. A producer from *Newsnight* had invited him onto that evening's show.

Romily Dawson from the communications team was now sitting opposite him in his Westminster office, drafting a statement.

'We'll keep it short and to the point. Apologize for your remarks, explain you were being flippant and reiterate your desire to get on with the job, citing the rehabilitation of prisoners as your priority. Yes?'

The Justice Secretary wasn't the sort of man who believed in apologies. 'Can't you just make it' – he flapped an impatient hand – 'go away?'

Romily stopped typing and raised one perfectly shaped eyebrow. 'You know better than that.'

'But don't you think it will blow itself out? There'll be a bigger story along soon enough. What about the weather? Or Brexit? Or the fucking Prime Minister?'

'You *are* the bigger story, Geoffrey.' Romily's phone pinged and she glanced at it. 'The *Guardian*. Another interview request. I think it's best you keep a low profile for now. We'll release this statement in a couple of hours, in time for the evening bulletins. Let's hope it snows heavily overnight. Snowmageddon might knock you off the front pages.'

Romily Dawson had handled – with an enviably cool head – leadership challenges, sex scandals, the furore over parliamentary expenses and perjuring MPs. She knew the interest in the minister would fade as the news agenda moved on. It was inevitable. But it was also a balancing act. Heathcote was at the mercy of a capricious media. She would do what she could to head off a crisis, but the story could blow up into something bigger, rumbling on for days. If the headlines became too damaging, he would have to resign.

Geoffrey Heathcote, who had survived seven years as an MP without a whiff of impropriety, had seen Cabinet colleagues caught in the eye of a political storm. He, too, understood it was simply a question of crossing his fingers and holding his nerve.

But some news events cannot be predicted. The timing of the ITV documentary coupled with Heathcote's radio gaffe was about to trigger a chain reaction of events that neither of them could possibly have foreseen. For all their experience, they had both underestimated the tenacity of journalists and their nose for a story.

Especially when that story featured a dishonourable politician and a poppet dubbed the Angel of Death, whose act of parricide was as embedded in the nation's psyche as the scissor blade in Dr Carter's neck.

*I'm so sorry to hear about your loss. It must have been awful. Perhaps now is the time to share something deeply personal with you. I don't tell many people this. My mother died in a terrible tragedy. It destroyed my family. We never recovered from it. At times, I feel lonely for the me of the past, but I have learned to exist alongside the pain.*

*I know exactly what you mean. Some days, I am so full of questions, I think I might go slightly mad from it all. Like you, there's no one in my life who understands what it is to be me. No one to talk to about all these feelings that have nowhere to go. How strange there are so many similarities between us.*

# 17

Early afternoon, and I'm in my room at the Hope and Anchor, laptop open, stomach tying itself into knots.

Lawrie is keeping the rest of the press pack on side and distracted while I finish writing tomorrow's exclusive splash.

The newspaper is using my first-hand account of the night of the murders and a photograph of me with both Carter sisters. I haven't mentioned the notebook to Lawrie yet. I'm still processing what it might mean.

Garth, the photographer, has taken some shots of me outside Hilltop House. I told him I didn't want my picture in the paper, but Colin got on the phone and said he'd spoken to the editor about a pay rise, and perhaps it was time for me to have more responsibility, and how he was so proud of how I'd come through. Even though I knew I was being manipulated, I couldn't handle the pressure of refusing, and so I said, 'No, it's fine.' Tomorrow I'll be on the front page of a newspaper that nearly a million people read.

I spellcheck my story, add Lawrie's byline to a piece I've written about the timeline of events on Saturday, 19 April 1997 – we're a team, after all – and press send.

Then I go downstairs for a drink.

The pub smells of spilled beer and woodsmoke. A fire burns in the grate, and snow has started to fall again. An old man with a scarf and flat cap sips his pint. It's warm and I yawn, overcome by an urge to close my eyes and drift off. Sleep proved elusive last night. The bed was comfortable, but I stayed awake, blinking into darkness, watching morning colour in the sky.

I tried so hard to forget what I knew. For years, I carried the scars of our estrangement, deeply hurt that, in spite of everything, it was Shannon who cut all contact with me. As I grew older, I distanced myself from other girls, never quite trusting the fool's gold of friendship. I told myself I was a child, misremembering the truth of that night. We all have a past and this was mine. Put it away. Don't think about it.

But now I'm back in the place that has haunted the hollows of my life and the ghosts of my childhood walk alongside me, murmuring in my ear.

When tomorrow's edition hits the news stands, I'll be the story too.

Ten minutes later, when I'm sipping soda water flavoured with too much lime, Lawrie appears in the pub. He's on the telephone again, and his face is radiant, like the sun is rising in it.

He catches my eye and gives me a thumbs up. While I wait for him to finish, I text Aunt Peg and tell her I miss her. *Courage and caution, Brinley Ada Booth*. That's what she'd say if she was here. Except this time I've thrown caution to the wind and I don't feel brave at all.

I'm expecting Lawrie to say I've done a great job, that Colin is cock-a-hoop at my copy, and already I'm smiling inside because a perverse part of me *wants* to impress them, but instead he finishes his call, slams the table with his hand and says, 'Yes!

'You have checked out of the hotel, haven't you?' He's not looking at me when he says this, his fingers flying over the touchscreen of his phone.

'I've just done it. My bag's in the car. Why? What's going on?'

Lawrie looks around to make sure none of the other journalists are in the pub and leans in, his mouth close to my ear. 'Drink up. My police contact has come through.'

I stare at him, not certain what he's driving at.

He gestures at me to hurry up. 'But we need to get a move on. I think the *Daily Mail* is on to it too.'

'On to what?'

He grins, suddenly wolfish. 'I've only got a bloody address.'

The penny drops with a loud clunk. 'For Shannon Carter?'

But the energy coming off him tells me I'm wrong, and now I understand why Lawrie Hudson is chief reporter. His police contact – cultivated over months and years of pints down the pub and rounds of golf – has slipped him the information every major news organization has been chasing down since the Justice Secretary's balls-up on national radio. This is potentially career-making. For both of us.

'Even better than that.' He glances at the clock above the bar and I can tell he's impatient to leave. 'We're going to have ourselves a little road trip to Essex. Pay a visit to the other Carter sister.' He consults his notepad, a look of triumph on his face. 'She's called Catherine Allen now.'

*Thank you for replying so quickly. Things are difficult right now. It was a comfort to wake in the night and see your message waiting for me. It feels like we are friends, even though we have never met. I wonder if we will one day?*

# 18

The sky was darkening, and when Catherine breathed in the cold air, it made her chest hurt.

The wood basket was empty again but Edward had gone out without saying goodbye, slamming the front door behind him, so Catherine slithered down the icy path alone to retrieve more logs.

She stood in the front garden, silence filling up her heart and her lungs. Bushes and branches and wooden furniture were obscured by a thick, white covering. The smell of winter was everywhere, sharp and clean. It lent a clarity to her thinking.

Something was wrong with her husband.

A flock of birds spread their wings against the bruised clouds, their silhouettes rending the sky. It made her think of someone taking a knife to her life, tiny nicks here and there until only a gaping hole was left.

She and Edward had exchanged approximately thirty-five words all day, and only by chance. She'd been in the hallway, dusting, when he'd emerged from the study to go to the toilet.

Catherine (friendly): 'Hello, love. How are you getting on?'

Edward (brusque): 'Do we have any milk?'

Catherine (taken aback): 'Loads. I bought some earlier because of the forecast.'

Edward (abrupt): 'I think we need more. I'll go and get some in a bit.'

This was not the Edward she knew. Her Edward was warm and engaged, a family man. Full of jokes and laughter and proclamations of love. A planner of adventures, a scaler of challenges, brimming with dynamism and the unbridled joy of being alive. A man filled with empathy and generosity, of not following the crowd, but choosing his own path. A man comfortable in his skin.

The first time he offered to cook for her, he sent an email asking for a list of her favourite foods. When she arrived at his house, he had filled his fridge with her most decadent choices. Throughout their twelve-year marriage, he'd often bought her books he thought she might enjoy, or a portion of tiramisu from the Italian deli near his office, or a tub of fat olives or expensive red wine. Postcards and unusual artwork, and once, a vintage record player with a box full of seven-inch singles. But for the last few days, he'd spoken to her in a mechanical fashion, stripped of emotion.

Perhaps the pressure of work was getting to him. For all his affability, he was not one to discuss what was bothering him, preferring to work through any issues on his own and waiting until he was sure about his facts. Maybe he was concerned about money. She hadn't had a chance to tell him yet, but she'd made a substantial amount at the kitchen table that morning, selling some shares. Christmas was an expensive time of year. The news might lighten his load.

But, in truth, there was no need for Edward to leave the house that afternoon, and yet he had.

The porch light picked out his boot prints as they tracked down the path and through the open gate. Catherine hesitated, uncertain about leaving Honor alone. But her daughter was in her bedroom, glued to her mobile phone, and would barely notice she'd gone.

Determined to repair whatever was wrong, she zipped up her old garden coat and followed her husband. Perhaps the open skies and fresh air would allow them to explore the dusty corners of their relationship, away from the confines of home and parenthood.

The village was deserted, the weather driving families indoors. His stride was longer than hers, and she had to stretch to place her own boots inside the prints left by his. She reached the end of the lane and turned right without checking because that was the way to the corner shop. But the snow was unmarked, and when she looked around, she noticed his boot prints were leading down to the river.

She set off in the same direction.

The trees were thicker on the towpath, and they bent towards her, bowing in deference. A water vole darted out from under a bush, heading towards its burrow at the river's edge. The Blackwater, sluggish and inky, might freeze tonight, the forecasters said. It hadn't done that for years.

Catherine heard him before she saw him, his voice warming up the ice-tinged twilight. He was sitting on a bench, his shoulders bent, one hand clutching his phone, the other playing with a scrap of paper in his hand. She felt a rush of affection at the sight of him and almost called out, but instinct stopped her, and then she was glad because the tempo of his voice changed and became agitated, almost ugly.

'I'll leave tonight if you tell me the truth,' he said.

A silence followed, so still that Catherine could hear the sound the snow made as it settled on the ground.

'I can't discuss it with her.' He was shaking his head. 'Not yet. I don't want to.'

Her world tilted. Edward was talking about her, she was almost certain of it. But to whom? Catherine took a step towards her husband, to ask what on earth was going on. But there was a hardness to him she'd never encountered before and it frightened her.

'Do I love her?' A bitter laugh. 'Of course I do, Eliza. I wonder, though, if she loves *me*.'

Eliza? *Her* Eliza? Catherine's stomach turned over. For what possible reason could Edward be talking to her? The reality of what this might mean – and the repercussions, especially for Honor – made her restless with fear.

Her toes were so cold, almost numb. If he turned around now he would see her. A compulsion to get away from him, to unhear what had been said, took hold. Anyone but Eliza. She stepped backwards and then she was running through the snow, away from the crack in her marriage, the disdain of her daughter, the collapsing walls of her life.

The house of straw she had staked everything on was about to fall down.

# 19

We arrive in Coggsbridge just after six.

The snow made driving slow and difficult, but not impossible. Lawrie left his car in Kent and travelled with me because he needed to make calls and chase up addresses. Almost four hours together in an enclosed space. Be still my beating heart.

The travel department has booked us into a guest house on the main street, and after we've been shown to our rooms, I check my mobile phone.

Still no message from Aunt Peg, but then I remember it's Wednesday. Bingo and ballroom dancing at the church.

'What shall we do now?' I ask Lawrie when we meet back in reception, but I know what his answer will be. Some reporters prefer a good dinner and an easy life. Lawrie is not one of them and neither am I.

'Let's go straight to the house,' he says. 'See what Catherine Allen has to say for herself.'

He's worried the *Daily Mail* will have got there first. Colin is counting on us to sign her up and get her under contract. He's so determined to splash on the reunion between the Angel of Death and her sister that he tried to send an agency reporter ahead of us, but Lawrie was adamant: his contact, his story. He refused to give away the prize of this address, especially to an agency, who might sell it on to a rival news organization at an inflated price.

*4 Hawberry Lane, Coggsbridge, Essex.*

Her name is Catherine Allen now. Married to Edward Martin Allen, who was born on 15 April 1979.

During the long and treacherous drive from Kent to Essex, Lawrie also pulled the birth and marriage certificates of their extended families, and scoured the electoral roll. We now know that Mr Allen's parents – Carol and Stephen – are still alive and based in Brighton. He has a sister called Hannah in Bassenthwaite, Cumbria, living with a man named Mark Ashton. Lawrie used the details in today's *Sun* story to trace Pamela Carter's mother in Yardley, Birmingham, and with that information, an aunt in Nottingham and a cousin in Tring.

We know that Catherine Allen has a daughter, Honor, who is twelve years old.

We know that the youngest Carter sister has no social media accounts, no employment history and has been living under the radar for thirteen years.

We know everything now.

The house is not a house at all, but a cottage. There's a light in the window and a holly bush on the front lawn covered in red berries. It looks homely and wonderful.

A car is parked at the end of the lane. Ordinarily, I wouldn't give it a second glance, but its windows have steamed up which means someone's inside. My antennae twitch. Another journalist.

# WHEN I WAS TEN

Lawrie has wound down the car window and is looking up and down the street, sizing up the competition. This is the part of the job I dislike the most. Knocking on doors, intruding into private lives. But it's a necessity today, a justifiable public interest in this story that's lacking in celebrity bikini shots and bankruptcies.

As we're contemplating our next move, a woman with a dark fringe, wearing flowery wellington boots, hurries into number four.

She's halfway up the garden path before we react, and then Lawrie is out of the car and running after her, calling out her name.

She spins around, her mouth forming a circle of surprise, and I can't help thinking how vulnerable she looks. Her hair is a different colour, but I can see in her face the child she was. She doesn't see me, but I'm not sure she would recognize me these days. She hesitates for a few seconds, and then lowers her head and disappears into the house.

The car door up the lane has opened, and I spot a journalist from the *Daily Mail*. It's not the same guy who was in Kent, but I've seen him on jobs before. He joins us on the pavement.

'Did she say anything?' He's got a sandwich in his hand, mayonnaise at the corner of his mouth, and anxiety pulses from him, like he's missed something vital.

Lawrie gives a defeated shake of his head. He's swearing because our photographer isn't here yet, and he wasn't quick enough with his mobile phone camera.

The *Daily Mail* journalist swears too. 'I've only just got back here myself. She must have gone out while I was getting something to eat.'

'Got anything decent yet?' says Lawrie. 'You don't have to tell us what it is, but can you let me know if we should be worried so I can tell the news desk, at least.'

'Fuck all,' says the *Daily Mail* reporter. 'We've been here since yesterday, but we only confirmed the name and address a couple of hours ago. I knocked once, but there was no reply. I was planning to wait a bit longer, let them get nice and comfortable, defences down, and then, bam.'

'Well, if you're here and we're here, it won't be long before the others start showing up,' says Lawrie. 'Why don't we do it now? Get it in the bag.'

The *Daily Mail* reporter takes another bite of his sandwich. 'Or should we leave it? Try again in the morning. We don't want her calling the police, banging on about harassment. If she didn't say anything just now, she's hardly going to invite us in for a cup of tea and spill her guts. We want to keep her on side.'

They're arguing amongst themselves, back and forth. They don't ask me what I think, but if they did, I would say that news travels too quickly these days. That nothing stays secret and the old rules of reporting no longer exist. That while we were travelling in the car this afternoon, there would have been other leaks and whispers, half-truths and speculation, blown across the internet like spores in the wind.

Yes, the public has been transfixed by Shannon Carter's testimony, but its appetite for scandal is never satiated and there's a rising hunger, a *demand*, to hear from her sister. That Heathcote's unguarded remarks have fuelled the fire of the news agenda, which blazes unchecked across our newspapers, televisions, radios and social media channels. Consume it before it consumes us.

Smartphones have made journalists of everyone. And voyeurs, too. Posting footage of burning buildings and terrorist atrocities and the dying bleeding out on the pavement. Instant gratification. Desensitization. A sense of righteousness. Of outrage. An unquenchable thirst for more, more, more.

I consider walking up the pathway and knocking on her door myself, but my phone is vibrating, and I smile because it's probably Aunt Peg, but instead it's a Google Alert.

My heart is in my mouth. I blink twice, and then I'm calling out to Lawrie, thrusting my phone at him.

'Oh, God, look at this.'

Someone has posted Catherine Allen's name and home address on Twitter.

# 20

The Right Honourable Geoffrey Heathcote was thinking about his imminent dinner reservation at the Members' Dining Room in the House of Commons.

More specifically, he was thinking about the woman he was about to dine with, and what kind of underwear she might be wearing.

He had told Barbara he would be home very late because there was a debate and vote that evening, which was true. Except he had no intention of attending, and had, instead, booked a room at a hotel around the corner where he was planning to fuck his mistress stupid.

It was a risk, of course. The eyes of the nation were upon him. But Heathcote thrived on risk. He was counting on the fact most photographers were too lazy to hang around until the vote was over. In the unlikely event a couple of the more tenacious buggers decided to wait for him, he knew a back route to the hotel that would allow him to avoid them.

He popped a tablet of Viagra from the blister pack in his drawer.

His mistress – Anna – would distract him for a few hours. His wife would get a few hours' peace. The old girl certainly deserved it after the week they'd had. With a bit of luck, the story would have moved on by tomorrow. *Everyone's a winner, baby.*

He loosened his polka-dot tie and slipped on the blazer required for Members' dining. Anna would be here any minute. He'd persuade her not to bother with a starter or dessert. After all, it wasn't an expensive meal he was paying for.

The minister shut down his computer, placed his papers in a tidy pile and was just about to switch off the light when his desk telephone rang, signalling an internal call.

He almost ignored it, but his conscience wouldn't let him.

'Yes,' he said, his brusqueness a deliberate attempt to intimidate the caller into ringing off until tomorrow.

'Geoff, it's me.'

He recognized the gravelly tone of the Attorney General, Sir Stanley Townsend. The Secretary of State for Justice sank back down into his chair. It was 8.26 p.m. on a Wednesday in December. This was not a social call.

'What's up, Stanley?'

He had known Sir Stanley for four years. Technically, the Attorney General was his subordinate, but they worked closely with each other on a day-to-day basis.

'The Angel of Death case.'

Heathcote groaned. Was there no escape from this? 'Oh, sweet Jesus. What now? I've been trying to shut it down all week.'

'Unfortunately, it's taken on a life of its own.' Sir Stanley outlined the facts, most of which Heathcote already knew and some he did not, including Shannon Carter's continued

television appeals for a reunion with her sister, the inten-
sifying interest from the national press and the wide dissem-
ination of information and speculation across all social media
channels relating to his constituent. The Attorney General
cleared his throat before ploughing on. 'Not surprisingly,
I've just taken calls from the Home Office, UKPPS and the
probation team in question.'

Heathcote ran his fingers around his collar. The room
had become unbearably hot. Someone should turn down the
heating. Bloody ridiculous – and a waste of taxpayers' money.

'So what happens now?' he said.

As the Attorney General explained in detail the costly
and devastating repercussions of his slip-up on Radio 2,
Heathcote forgot about dinner with his mistress, his wife
waiting for him at home and the fact his American grand-
children were due to arrive for Christmas next week. Instead,
he saw his political career catch fire before his eyes.

# 21

Catherine peered through a crack in the curtains.

Two cars squatted on the lane, their engines running. She hadn't heard what that man had called out to her, but instinct had propelled her up the garden path and into the sanctuary of home. She could guess, though. He was a journalist, she would stake her life on it.

Oh, God.

She hurried up the stairs to check on Honor. *One. Two. Three. Four.* Her daughter had changed into her pyjamas and was sitting cross-legged on her bed, listening to music on her phone, exactly where Catherine had left her.

'Mum!' She took out her earbuds. 'Haven't you heard of knocking?'

Catherine offered a weak smile. It was clear Honor hadn't moved from the bedroom. She was determined to keep it that way. 'Sorry, love. Just saying goodnight.'

Honor proffered her forehead for a kiss. 'Bit early, isn't it?'

'I don't feel very well so I'm going to bed myself. Lights off in half an hour, OK?'

Her daughter rolled her eyes. 'I'm not a baby.' Then a flash of compassion. 'I hope you feel better tomorrow. Night.'

Catherine shut Honor's bedroom door behind her. With a bit of luck, she wouldn't emerge until morning.

Edward was walking through the back door as she entered the kitchen, and Catherine froze, uncertain how to talk to the man she'd trusted for so long. A part of her wanted to demand answers from him. Why had he called Eliza? What had she said? But after overhearing him on the phone, their marriage felt as fragile as river ice. Now, seeing him in the warmth of their home, brushing the snow from his hair, her heart squeezed with a painful kind of love.

His hands were empty.

'Where's the milk?'

Edward looked startled but recovered quickly. 'Sold out,' he said. 'The shelves were bare.' He laughed awkwardly. 'It's the snow. There's been a run on bread too.'

Half an hour ago, she would have believed him.

But it was a relief he'd walked home the back way, along the towpath, past the farmer's field and through the gate in their rear garden. Whatever else was going on, it was clear he hadn't been accosted by journalists. Yet.

She took a deep breath and was about to ask if he'd like a glass of whisky or a cup of tea – anything to prolong their connection and find a way to raise the difficult subjects of his phone call to Eliza and the reporter outside their house – when his eyes slid from hers and he turned to hang up his coat.

'I'm tired,' he said. 'I'm going to read in bed.'

Catherine watched him take off his scarf and hook it on the peg, arms hanging by her sides, pinned in place by a sense of impotence. Most nights, her husband fell asleep quickly with a book across his face. Once under, he was a heavy sleeper. But what if he looked out of the window and noticed the unfamiliar cars outside? She needed to prepare him.

'Ed—' she began. But he was already on his way out of the kitchen. As he passed his wife, he bumped her shoulder with his own and swung around to face her, closing his hand around her wrist so she couldn't pull free.

'You wouldn't lie to me, would you?' he said.

His fingers were grinding her bones against each other, bruising the paper-thin skin. In twelve years of marriage, he'd never used his strength against her. She wanted to cry out because he was hurting her, but she deserved it, didn't she?

A few minutes earlier, as she had kissed their daughter goodnight, Catherine had made a promise to herself. She would confess to Edward – as soon as possible – the truth about her parents' murders. The whole truth and nothing but the truth. But in the glare of his contempt, her vow of honesty turned to ash.

'Of course not,' she said, the denial spilling from her as easily as blood from an open vein.

# 22

## Thursday, 13 December 2018

It's so cold inside the car, my scar feels like it's on fire.

Most of the time it doesn't bother me. The lightning strike destroyed so many of my nerve endings the skin on my back remains numb, even now. But for the nerve endings that survived, extremes of temperature can set them alight. The pain makes me twist in the driver's seat.

It is minus four degrees outside and gone midnight. Lawrie is bundled up in his coat, and every now and then I turn on the engine to keep us warm, but the noise breaks open the silence of the street, so I don't keep it running for long.

The *Daily Mail* reporter is parked behind us, our photographer behind him.

'This is pointless,' says Lawrie.

But he's wrong. The air is humming with tension. Something will happen tonight.

If the family slips out under cover of darkness, we'll never track them down. Fleet Street's old guard might have got their stories by blagging credit card details or hacking mobile phones, but those dark arts belong to the past. These days it's all GDPR and being the first to update Twitter feeds with the latest breaking news.

In any case, the armchair commentators, the armies of the self-righteous and professionally outraged have posted and commented and retweeted until the address is plastered all over social media. We couldn't leave now even if we wanted to. The story is here.

The upstairs lights in the house went out while we were still bickering about the best time to knock, and the decision was made for us. No one wants a complaint to the press regulator on their record.

The *Daily Mail* reporter offered to keep an eye on things while we went back to the guest house for some sleep, but Lawrie refused. After Russell from the *Sun*'s stunt, he doesn't trust the opposition.

So all three of us are here. Watching. Waiting.

The front pages of tomorrow's newspapers are now online. My name up in lights. I tried calling Aunt Peg a couple of hours ago, to tell her what I'd done, but there was no reply, the phone ringing out until I hung up. Some nights, she pops into the flat next door for a sherry, but I've left Pearline's number in my address book at work. I'll try her again in the morning.

Snow collects on the windscreen. My feet are freezing. Lawrie is on his phone, texting. At one point, he sighs and puts it in his pocket.

'Does your boyfriend mind you spending the night with another man?' He laughs to show it's a joke.

'I don't have a boyfriend.' *But I'd like it to be you.* Thank

God I don't say that aloud because his next comment is this: 'My girlfriend gets so jealous. I tried to explain we're sitting in a freezing car in the middle of nowhere, but all she keeps asking is if you're pretty.'

A silence stretches between us.

'Do you like hummus?' Admittedly, it's not the catchiest of lines, but I've got a pot of it and some carrots in a Sainsbury's bag in the boot of the car, and it's the only thing I can think of to say.

He gives me a strange look. 'Sure.'

Cold air slaps my cheeks and the snow crunches underfoot, a crust of ice already forming on top. As I open the boot, headlamps light up Hawberry Lane, casting shadows across the nightscape.

Two cars are inching through the darkness towards us.

Lawrie steps out to join me. He rubs his hands together. 'Looks like we've got company.'

The cars slide slowly to the kerb's edge. After a minute or two, a man and woman emerge. 'Evening,' says the man, snowflakes settling on his shoulders. 'We're from Essex News. Fuck me, it's cold.'

Lawrie and I exchange a look. Essex News is the agency that supplies stories and photographs from this county to the national press. We might as well wave goodbye to our exclusive.

But it's only the beginning.

An hour later, three more news organizations have arrived in Hawberry Lane, their vehicles parked haphazardly across grass verges. 'ITN' is emblazoned across one of the vans.

By 2 a.m., Hawberry Lane is clogged with media outlets.

With no room to park by the kerbside, they are now blocking off the narrow street. One or two of the camera crews are staking a claim on the pavement, bagging the best positions in readiness for the morning.

'What the hell is going on?' I say to Lawrie. We both recognize the significance of the story, but the number of media organizations at this time of night is baffling.

We wander over to one of the TV news crews. A producer is scribbling notes on a pad. In the last few hours, there have been significant developments, she tells us. The tweet has gone viral. News organizations both abroad and in Scotland are intending to reveal Catherine Allen's real identity. The Official Solicitor and the Attorney General are now involved.

A police car crawls into the melee.

You want to meet me? I don't know what to say except it's a wonderful idea and why on earth didn't I think of it myself? When can you get away? Where shall we meet?

Forgive me if this seems a little forward, but why don't you send me your address?

# 23

In one minute and twenty-six seconds, Catherine Allen will be dead.

She smooths back Honor's hair, her heart full of love and hope and despair, and sits on the edge of her daughter's bed.

'There's something I have to tell you, sweetheart. It's going to be a difficult thing to hear, so I need you to prepare yourself.'

Another hammering at the front door, a dark threat in the eye of the night.

Honor yawns again, propping herself up against the pillows. 'What's going on, Mum? Why is there a rucksack in my room? Who's at the door?'

'We have to leave now,' Catherine says. 'I need you to get out of bed, put on a warm jumper, and then we're going downstairs. I'm going to put a blanket over your head, and we're going to walk out to the car.'

'What?' Her brow furrows. 'Why?'

Edward is leaning against the door frame of Honor's room. He is barefoot and wearing a shirt and jeans, a belt dangling loosely in his hand.

'Yes, Catherine. Care to elaborate?'

His voice is cold against the sudden heat behind her eyes and then, tears almost blinding her, she begins to speak.

'A long time ago, there was a family called the Carters. There was a mother and father, and two daughters, and they shared a beautiful home called Hilltop House.'

'Wait . . .' says Honor. 'They were on the television the other day.'

'That's right, sweetheart,' says Catherine. 'But the Carters weren't kind to their daughters, and one winter's night, one of their girls, an unhappy little thing, was so upset by something they had done to her that she killed them.'

Honor's eyes are saucer-wide. It makes her look so young, and Catherine mourns the loss of her innocence. Edward is still leaning against the door frame, the leather belt passing through his fingers, his face as hard as rock.

'That's sad,' says Honor.

'It *is* sad,' says Catherine, taking one of her daughter's hands. 'Terribly, terribly sad. Now, do you remember me telling you that my parents and sister were killed in a house fire?'

Honor nods. 'Of course. But what's that got to do with this?'

'Sweetheart, I'm so sorry, but I wasn't telling the truth. They didn't die in a house fire.'

Catherine, tears spilling down her cheeks, waits for Honor to puzzle it out. The bedside lamp bathes the room in its gentle light, picking out books, make-up, jewellery, the paraphernalia of a young girl whose life will be upended in a matter of seconds.

'Are you saying . . . ?' Honor shakes her head. 'No, that can't be right.'

'What can't be right, darling girl?'

'That your parents – I mean, no, it's stupid – but were they the Carters?'

Tears are trickling into Catherine's mouth, filling it with bitterness. This is it. The moment she has spent the last thirteen years hoping would never come. This is the moment that will change everything.

'That's right.' Her voice cracks like breaking ice.

'So, that woman on the television—'

'—Shannon Carter—'

'—is your sister?'

'That's right.'

'So your sister *is* alive.' Her face lights up, and then, wonderingly, 'I have an auntie.'

Catherine breathes out slowly. Her hands are trembling so much she cannot control them, and so she squeezes Honor's fingers again, but an incredulous expression passes across her daughter's face and she pulls sharply away.

'So what about the other sister? The one Shannon Carter is looking for, the one who stabbed her parents fourteen times with a pair of scissors. What happened to her?'

The question hangs in the air. Catherine's throat closes up. Honor starts to cry, because she knows the answer, even though she doesn't want to.

'That little girl was called Sara Carter and she spent eight years in a secure unit for children. Thirteen years ago, she was released and given a new identity so she could have a fresh start without everybody knowing about her past. She cut all contact with her family, all her old friends. Sara wasn't a bad person, love. She was very sorry her parents died. She was given a probation officer called Eliza, who helped her to cope with the outside world. She wanted nothing more than a family of her own, and a chance to live a normal life.

'She moved to a quiet village, got married and had a beautiful daughter, and she was so happy and grateful for her second chance, but then the newspapers got hold of her name and they wanted to tell the world who she was.'

The air in the room is heavy with tension. It is there in the stretched leather of Edward's belt, the disbelieving look on Honor's face, the bated breath of the reporters waiting outside, preparing to expose her true identity.

'Are you' – Honor's voice is small and scared – 'Sara Carter?'

'Yes, my love, I am.'

And just like that, Catherine Allen was dead.

# PART TWO

*WHY?*

# 24

## Saturday, 19 April 1997

When ten-year-old Sara Carter opened her eyes on that fateful spring morning, she had no inkling that within forty-eight hours her family would be on the front page of every newspaper in Britain.

The year would fill up with major news stories and cultural milestones. Tony Blair elected Prime Minister in a Labour landslide. The Hong Kong handover. The birth of Harry Potter. The death of Princess Diana.

But no news event – except perhaps that car crash in a Paris tunnel – would quite manage to replicate the nation's collective intake of breath at the Hilltop House murders and the Angel of Death, a blonde-haired moppet who stabbed her parents fourteen times with a pair of scissors.

A local freelance photographer who couldn't sleep was making himself a cup of tea and idly listening to his police scanner when the initial report came in. He was the first of the news media on the scene and captured the images that shocked a generation.

Sara Carter, strands of fair hair darkened by spatter, a stunned expression in her eyes and – the heartbreaking detail that elevated this photograph into the stratosphere – a blood-stained rag doll clutched in her small hand.

Followed moments later by her traumatized older sister Shannon, dressed in too-small pyjamas, being comforted by police.

Captured in colour on a Nikon F4, those pictures – published in news outlets across the world when the judge lifted reporting restrictions after the twelve-day trial – paid for the photographer's new house and put his sons through university. A career-defining moment.

A defining moment for them all.

But on that particular morning, when the sky was pastel blue and the sun was its beating heart, there was no hint of the darkness that would tighten its grip around the neck of the Carter family.

Dr Carter was holding a general clinic at his surgery ten minutes' walk from their grand house in a pretty Kent village. Pamela Carter was knitting blankets for the neonatal intensive care unit at the hospital in Canterbury.

Shannon Carter, aged twelve, was still asleep.

Sara squeezed her toes and relaxed them. She was sleepy and warm beneath her duvet, despite the hollow feeling in her stomach that came from going to bed without dinner.

She screwed up her eyes, as if closing them could switch off her memory of last night. She didn't want to sully the quiet joy of just-waking-up by replaying the confrontation with her father. He was at work now, and for a few precious hours, there was the promise of peace.

Despite the sunshine bleeding through her curtains, the spring air had bite. Sara pulled on her dressing gown and slipped across the landing to wake up her sister.

Because Shannon was the eldest, she had the biggest bedroom. Sara didn't mind, though. Shannon's room was always cold, the sun never reaching the back of the house.

Her sister was a hump beneath the duvet, a flash of white-blonde hair the only sign she was there at all. Giggling to herself, Sara climbed into bed beside her.

'Get off!' Her sister gave a shriek. 'Your feet are freezing.' She shoved Sara away, but she was laughing too. She rolled over so they were face to face.

Sara grinned at Shannon, whose features were still softened by sleep. Despite their differences in personality, she idolized her older sister. The winter blue of the eyes. The mole on her cheek. Hair as pale as a ghost in snow.

'Shall we make pancakes for breakfast?' Shannon's breath was warm against her face. 'With banana and chocolate spread—'

'—and golden syrup and lemon.' Sara finished her sister's sentence with a smile. 'Move up a bit.' She poked her in the ribs. 'I'm falling out of bed.'

Shannon obliged by shifting closer to the wall. As Sara settled herself into a more comfortable position, her leg brushed against a cold, damp patch on the sheet. Instinctively, she jerked away, but she didn't cry out or ask questions or tease. She knew exactly what it meant.

Shannon caught the movement. Her eyes filled with shadows and she burrowed her face in her pillow, cheeks aflame.

'Don't worry,' said Sara, pressing a cool palm to her sister's burning skin. 'We'll put on a wash before Pamela notices.'

Downstairs, the bundle of laundry stuffed under her arm, Sara tiptoed into the utility room while Shannon approached the sitting room with the air of someone about to enter the lion's den. Sara had instructed her sister to distract their mother by asking if they could make pancakes, even though they both knew what the answer would be.

'Your father said no breakfast this morning,' said Mrs Carter, eyes downward, examining her knitting. No holes were permitted in blankets for premature babies in case their tiny fingers and toes became entangled and she was meticulous about this detail. Sara often thought their mother cared more about other people's children than her own.

While Shannon pleaded unsuccessfully with Mrs Carter to change her mind, Sara loaded up the washing machine and foraged in the kitchen for something to eat.

She had learned, over time, to be careful about what she took, because her mother kept an inventory of food. Pamela Carter used a ruler to measure the length of each loaf of bread from the village bakery and knew if her daughters had cut off a slice. She regularly weighed the expensive ham from her once-a-week trip to the deli and kept a tally of eggs and cheese. The amount of milk in the plastic bottle in the fridge was carefully measured with a black marker pen.

But Sara, ever sharp, had noticed that while her mother counted the biscuits in the tin, she did not detect the pilfering of an occasional unopened packet. Imperfect fruit and vegetables were always discarded in the rubbish bin, and because

Mrs Carter was inclined to avoid the messier side of life, she never noticed when Sara retrieved them.

The sisters were greedy. That's what their mother told them. That's why she had to keep such a close eye on what they ate. But Sara found it difficult to understand how it was possible to be greedy and so hollow with hunger at the same time.

'Morning, Pamela,' said Sara, poking her head around the sitting room door, arms hidden behind her back. Mrs Carter had insisted the girls address her by her first name since they were old enough to talk.

Mrs Carter didn't bother to raise her head for her youngest daughter either. 'Good morning, Sara,' she murmured, but she was counting stitches and did not see the look of complicity that passed between the girls.

The Carter sisters waited to be dismissed. Their mother was a disciple of old-fashioned family values. Their father was the head of the household, its disciplinarian, while Mrs Carter's role was to support her husband and enforce his strict standards of conduct. She spoke in a flat tone, even when she was angry. Despite this, the girls had learned to read her moods. This morning, the waters were calm.

'You may go and get dressed,' she said.

'Thank you, Pamela,' said Shannon, and the sisters ran up the stairs, tumbling over themselves like puppies, fear escaping from them like steam from a pressure cooker.

Without the need for discussion, they settled on Sara's bedroom because it was warmer, closing the door behind them. Sara unloaded her spoils onto the carpet. Two apples – one bruised, one pock-marked with blemishes – and a packet of McVitie's digestives.

'Well done,' said Shannon, grabbing the least damaged apple. Sara didn't mind. She was less fussy than her sister and ate around the brown patches of rot on her own piece of fruit.

Silence for a few moments.

'What shall we do after ballet?' Shannon wrapped her apple core in a tissue and stuffed it in the rubbish bag hidden under Sara's bed before tearing open the biscuit packet. Crumbs fell down her pyjama top as she crammed one into her mouth.

Sara took her own digestive and nibbled its edges delicately. 'Go and see Brinley?'

Shannon grinned. 'Yes! I want to know what she's wearing tonight.'

'Are you excited about the disco?'

Shannon shoved in the last of her biscuit and wrapped her arms around her knees, feigning nonchalance. 'Kit said he's going to be there.'

Sara mimed exaggerated kissing on the back of her hand. Her older sister nudged her harder than was strictly necessary. 'Stop that right now, Sara Catherine Carter.'

'So have you?'

'Have I what?'

'Kissed him?'

'Of course not.'

'But you want to?'

Shannon's cheeks were aflame again. She gave the sort of shrug that suggested she didn't care, when the truth was she cared very much. 'I suppose so.'

Sara's eyes widened, and she edged closer to her sister, cross-legged and leaning forward, as if about to hear a story. 'Are you going to?'

Her sister fixed her with a stare. 'That's for me to know and for you to find out.'

'Girls?' Their mother's voice drifted up the stairs. Shannon and Sara froze, listening for her footsteps. 'Are you nearly ready? We're leaving in twenty minutes.'

Their eyes met, and both grabbed a couple of extra biscuits before hiding their contraband under the bed and getting dressed for their Saturday morning class.

Although they didn't know it yet, giggling and chatting as they slid on their white tights and pink leotards in the familiarity of Sara's bedroom, the Carter sisters would never eat breakfast together again.

# 25

My mother is dying.

At least, that's what my father says, but he said Take That weren't going to split up, so I expect he's wrong about this too. I don't want her to leave me. I won't let her. But the nurse is here again, and when she comes, she gives her something that makes her all sleepy, and when her eyes shut, she looks like she's dead, but she's not yet. She's not. I won't let her be.

Everyone wants me to talk about it. Aunt Peg asks endless questions about how I'm feeling. My headteacher dragged me out of English yesterday to see how I'm coping but I didn't *want* to go because a) Travis Lane was sitting next to me and b) I was enjoying the class discussion about *The Day of the Triffids*.

My father's no good at all. He walks around with a glazed look in his eyes, and sometimes he forgets to buy bread for my packed lunch. The only time he cheers up is when Maureen Connolly from the pub brings us casseroles and cottage pies, which my mother refuses to touch because they're made by *that woman*, whatever that means.

Mum's bed is downstairs now, so I'm quiet as I eat my

breakfast, sitting behind her door, because she forces her eyes open when she knows I'm there, and I want her to sleep so she can get better, but I want to be near her too.

It is Saturday. The worst day of the week.

I like it best when it's just me and Mum, when I come home from school and Dad's at work and the nurse has left. I feed her tiny spoonfuls of Complan and tell her about my day, and she smiles, and sometimes – not often – she sings, and I join in, and my heart feels happy.

But when my father's here, it's like the world has hard edges and the air is filled with things that no one says. Like now. The nurse is speaking to him, but I can't hear what she's saying because he's shoving plates into the kitchen cupboards. The crashing sound is going to wake my mother, but if I tell him to be quiet, he'll grab my shoulders and shout at me for being uppity, and Mum will ask him to stop and a tear will slide down her cheek, and I can't bear it when that happens, so I bite my lip and carry on sitting on the floor, eating my cereal.

The carpet is heavy and red, full of swirls. A drop of milk has landed on the pile, and I rub it in so my father doesn't see.

The nurse comes out of the kitchen and her face is sad, but when she sees me, she rearranges her expression into a smile. I like her because she doesn't ask me how I am.

'Wouldn't you be more comfortable on a chair?' Her eyes crinkle as she says it, so I know she's not telling me off.

I pick up my bowl and drink the milk straight from it. It's full of sugar and tastes delicious. 'I've finished.' I stand up. 'Are you going now? Is Mum OK? When do you think she'll get better?'

Her eyes flick towards the kitchen, where my father has just slammed a cupboard door and is now tossing cutlery into the drawer. The sound of forks and spoons hitting each other is a percussion of anger and sadness.

'She's comfortable, petal,' says the nurse. 'I'll come back a bit later, all right?' She opens her mouth as if to say something more, but squeezes my shoulder instead. We stand in silence for a minute. 'Talk to your dad,' she says.

But I don't want to talk to him so I stand at the sitting room window and watch her drive off. Her little car disappears around the corner and then the front door of Hilltop House opens and Shannon and Sara walk down the steps, clutching their ballet cases.

Shannon gives me a wave and mouths something at me, but I can't work out what she's saying. I expect she'll be over later with Sara because they always come over on Saturday afternoons, or I go there.

Our house is the smallest on the street. It's not grand like Hilltop, or as neat and tidy as Mr and Mrs O'Toole's next door. There are cracks in the paintwork and weeds on our front path. We don't have a gardener or a window cleaner like the Carters. But our view is just as pretty.

A river runs through the heart of the village like an artery (we've been doing the circulatory system at school) and Saltbox Hill rises behind it. My mother is going to take me there for a picnic when she gets better, like she used to when I was little and her clients had all gone home. We would roll down the hill, full of sandwiches and lemonade, grass in our hair.

If I close my eyes, I can feel the heat of the summer sun on my cheeks, and hear the violin legs of the crickets, and my mother is singing, a low, sweet song about a boat and a bird on the wing.

'Brinley, can you come into the kitchen for a minute?'

My father is framed in the door of the sitting room. I don't know how long he's been standing there, but before I can answer him, he's already turned away. He doesn't wait for me to follow because he knows I will.

When I enter the kitchen, he's sitting at the table, head in his hands. His shirtsleeves are rolled up and I can see his tattoos, and there's dried paint on his forearm and dirt beneath his nails. I drag out a chair and sit opposite him. The kitchen clock ticks on and on, and I count in time to its beats, because the air feels loaded with something and I don't know what else to do.

A minute or so passes. I trace the grain of the wood with my finger. Eventually, the silence becomes too much for me.

'Dad?'

He lifts his head and his eyes are red-rimmed and watery. My father never cries, so this is an alarming development.

'Brinley, love . . .'

The last time he called me 'love' was when I broke my wrist falling off the monkey bars in the park two years ago.

'You know how poorly Mum is, don't you? That she's not going to get better . . .'

I don't answer. I don't want to make it easy for him. He reaches his hand across the table. His arm is smooth and strong. I can see a vein pulsing through his skin.

'Well, the nurse who came today, love, she doesn't think it's going to be long.'

I meet his eyes, a challenge in my own. 'Until she gets better?'

He exhales my name in frustration and tenderness, but I can hear the jagged edges of his impatience too, and something else: sorrow.

'Until the end.' The words hang between us. I stare at him. 'She thinks your mum has only got a few days left, possibly less. I'm sorry, love.'

I put my hands over my ears.

'Brinley,' he says sharply. 'Do you understand what I'm telling you?'

I press my hands in harder until all I can hear is the humming echo of my blood.

'Mum is dying.' He speaks slowly, as if I'm stupid. 'Do you understand that?'

To understand it, I would have to accept it – and I'm not doing that. I'm not giving up on my mother, even if he is.

Hands still over my ears, I start to sing and I don't stop until my father sweeps my cereal bowl off the table with the back of his hand and stalks out of the kitchen, leaving broken bits of china all over the floor.

# 26

The whispering started as soon as Shannon walked into the changing room.

Sara glanced at her sister to see if she had noticed, but she was staring ahead with a fixed expression that indicated she knew exactly what was going on, but was choosing to ignore it.

The ballet school was a jaunty sort of a place. The walls were painted in vivid hues of purple and hot pink. Framed black and white photographs of Rudolf Nureyev and Margot Fonteyn lined the corridor that led from the entrance to the rabbit warren of changing rooms at the back of the building. It was the sort of place where appearance mattered, but the glossy smiles and not-a-hair-out-of-place buns hid a diseased heart.

The Carter sisters had pleaded to give up ballet but their mother wouldn't let them. It was good for their posture, apparently. For discipline.

Sara placed her ballet case on the bench that lipped the far wall. Her older sister opened a locker and hung up her coat. As Shannon bent to untie her trainers, a hairbrush bounced off her back.

The older girl straightened up, anger tugging at her features, narrowing her eyes and thinning her lips. 'Who threw that?' Her eyes, hard as slate, swept in a slow half-circle around the room, but all the girls were looking away, busying themselves by taking off their outdoor clothes or tying up the silken ribbons of their shoes. Someone giggled.

'Are you OK?' Sara pressed closer to her sister. 'Did it hurt?'

Shannon dismissed her sister's concern with a head shake and a couple of strands of white-blonde hair worked themselves free. She bit her lip. For a second time, she bent over to untie her laces, her gaze flicking warily upwards every now and again.

From across the changing room, a foil package of sandwiches hit the side of her face. Followed by a cereal bar. A banana. Two packets of crisps.

'Stop it!' Sara shouted. Even though Shannon had warned her to stay out of it. Even though Shannon had side-stepped the small pile of food and was calmly pulling off her jeans. 'Just stop it.'

'Ickle sister's fighting your battles now,' said a tall girl with acne. She smirked as she adjusted her leotard to stop it from cutting into her inner thigh. 'Can't you speak for yourself?'

'Yeah, Shannon,' said another girl. 'Are you' – she adopted a baby voice – '*scared*?'

Shannon slammed the locker door. It made a loud, metallic clang that demanded attention. Her shoulders rose as she drew in a breath. She swung around to face them.

'Shut your mouth, Orla Brookes.'

Sara put a hand on her arm to calm her, but Shannon shook it off, eyes like stones.

'She speaks,' said Acne Girl, looking around at the other girls, inviting them to be complicit in her baiting. 'The creature actually speaks.'

Acne Girl – Sara didn't know her name, but recognized her as a pupil from Shannon's school – whispered something to Orla, a wiry, muscular girl.

With barely a pause, Orla crossed the room and grabbed hold of Shannon's wrists. Shannon, who was underweight and unused to physical confrontation, struggled to free herself, but she was no match for her tormentor, who boxed as well as danced.

Sara flew forward to prise apart Orla's fingers, but another girl, who had so far been quiet, forced her back.

Acne Girl retrieved the foil-wrapped sandwiches from the floor and opened them up. The changing room filled with a distinctive aroma. 'Mmmm. Smells like egg mayonnaise to me. Do you like egg mayonnaise, Shannon?'

She grabbed half of the sandwich and pressed it hard against Shannon's closed lips. Chunks of half-mashed slippery egg slid from between the bread and down the front of Shannon's leotard.

'Eat up, you anorexic bitch,' said Acne Girl.

Sara yanked herself free from the girl who was holding her back. At the same time, Shannon stamped on Orla's toe. In her ballet tights, it wasn't hard enough to do much damage, but it startled Orla, who loosened her grip, allowing Shannon to break free.

Shannon planted two hands against Acne Girl's chest and shoved her. 'Fuck off, Danielle.'

As the expletive spilled from her, the door to the changing room opened.

Mrs Carter's intake of breath was audible in the pin-drop silence. She glanced at the floor and the collection of discarded food. Sara's heart stuttered at the sight of her mother. From an early age, Mrs Carter had instilled in them the importance of impeccable behaviour in public and how their actions might impact on their father, a bastion of the community. Danielle burst into noisy tears while the other girls clustered around her.

Mrs Carter moved swiftly across the room and gripped Shannon's shoulder. Tiny flames of anger burned in the woman's eyes. 'What on earth do you think you're doing?' Her words were darts of poison, pointed and corrosive.

'It wasn't Shannon's fault,' said Sara, pulling at her mother's arm. 'They started it.'

'Be quiet,' said Mrs Carter, without taking her eyes off her oldest daughter. Her gaze searched Shannon's face, settling on the smear of mayonnaise at the corner of her mouth.

Her hand snaked out, pinching her daughter's stomach between her fingers. To an observer, it might have looked as if she were drawing the girl into a hug. But she twisted sharply, spandex and skin, and pressed her mouth to Shannon's ear so the others couldn't hear.

'Greedy little pig.'

Each word was spoken with softness – their mother never raised her voice – but enunciated as precisely as a knife-cut across the wrist.

Tears of pain and humiliation filled Shannon's eyes, but she did not cry out. Sara heard a stifled titter from one of the watching girls. The tension in the changing room sharpened.

'Apologize.'

Shannon stared incredulously at her mother, a plea in her eyes. Even though she knew it was safer to stay quiet, Sara, who hated injustice, could not contain herself. 'But she didn't do anything wrong.'

Mrs Carter did not appear to have heard.

'I'm waiting, and so is Danielle.'

Danielle, with an ostentatious, shuddering breath, wiped her eyes. Sara caught a glimpse of her grin before it was lost again behind her hand.

Sara knew how much it would cost Shannon to apologize. Not only here at ballet, in front of these girls with their taste for cruelty, but in the day-in-day-out relentlessness of the school playground, the classroom, the bus journey home.

'Pamela—'

'Don't,' said her older sister. She fumbled for Sara's hand and squeezed it, but she didn't look at her. 'It's fine.' A hoarse whisper. 'I promise.'

Heat stung the back of Sara's eyes. The strains of music from one of the dance studios filtered through the door, up-tempo and incongruous. Mrs Carter folded her arms. The group of girls surrounding Danielle parted to let Shannon through. She might as well have been walking to her execution.

The two girls stood opposite each other.

Danielle's face was tear-stained and she was shorter than Shannon, but her arrogance was written in the forward thrust of her shoulders and the upward tilt of her chin. She smirked at Shannon, but couldn't quite meet her eyes – that hint of cowardice, the hallmark of all bullies.

Shannon, although taller, appeared reduced. Her shoulders were slumped, her head bowed. Her badges were shame and humiliation.

Neither girl spoke.

'Haven't you got something to say?' Mrs Carter's tone was as sharp as the jut of her clavicles.

Shannon's lips parted and then closed again. Danielle's smirk widened. The girls in the changing room drew in a collective breath, greedy for the finale.

Only Sara sensed what was coming, and she closed her eyes.

Shannon shuffled closer to Danielle. She looked beaten down, an apology in every step.

An expression of triumph lit Danielle's face. She had cemented her victory in the dog-eat-dog world of schoolgirl rivalry.

Shannon stuck out her hand, offering to shake, and Danielle was surprised into acceptance. But as the older Carter sister's fingers closed around the hand of her nemesis, she jerked and twisted her own hand sideways, bending back Danielle's wrist until she cried out in pain.

Sara was aware of several things happening at once: her mother's controlled exhalation of fury; the gasps of outrage from the girls; a sense of her own excited terror.

But mostly, the sound of Shannon's voice, clear and cool.

'Why should I say sorry to a bitch like you?'

# 27

Maureen Connolly has arrived with fish pie.

I despise fish pie.

It's on the kitchen table and the smell makes me feel sick. I drag a chair over to the worktop and use it to stand on to reach the top cupboard. My hand pats the tins and packets until I find what I'm looking for. Pink wafers, my favourite. I stuff four in my pocket and shove the torn packet to the back behind the baked beans and tuna chunks.

Maureen Connolly is in the sitting room, murmuring to my father. I listen for a while, my ear pressed to the door, the cloudy biscuits melting on my tongue, and when the murmuring stops for longer than a minute, I open it without knocking.

My father jumps as if I've spilled hot tea on him. Maureen Connolly's face is flushed and there's a pinkish chafing around her mouth and chin. There's a feeling of something in the air, but I don't know what it is.

'Shouldn't you be back at the pub by now?' I plant my hands on my hips.

Maureen Connolly looks at my father. My father looks at the carpet. He scratches his beard.

'Don't be rude,' he mutters.

'I'm on my break, love.' Maureen Connolly tries on a smile. 'I've popped your dinner down.'

'Doesn't your husband wonder where you are?'

To my surprise, Maureen Connolly throws back her head and laughs, a rough, earthy sound. 'I haven't got a husband, love, and thank God for that.'

This news makes me feel anxious, although I'm not sure why.

'Look, why don't you go out and play?' My father sounds hopeful, but I disappoint him by shaking my head. He burrows through his pockets and produces a fifty-pence coin, twirling it between his fingers like a magician. 'What about some sweets?'

I hesitate, briefly tempted.

But I don't want to leave my father and Maureen Connolly alone.

'No thanks,' I say.

We stand there, the three of us, on that Saturday morning with the promise of spring lighting the sky and my mother sleeping in the next room, skin as dry as sawdust.

'Brinley . . .' There's a warning in my father's voice that I know I should heed, but instead I cross the room and grab hold of his arm, like I'm five instead of twelve. He tries to shake me off, his tone hemmed with affection, but mostly impatience. 'Get off, you're too heavy for this now.'

But I don't let go. I want his attention. On me. On my mother. On anything but Maureen Connolly. 'Can we go to the park?' I tug harder. 'Or we could feed the horses. No, wait, what about the library? I need to get some books for my homework.'

He prises open my fingers, rougher than he usually is. 'No,' he says, 'I can't leave your mother.'

Maureen Connolly is watching us. At one point, she rolls her eyes. A rush of hatred boils up inside me. Maureen Connolly with her stupid face and dark curls. My mother has no curls left, just a fuzz that barely covers the pale contours of her skull.

My father puts both hands on my shoulders and propels me towards the door.

'Off you go now. Maureen and I need to have an adult conversation.'

His tone is clipped, boxed-off. No room for argument. No room for me.

I'd like to say I drift from the room with all the dignity of Princess Diana, but I don't. I tut loudly and slam the door, but not before I catch a glimpse of the smile on Maureen Connolly's face.

It says: *I win.*

I grab my coat from the bannister and tie up the laces of my trainers. Then I run back to the kitchen, lift the dish of fish pie off the table and drop it into the bin.

# 28

The car filled with the noise of silence.

Shannon stared out of the window, hands folded in her lap, watching the fields flash by. Spring was everywhere, in the pastel streaks of sky and the hedgerows anointed with blousy flowers. The car twisted down the narrow country lane that led back to the village, past the pond and the church and the Hope and Anchor pub to the rolling greenery of Saltbox Hill and beyond.

Shannon had not spoken a word since their mother had frogmarched her out of the changing room, Sara scurrying behind them, weighted down with coats and ballet cases. Sara disliked ballet so much she hadn't minded missing her class, but the look of triumph on Acne Girl's face as she'd gathered up their things had still felt like a stab in the back.

Mrs Carter's hands gripped the steering wheel. She pressed her lips together until they were thin and bloodless. Sara could almost see the anger pulsing from her mother, like heat shimmer on summer days, but Shannon was lost in the landscape blurring the car window.

'Shall we go over to Brinley's when we get home?' Sara looked hopefully at her sister. Even though they were all friends, Shannon could be possessive and considered Brinley *hers*.

Shannon kept her eyes on the view outside, but at least she answered. 'If she's in.'

'I don't think so,' said Mrs Carter, although it was clear from her tone there was no 'thinking' about it. 'You're not going anywhere, my girl.'

'It wasn't my fault!' The words sprayed from Shannon, a broken pipe that could no longer contain the leak. 'They started it.'

'Really?' Mrs Carter's reply was coated in scepticism.

'Why don't you ever believe me? Why can't you, just for once, be on *my* side?'

'I *am* on your side, and that's why no daughter of mine will be permitted to assault her classmate and use foul language.' A deliberate pause for impact. 'Wait until your father hears about this.'

'No!' The Carter sisters cried out in unison. A tear trickled unchecked down Shannon's face. Mrs Carter glanced at the older girl in the rear-view mirror. For a moment, the hard set of her features softened, a curtain pulled back to reveal herself. 'I *have* to tell him,' she said. 'Before he hears it from someone else.' Sara scrabbled for the right words to appeal to their mother. 'Please, Pamela,' she said. 'The girls are always mean to Shannon. It's been going on for ages—'

'Shut up!' A hiss from Shannon.

'You should tell her,' she hissed back.

'As if that will make a difference.'

'Whispering is very rude.' Mrs Carter's voice cut through their exchange, the curtain falling back into place. 'Is there something you'd like to share, girls?'

'No, Pamela,' they said in unison again. Shannon turned back to the window; Sara smoothed out the fabric of the tartan skirt she'd pulled over her leotard, counting its squares.

The car journey continued in silence.

Hilltop House straddled the crest of Hanging Hill Lane, overlooking the village. It was a double-fronted, Georgian-style house with immaculate paintwork and perfectly kept gardens. Dr and Mrs Carter were well respected within the community and were keen on maintaining appearances.

A window cleaner came twice a month and the lawn was scarified every autumn. Seasonal flowers filled the vases and, in the summer, Dr and Mrs Carter hired a marquee and a big band and invited the whole village. They were known for their charity work, their patronage of the village's local shops, their inclusivity and generosity.

But appearances can be deceptive.

Dr Carter's personalized Mercedes SLK was parked in the driveway when Mrs Carter pulled in, his two-hour morning surgery finished.

The Carter sisters glanced at each other and Shannon pointed upwards with her finger. Over the years, the girls had developed an unspoken language. This meant: *Let's go upstairs as soon as we get in.*

The house was quiet and smelled of lemons and furniture polish. With luck, their father would be in his study, catching up on paperwork. Their mother strode ahead, dropping the car keys into a dish on a bureau in the hallway. 'Richard, where are you?'

Both girls removed their shoes and put them in the downstairs cupboard, as they had been taught to do since they could walk. They shared another shorthand glance which said they should get changed out of their leotards and wait for Brinley to come to them.

For all her hauteur, Mrs Carter was careful to be kind to the girl next door because her mother was dying and her father painted the outside of Hilltop House every spring, and, most importantly, Mrs Carter knew that gossip spread like seeds on the wind. She wouldn't send her away.

Shannon was already on the ninth step, light-footed and quick, Sara just behind her, when a door opened downstairs. The click of the latch and the rush of wood pushing against carpet made Sara's stomach fold over and her knees loosen.

'Shannon?' Their father's voice drifted upstairs, pleasant and low.

Shannon's whole body tensed, like someone had pressed pause on her life. Sara could not stop in time and bumped into the back of her older sister's knees.

'Come here, please.'

Sara's hand groped for Shannon's. She squeezed it and Shannon squeezed back. Then her sister turned around and made her way back downstairs.

The study door shut again.

Sara sat down on the eighth step, a pain in her stomach. Knowing Shannon was in the study alone with their parents frightened her. But the last time she'd stood up for her sister, she'd received a punishment of her own. Dr Carter liked to hand out punishments. He believed they were character-building.

She wrapped her arms around her knees and waited.

\*

After what felt like a long time, but was about twenty minutes, the study door opened. Shannon flew up the stairs and did not stop. Sara glimpsed a shock of white-blonde hair, the stain of tears on her sister's cheeks and a crack in her expression that had been levered apart by the cruelty of their father.

Her sister's bedroom door closed.

Sara hesitated, not sure what to do next. She loved her sister with everything she had, but Shannon did not always welcome spectators to her most degrading lows.

She could hear her mother and father talking and laughing in the kitchen, the clink of mugs and the grind of coffee beans. Not once had they raised their voices, but that was worse. Their controlled viciousness was a thousand times more painful than the bluster of Brinley's father or the sweep of Mrs Aggarwal's broom against their ankles after Shannon, hungry as usual, had thieved a chocolate bar from her shop.

After a few seconds of painful indecision, Sara ran up the stairs to her own bedroom, gathered up the half-eaten packet of biscuits and knocked on Shannon's door.

A muffled voice. 'Go away.'

'It's me,' she said, and without waiting for Shannon's reply, let herself in.

Shannon was lying on her bed, her face buried in her pillow. Sara put her hand over her mouth. Her sister's hair had been hacked off and stuck out at ugly angles. The back of her neck was exposed, the milky white skin as vulnerable as an unbruised heart.

Sara crouched by her sister's bed and laid her head on the pillow next to her.

They stayed like that for several minutes, amidst the sound of quiet breathings, of love and hurt and fear, of knowing without speaking.

Eventually, Shannon pulled herself upright. Her cheeks were blotchy from crying and her eyes were glassy, an injured animal on the cusp of death.

She gestured to her hair, her voice a thin break. 'Look what he's done to me.'

Sara reached for her sister's hand. 'You still look beautiful.'

'They said I can't go tonight, even though I promised Kit I'd be there.' Her lip trembled. 'He'll be waiting for me. But I don't want to go now, anyway. Not like this.'

Sara didn't know what to say. She didn't care how she looked and couldn't think of any boys she liked in the way Shannon liked Kit. She was in the last year of primary school, still clinging to childish things. She enjoyed sketching animals, roller skating and collecting shells. Shannon was only two school years above her, but light years away.

'It's all my fault,' said Shannon, shaking her head in despair. 'I should never have sworn at Danielle. If only I'd ignored her, Pamela would have had nothing to tell Richard.' She wrung her hands. 'If only I could do something right for a change. They'd love me then.'

She got off the bed and stared at herself in the mirror. Fresh tears, and something else. Anger. She tugged at the uneven tufts of her hair and her eyes were dark as night.

'I hate them,' she said. 'I fucking hate them.'

# 29

The trouble with storming off is I don't know where to go.

I consider walking to the village shop, but my purse is empty – I kick myself for refusing my father's fifty pence – and despite the blue skies, it's even warmer than it looks, the sun having burned off the early-morning chill.

By the time I've reached the end of our path, I've already changed my mind, but it's too late to go back, and I wouldn't want to anyway, not while *she's* there, so I decide to go down to the river.

As I turn left, I see Mrs Carter's car on the driveway, which must mean Shannon and Sara are home from dancing. I change course and head up the way to Hilltop House.

Although we're neighbours, our houses are separated by a stretch of pavement, a hedge and a bank of trees. We've lived next door to each other since I was born, and I've never noticed the difference between us, but lately I've started to mind that their house is three times the size of mine, and our house is three times as shabby. I rub at a speck of dried mud on my coat and ring the bell.

Mrs Carter opens the door. She's wearing a pale pink

sweater and her nail polish matches, and she looks so pretty and put-together, I feel homesick for the woman my mother used to be.

'Hello Brinley, how lovely to see you. How's your mother, dear?'

'She's getting better,' I say. 'Is Shannon in?'

Mrs Carter's face clouds over and she leans forward, conspiratorial. 'She's a bit upset, dear. An accident at the hairdressers. Perhaps you can cheer her up.'

She takes my coat and I leave my trainers by the front door. As I climb the stairs, Mrs Carter lines them up until they're perfectly straight. In my house, no one cares if you're wearing shoes or not. That's probably why the floors are so dirty.

Sara's bedroom door is open so I know they're not in there. I knock hard twice on Shannon's door, then tap twice and then repeat the whole thing. I'm supposed to do it three times, but it takes too long. We're a bit old for secret codes, but Sara likes it, and we indulge her.

Sara opens the door. From the look on her face, I can tell something is terribly wrong. When I glimpse Shannon, I know exactly what it is.

But I'm careful. I've learned not to react, even though no hairdresser would have left my friend in this state. I don't ask questions because Shannon never asks questions about my mother and father, and that's the way I like it. Instead, I ask for a pair of scissors.

Sara runs to the bathroom to get them while I persuade Shannon to sit on her dressing table stool.

'What are you doing?' she says, her eyes, fearful, meeting mine in the mirror.

I raise my eyebrows in what is supposed to be a comical fashion, trying to make her smile, anything to rid her face of its dead expression. 'Remember what Mum did before she got ill?'

'I'm not sure this is a good idea,' she says.

'I'm your best friend, aren't I? Trust me.'

I know I can do it. I've spent hours sweeping up hair and watching my mother at work in our dining room, absorbing the way she holds the scissors, the feathering and layering, the thinning and over-direction. Shannon is my oldest and dearest friend, a sister in everything but name. Sadness rises from her and I want to blow it away, to lift the shadows from behind her eyes, because I love her – I can't imagine ever *not* loving her – but mostly, I want her to be happy again.

'I don't suppose you can make it any worse.'

I gather a hank of white-blonde hair between my fingers, say a little prayer and cut. The scissors are blunt but work-able. Sara is watching, her mouth hanging open a little, but this requires my full concentration, and so I don't look at her again, or think about Maureen Connolly, or my mother, but instead picture all the models in my magazines, the pop stars and actresses, and I snip and snip and snip.

When I've finished, there's a pile of hair on the carpet.

I'm almost too scared to look up.

But Shannon is staring at herself in the mirror, and there's a smile tugging at the corners of her mouth.

It's not perfect, of course it isn't. I'm twelve and the only hair I've cut before is synthetic and belongs to my dolls, and it's not as tidy as I'd like, or as sharp-edged as when my mother does it, but Shannon's eyes look much bigger and the cut exposes the definition of her jawbone and the pale skin on the long sweep of her neck. She looks different – older, more elegant.

'Wow,' says Sara, and I know exactly what she means.

Shannon places her hand on the nape of her neck. She shakes her head two or three times, as if it feels unexpectedly light. Then she gets up from the stool and puts her arms around me.

'Thank you,' she says. 'Thank you.'

The morning creeps into afternoon. We lie on our stomachs on Shannon's carpet, and we talk and talk. About Maureen Connolly and disgusting fish pie. About my urge to run and keep running. She tells me what happened at ballet and I offer up words of comfort, but we know that Monday morning will be awful for both of us.

Because I'm friends with Shannon, the girls at school are cruel to me too. *Is your mum dead yet? You're so ugly you should kill yourself. Why do you always wear such terrible clothes?*

Neither of us mentions our parents.

'I wonder what Kit will think of your hair,' I say, changing the subject. This is safer ground. Shannon likes talking about Kit.

'Doesn't matter now.' She blows on her nails, freshly painted in black varnish. 'I'm not allowed to go.'

I sit upright, heart jumping. This is news to me. Despite everything, we've been looking forward to the disco for weeks.

'What? Why?'

She doesn't look at me. 'My father.'

'Well, I'm not going if you're not.'

But I want to go. I don't want to spend the evening at

home with my mother, who sleeps nearly all the time, and my father, who's distracted by a woman who works at the pub. I want to wear lip gloss and dance with my best friend, hide in dark corners and talk about boys.

'Why don't we sneak out? Remember that time we tried to go to the Radio 1 Roadshow?' Sara is lying on Shannon's bed and she's lifting one leg and pointing her toe. 'We didn't get caught then.'

It's an idle comment, a barely-even-thought-about comment. It was the first and last time we'd done anything like that, and we only got as far as the train station before we lost our nerve and came home again. For a minute, I think Shannon hasn't heard, but then she glances at me, and it's a look that changes everything. There's excitement in it, a touch of defiance.

'You could get ready here,' she says. 'Pamela leaves us alone when you're here. We could pretend you're staying the night.'

'*Can* I stay the night?' I don't want to go home, to the smell of disease and disinfectant, and my father's disapproval.

'*Stay the night, stay the night, stay the night.*' Sara flexes her ankle in time with her chanting, then rolls on her side, rests her chin in her palm and smiles at us.

'Are you sure your parents won't mind?'

Shannon's face closes up. Sara's is a mirror image. The atmosphere shifts. It's swollen with sorrow and something I recognize as resignation, as if the sisters are to blame for the dark places they find themselves and there is nothing they can do about it.

'They won't care,' says Shannon.

'They don't care about anything,' says Sara.

'Except what other people think of them,' says Shannon.

'They might give us money for pizza if you're here,' says Sara.

'It's safer when you stay,' says Shannon. 'Please stay.'

And what they say, in their matter-of-fact way, is horrifying but true.

I may not be a straight-A student but I'm not stupid. Or blind. Over the years we've lived next door to each other, I've played with the Carter sisters for hours and hours, and stayed the night at least half a dozen times. I've caught glimpses of the darkness that edges their lives, although the girls rarely talk of it.

When we were ten, Shannon's mother sent her on a school trip to the British Museum with a water bottle laced with spoonfuls of salt. At lunchtime, I found her being sick in the toilets. My best friend was crying and the truth came tumbling out. It was not the first time Mrs Carter had pulled this particular stunt, but she was clever, leaving months between each episode until Shannon had lowered her guard. She swore me to secrecy, insisting she deserved this punishment for breaking a plate or forgetting to practise the violin or whatever minor infraction had occurred. It took weeks of encouragement to persuade her to confide in our teacher. But when she'd finally plucked up the courage to tell him, he'd thrown back his head and laughed, dismissing her 'silly attention-seeking stories'. In that moment, Shannon had lost the last of her faith in grown-ups. What was the point if no one believed her?

And Mr and Mrs Carter are careful. They take great pains to be kind to me and to others, even if they're not kind to the Carter sisters.

'You can borrow my black top with the beads,' says Shannon, a knowing smile playing about her lips.

I've coveted that top for months. 'Deal.'

My name is Brinley Booth and I'm twelve years old. I don't think about consequences. I don't think about what-ifs and maybes and regrets. About cause and effect. I think about the here and now. The disco. The sleepover. The *thrill*.

That's the terrible truth about mistakes. We never know when we're making them.

# 30

It was all agreed.

Sara would be the one to ask because she was the bravest, but Brinley had to go with her because Pamela and Richard Carter were more likely to say yes if she was standing there.

The Carters were in the conservatory, listening to classical music and drinking red wine. It wasn't dark yet, and the gardens of Hilltop House were bathed in the muted light of early evening. It lent the place a timeless quality.

The music carried on the air, which was edged with warmth, and it made Sara wistful for something she didn't understand. Her mother popped an olive into her lipsticked mouth and sipped her wine. Sara's stomach rumbled. Brinley stood awkwardly next to her.

Mrs Carter flicked over the page of her magazine. 'What is it, girls?'

'Can Brinley sleep here tonight? We won't be any trouble, we promise. We'll stay upstairs and out of the way.' Nervousness made Sara stumble over her words. She was never sure how her parents would react to the simplest of requests and that uncertainty fostered a climate of fear.

Mrs Carter licked her finger and turned another page.

'Please,' said Sara. Her mother was a stickler for good manners.

'I'm sure Brinley's father will be expecting her home soon.'

'He isn't,' said Brinley quickly. 'He's busy looking after my mother.' She smiled at Mrs Carter. 'He said I could stay. If I was invited, I mean.'

Mrs Carter took another sip of her wine. Dr Carter placed his glass on the table next to his chair, a fatherly twinkle in his eyes.

'Well, I've got no problem with that. What about you, Pamela?'

Mrs Carter smiled thinly. She had a speck of black olive caught in her front tooth. 'I don't mind either, as long as you behave yourselves.'

'We will,' said Sara and Brinley together.

Dr Carter fished about in his pocket for his wallet and withdrew a ten-pound note. He pressed it into Sara's hand. 'Here you go, girls. Treat yourselves to pizza.'

Sara and Brinley could scarcely believe their luck. The scenario had played out exactly as they had planned. They thanked Dr Carter and disappeared upstairs before he had a chance to change his mind.

Sara ordered pizza on the upstairs phone and rubbed her wrist while her sister and Brinley discussed their outfits.

The younger girl understood that this evening – the takeaway and sleepover – would come at a price, although she didn't yet know what it would be. For all his pasted-on smiles, their father did not appreciate being put on the spot.

As he had given her the money, he had held on to her

wrist and twisted his hand, pinching the delicate skin. Sara had known better than to cry out. She should have expected it. A part of her *had* expected it. Her father frightened her in a way her mother did not. But like most ten-year-olds, she had a short memory. She was young and impulsive and lived in the moment. It was a simple equation. Like her sister, Sara had wanted Brinley to stay over and that had meant facing down her fears, even if it was only for a few hours.

Years later, when she was in the unit, looking back through the thickened glass of memory, she would remember the early part of that night as one of the happiest of her childhood.

Music. The smell of pizza grease and cheap perfume. Watching her older sister change from jeans to a dress, and back again. Laughter and shushing and the air trembling with the thrill of standing on the edge of something important, the road of life unmapped and full of possibility.

'What do you think?'

Shannon spun in a circle in front of them both. She was wearing black jeans and a vest-top. A choker circled her neck. Brinley had helped with her hair, and the effect was startling. She looked edgy and grown-up. Beautiful.

Sara, in her plain polo neck and tartan skirt, was fascinated by the transformation, by this glorious stranger who looked a bit like her older sister.

'Repeat the plan back to me,' said Shannon, smudging black eyeliner beneath her lashes with her finger.

Sara sighed theatrically but did as her sister instructed. 'Pamela will never come upstairs, but in case she does, lay out the spare mattresses, put pillows under the blankets, and if she asks where you are, tell her you're both in the bathroom.' She watched as Brinley applied a sticky layer of lip gloss. 'But she won't.'

'What else?'

'Have the radio on to make it seem like you're still in the room,' said Sara. Shannon nodded in satisfaction.

'What about my shoes?' said Brinley, smoothing down her skirt. 'They're downstairs. What if Pamela notices they're gone?'

Shannon scrabbled in her wardrobe for a pair of low-heeled black boots and chucked them at her friend. 'Borrow these.'

A skein of faint stars was scattered across the night sky when Shannon opened her bedroom window. The air was cooler now the sun had gone down, but it was still warm and the scent of possibility was everywhere. She hefted herself onto the sill and swung her legs around until they were hanging out of the window.

She turned and grinned at Sara, impish. 'Wish me luck.' And then she was gone.

Shannon's bedroom, while at the back of the house, did possess a single advantage, and that was a narrow balcony that overlooked the garden. From the balcony, it was possible to drop comfortably onto the flat roof of the garage and scramble to the ground, out of sight of the conservatory.

Brinley peered out of the window. Shannon had already made her way down and was opening the back gate.

'Good luck,' said Sara softly. Brinley gave her a quick hug, and then she, too, was gone.

# 31

The girls held hands as they ran down the lane and through the village, the night sky unfurling above them, a roll of navy silk.

They laughed as they ran, wrapped up in the joy of being young and unfettered, trembling on the edge of adolescence, when feelings, not reasons, were enough.

Shannon stuck close to Brinley, hugging the river and the wide bank of trees that wound through the village to avoid being seen by friends of Dr and Mrs Carter, who were out enjoying the mildest Saturday evening in weeks. When they passed the Hope and Anchor pub, Brinley turned her head away too – a glimpse of Maureen Connolly would have ruined her night.

Once they were through the main drag of the village, the girls slowed down to catch their breath. Shannon chewed on a nail, struck by a sudden wave of dread. 'What if Richard finds out we're gone?'

'We're here now,' said Brinley. 'If you're that worried, we can stay for half an hour and then head back.'

Shannon nodded, pacified. She would meet up with Kit,

as she'd promised she would, and slip home before her parents noticed anything was amiss.

The disco was in the church hall at the far side of the village, on the bend in the road that led to the secondary school and beyond.

As the girls turned the corner, music thumped across the quiet night, lights flashing against the wall in a fury of colour. Teenagers clutching plastic cups milled around outside, the boys play-fighting and peacocking while a handful of giggling girls watched them. One of the boys produced a plastic bottle of cider from behind a bush and refilled his cup.

'Ready?' said Brinley.

'As I'll ever be,' said Shannon.

The girls squeezed fingers, and then crossed the road and pushed hard against the double doors that led into the hall.

The music was so loud that Shannon considered turning round and going home, but Brinley was nudging her and jerking her head towards the empty dance floor in an unsubtle fashion.

There he was.

Kit hadn't noticed her yet. He was leaning against the DJ stand and had his back to her, disco lights playing across his T-shirt. He was talking to a girl – Shannon could see the cock of her hip and the pointed toe of a shoe, but not her face – and then he drained whatever was in his plastic cup and crushed it in his hand.

The girls loitered awkwardly on the edge of the dance floor. They were in the same class at school and shared one or two like-minded friends, but none of them had come tonight, preferring the company of their books to the agonies of a Year 8 school disco.

'Shall we dance or something?' said Brinley.

'No way!' Shannon's cheeks flushed. 'That would be so embarrassing.'

'OK, why don't you go and talk to Kit?'

'God, no. Not yet.'

Brinley laughed good-naturedly at her friend. 'What about a drink, then?'

'I suppose so.' Shannon ran a self-conscious hand through her newly shorn hair. A couple of pupils had whispered to each other when they'd seen her, but none had so far commented to her face.

They edged past clots of students, some gawky and shy, some preening and eyeing the opposite sex, and made their way to the kitchen hatch, where one of the PTA was serving non-alcoholic fruit punch.

'Bottoms up,' said the woman, all smiles and overdone bonhomie.

As they turned away, a girl from their class – Nicole Renton – bumped into Shannon's shoulder, splashing her drink all over her jeans.

'Sorry,' said Nicole, sounding bored. She looked Shannon up and down in a deliberate way. 'Oh,' she said, as if she'd only just noticed it. 'I like your hair.'

'Really?' said Shannon, a hopeful note in her voice.

'No,' said Nicole. Her laughter was edged with scorn. 'Oh, look,' she said, already walking off, 'there's Danielle and Orla.'

A whisper of moths flapped their wings in Shannon's

stomach. A lump lodged itself in her chest. She had hoped they wouldn't come tonight, but that had been misguided.

Danielle and Orla were surrounded by eager acolytes. She caught a glimpse of shiny hair, a cropped top and skin-tight trousers. Lipstick. Heeled boots. A leather jacket. Her own clothes seemed childish and unfashionable in comparison.

She exchanged a glance with Brinley. The joy that had filled them earlier was dimming. Both sensed an undercurrent of something darker to come.

'Shall we go?' said Brinley, low-voiced.

Shannon half heard the question but she didn't answer, transfixed by the scene playing out in front of her.

Danielle had broken away from her friends and was hip-swaying across the dance floor towards the DJ stand. She laid a proprietorial hand on Kit's arm.

Kit spun around to see who it was. Danielle draped both arms around his neck, but while he offered a polite smile, he placed his palms on her shoulders, maintaining a distance between them.

As he scanned the crowd filling up the church hall over the top of her head, he noticed Shannon standing in the corner, tugging at her hair. His face blazed with a fierce kind of pleasure.

He excused himself, and then he was moving across the hall towards the oldest Carter sister, leaving Danielle alone on the edge of the dance floor, a neon wash rinsing the stones of her eyes.

As Kit pulled Shannon into a hug, an unbearable lightness filled her up. She hid her face in his neck, uncertain about whatever this was, but willing it to last forever.

## WHEN I WAS TEN

Only Brinley noticed the way the light hollowed out the planes of Danielle's face, as hard and flat as flint.

If looks could kill, Shannon Carter would be sprawled across the floor with a knife sticking out of her back.

# 32

Sara stuffed another pillow under the duvet and admired her handiwork. At a glance, it looked exactly as if Brinley was asleep on the camping mattress on the floor.

She changed into her pyjamas and sat on the end of her sister's bed. The lamplight softened the starkness of the plain walls but threw up shadows that might have been monsters. She hugged her threadbare rag doll to herself and tried to concentrate on her book. She wondered if the girls were enjoying themselves and hoped they'd be home soon.

A draught nudged the bedroom curtains. Sara shivered in the thin breath of air and wandered over to shut the window. From downstairs, she heard the muffled ring of the doorbell but barely gave it a second thought. She peered into the dark garden. Would Shannon and Brinley be able to slip back in unnoticed? What if Dr and Mrs Carter heard them?

Concern pricked at her, questions needling her brain. Would the girls expect her to creep downstairs and open the front door rather than risk making a noise trying to climb through the window? She dare not think how her father would react if he discovered what they'd done.

She checked the clock. 9 p.m. At least an hour until the disco finished. No need to worry yet. Sara thumped Shannon's pillow and propped it up against the headboard, helped herself to a slice of leftover pizza and began to read again.

She couldn't be sure when she first realized something was wrong. Ten minutes later, perhaps fifteen. And it was more of a feeling than a knowing. She placed her book down, pages splayed across the duvet, and slipped off Shannon's bed, fingers trailing greasily across the cotton.

Sara stood in the centre of the bedroom, quiet as a mouse, and listened.

She could hear the drowsy night-time song of roosting birds and the occasional rumble of a car driving through the village, and the distant lowing of cows in the cattle shed down the lane. She could hear the shriek of a mating vixen and the groan of the hot water pipes, and the faintest drift of classical music.

A floorboard on the landing outside Shannon's bedroom creaked.

All at once, above the sounds of the night, she could hear a ringing in her ears and the push of blood through her veins and the quickening of her breath.

The noises in Sara's head were as loud as a rushing river and she willed her body to quieten itself. She stood as still as she could manage, straining to listen, trying to dismiss it as a trick of her imagination or the bones of the old house settling to bed.

After a few seconds – although to Sara it felt much longer – she began to relax, to assume that she must have been mistaken. She was fiddling with the make-up brushes on

Shannon's dressing table, dusting blusher across her cheek-bones, when something made her spin around, a crushing feeling in her chest.

Because there it was again, the creak of a landing floor-board that confirmed someone was standing outside the door.

Her gaze flitted to Shannon's bed, realizing too late she had forgotten to put back the pillow that was supposed to pass as her older sister's sleeping body. Too late to turn the radio on.

Fear tightened its cold fingers around her throat.

She had just enough time to pull shut the door to Shannon's tiny en suite bathroom before the bedroom door opened and Mrs Carter walked in.

She was carrying a glass of wine in her hand and an expression that Sara knew well.

'Hi, Pamela,' she said brightly, an antidote to the gathering clouds of her mother's anger.

Her mother stared at the pizza box on the bedroom carpet.

'Put that in the bin.'

Sara picked it up, the sickly taste of anxiety in her mouth. This was not going to end well. Alcohol sharpened the edges of her mother's personality until it cut her daughters to ribbons.

'Where's Brinley?' she said.

Sara made herself look at her mother. 'She's asleep. She was tired.' She gestured in the vague direction of the camping mattress.

Mrs Carter pursed her lips but did not comment. She glanced around the bedroom.

'What about Shannon?'

Sara's mouth dried. 'She's in the' – she coughed to clear her throat – 'bathroom.'

'I'll wait for her,' said Mrs Carter, putting down her glass. Sara noticed her lips were darkened by wine.

'She was going to have a shower, I think. She'll probably be a while.'

Sara kept her voice steady. She was good at lying and had perfected her technique over the years. She knew how to keep a story straight, how not to break under interrogation, and, most importantly, how to protect her older sister. But Mrs Carter's eyes were watchful and knowing. The flickerings of Sara's unease deepened into something more primal.

Mrs Carter raised her eyebrows. 'I see.'

The camping mattress had been made up and laid out under the window. Mrs Carter switched on the main bedroom light. Under its harsh glare, the duvet appeared lumpy and unconvincing, not human-shaped at all.

In three strides, Mrs Carter was across the room and kneeling by the pile of bedding.

'Don't wake her,' cried Sara, who could not bring herself to watch.

Mrs Carter ignored her. Propped in the corner of the room was Shannon's hockey stick and the older woman picked it up. With as much strength as she could muster, she brought down the weight of the wood on the soft mound beneath the covers. Once. Twice. Three times, she struck it. As hard as a hammer falling. As hard as an iron bar against flesh.

She pulled back the duvet to reveal a dented pillow and Brinley's discarded clothing.

Caught in a lie like a rabbit in a snare.

Her mother stood up, fluid and elegant, and headed towards the empty bathroom. Sara closed her eyes. Her mind was feeling around for ways she might warn her sister, but panic was whitening everything. In that blank space of fear, she couldn't think of anything useful at all.

Mrs Carter's back was to her youngest daughter. With controlled precision, she closed the bathroom door and turned to face her.

'Where are they?'

Her voice was soft, pleasant even. But Sara was not fooled. Dr and Mrs Carter were specialists in sleight of hand, the art of pretence, the cover story of loving discipline. The Carters were wonderful, *invested* parents, according to Sara's school teachers, her violin tutor, Brown Owl, the owner of the village bakery. According to everyone they knew. Except their children.

'I don't know,' she said.

A weighted silence settled over the bedroom. Sara had a lump in her throat and she kept swallowing, but it wouldn't clear. Her sister's bedroom represented comfort, but now the girl was cut adrift, alone and unprotected. Mrs Carter tipped her head to one side in a grotesque display of coquettishness.

'I think you do.'

Sara shook her head over and over again. 'I don't, honestly. I promise.'

In one swift movement, Mrs Carter smacked the hockey stick against the square of carpet in front of her daughter. Sara flinched. The room filled with the violence of torn air.

Tears slid from Sara's eyes, even though she was the

180

defiant one, the stronger of the two sisters. Mrs Carter repeated the action, interspersing each strike of the hockey stick with a word. She did not raise her voice.

'Where.' *Thud.* 'Are.' *Thud.* 'They?' *Thud.*

But fear muted Sara. She could not speak now, even if she'd wanted to.

Mrs Carter pressed her face up close to the girl. Sara could see where foundation had settled into her mother's pores and the rheum in the corner of her eyes, turned black by mascara. She smelled sour, of red wine and bitterness, and there was spittle at the edges of her lipsticked mouth. But the spark of joy that arced from Mrs Carter as she threatened her youngest daughter was the most terrifying part of it all.

'I will ask you one last time. Where are they?'

Marshalling every bit of her inner strength, Sara stammered out an answer. 'I don't know.'

The girl could not anticipate how her mother would react, but she did not expect laughter. Mrs Carter chuckled, throaty and amused. The delight that emanated from her was palpable.

She stroked the hockey stick, her fingers caressing its solid wooden curve.

'Get onto the bed. Face into the pillow, please.'

'No,' said Sara. *No.* And it wasn't a refusal, but a plea. 'No, please don't.' Her lower lip trembled. *Please don't.*

'Do as I say.'

Mrs Carter's voice was light, not a trace of anger or aggression. But Sara knew what her mother was capable of. The threat of violence, certainly. But its execution too.

And a doctor in the family proved useful at times. For

medication. Sutures. Proper dressings. But not *too* often. Not enough to raise suspicion. The odd accident here and there, a childhood rite of passage. A taster perhaps, but not the main course. Physical violence was too obvious, too easy to document, too difficult to explain away.

No, the Carters' stock-in-trade was fear and humiliation.

'Get onto the bed,' Mrs Carter said again.

Sara lay across the duvet, that same crushing feeling in her chest making it feel like all her organs were being squeezed until she couldn't breathe. She buried her face into Shannon's pillow, caught a trace of the scent of her sister's body spray.

She tensed, preparing for the strike of the hockey stick. Thirty seconds passed. A minute.

But it didn't fall.

Instead, she heard the soft tread of footsteps, a sense of moving air. The powerful smell of aftershave.

'What have we told you about lying?'

Dr Richard Carter, pillar of the community, much-loved GP and husband, father of two, had joined the proceedings.

Her bladder voided itself.

'Oh dear,' he said. 'You've had an accident. Shall we get you cleaned up?'

Sara didn't move. The last time this had happened, her father had given her antibacterial surface wipes to clean herself with. The insides of her thighs had been raw for days.

'Get up,' he said.

She dragged herself from the bed, her wet pyjamas clinging to her legs, her head bowed. Mrs Carter forced her to look at them by pinching the girl's cheeks between a polished thumb and forefinger and jerking her chin upwards.

'We didn't want you,' said Dr Carter conversationally.

'We should have got rid of you,' said Mrs Carter, squeezing harder.

'We don't love you.'

'You're disgusting.'

'Filthy.'

'No better than an animal.'

Sara's eyes glazed over. She looked beyond her parents to her sister's curtains, a jaunty gingham print. She counted the squares to distract her from the barrage of words. Their voices faded to a distant echo.

*One. Two. Three.*

'Worthless.'

*Four. Five. Six.*

'Pathetic.'

*Seven. Eight. Nine.*

'Ugly.'

*Ten. Eleven. Twelve. Thirteen. Fourteen. Fifteen.*

Mrs Carter kicked the pizza box that Sara had put back on the floor when she was ordered onto the bed. The corner of it grazed Sara's shin. 'Fat.'

*Sixteen. Seventeen.*

She pinched her daughter's arm. 'Are you listening to us?'

'Yes, Pamela.'

Dr Carter bent until he was at eye level with his daughter. 'Do you want me to take you to the shed?'

*No, no, no.*

Sara hated the shed because it was dark and cold, but mostly because of the spiders. The thought of them crawling into the hollow spaces of her body made her want to scream for the rest of her life.

'No thank you, Richard,' she said, not quite able to disguise the waver in her voice.

'Then you know what you need to do.'

'Where *are* they?' said Mrs Carter, dripping with honey. 'Tell us, sweetheart.' She put an arm around her daughter's shoulders. 'Come on, now.'

This was a common trick, to reel her in with endearments. But Mrs Carter's touch was surprisingly tender and Sara, starved of affection, leaned into her mother, confused by her feelings.

While Dr Carter peered out of the window into the darkness of the garden, Mrs Carter bent closer and whispered into her ear so he wouldn't hear. 'It will be better if you do as he asks. Get it over with quickly. Shannon will understand.' This kernel of humanity was so rare and unexpected that Sara began to cry again.

Dr Carter sat down on the edge of the bed and folded the girl's hand in his. 'Tell us, darling. It's cold in the shed. Too cold to spend a whole night there. There's a nest of spiders. And mice. I saw one earlier when I was getting the rake.'

*Eighteen. Nineteen. Twenty. Twenty-one. Twenty-two. Twenty-thr—*

When she didn't answer him, his voice hardened and he tugged on her hand. 'Have it your way then. Let's go.'

*No.*

*No, no.*

Her father pulled harder, anger soaking his words. 'Come *on*.'

*Twenty-four. Twenty-five. Twenty-six.*

He dragged her from the bed across the floor, towards

the door. She made herself as heavy as she could, but she was slight and he was strong, his temper making him rough with her. The carpet burned her skin. She hit the back of her head on the corner of the wall and cried out.

Her mother put a hand on Dr Carter's forearm. 'Go easy, Richard,' she murmured, but he shook her off.

'Tell us—'

*May my sister—*

'—where they—'

*—forgive me—*

'—are.'

*—for what I am about to do . . .*

'The disco.' She whispered it. He made her repeat it. A metallic bitterness flooded her mouth, the flavour of betrayal. She was not yet old enough to understand her parents had long since guessed the whereabouts of her sister, but got a kick out of manipulation and power play.

Dr Carter helped Sara to stand up. He gave her a flannel to wipe her face with. He kissed the top of her hair, murmuring his thanks. He coaxed her downstairs with promises of warm milk and biscuits.

And then he locked her in the shed.

# 33

I don't know what to do with myself.

Shannon and Kit are holding hands and grinning at each other, and I'm standing next to them, close but not *too* close. The spare part. The gooseberry. It's not like I'm not used to threes. Mother, father and me. Shannon, Sara and me. But in each of those triangles, I have my place. Not here, though. This is for them.

The disco pulses with noise and light and music. I've had enough. I'm ready to go home. But Shannon has lit up like a burning candle, and I can't ask her to leave now.

The crowd has loosened up. Five or six couples are shuffling around the dance floor, full of contraband cider and self-conscious smiles. Danielle has retreated to the corner, but she's still throwing venomous glances in Shannon's direction. My friend hasn't noticed. She's too wrapped up in Kit.

I can imagine what we'll be talking about all night, buried under our duvets. Giggling and whispering, replaying every word. But I'm not envious. I like seeing Shannon smile. She doesn't do it enough.

Monday morning will be a different story. The girls at school. But I can't think about that now.

Kit is leading Shannon by the hand to the dance floor, and there's something wholesome and old-fashioned in their interaction. They're delighted with each other. Even Danielle must see that.

But I can't stand here on my own any longer and I make my way through the throng towards the toilets – anything to kill a bit of time.

I push through the double doors and bump straight into Dr Carter.

He's charging into the church hall like he's on fire. His lips are pressed together, his jacket half unbuttoned. But when he sees me, he slows down. He smiles, but it's like he's forcing his facial muscles into an unnatural shape.

'Your father is looking for you,' he says.

I don't know what to say, but one panicked word flashes in my brain. *Mum.*

'Your mother is fine,' he says, reading my mind. 'But we assumed your father *knew* you were staying the night with us.' Dr Carter's tone is gently chiding. 'He was worried about you because it was dark and you're supposed to go home when the street lamps come on.'

He's still talking, but he's peering over my shoulder, his interest waning. 'He knocked on our door, looking for you. He was so relieved when I said you were up-stairs, but when Pamela went to fetch you, neither you nor Shannon were there.' He tries to smile again but it's not enough to hide his censure. 'Speaking of Shannon, where is she?'

That last sentence slips from him, casual as anything, but he's looking at me again, and there's an intensity in his expression that's unnerving.

I wonder what it cost Sara to give us up. And what Shannon's punishment will be.

But at least my father still cares enough to come and find me.

*My father.*

The penny drops, sending ripples across my self-awareness. A coldness takes root. The reason Dr Carter is here is nothing to do with my father – and everything to do with me. In my hurry to punish him for Maureen Connolly, for my mother, I didn't bother to tell him where I was. He's been so wrapped up in himself that I never thought he might come looking for me.

It's my fault Shannon's father is here.

It's my fault Dr Carter is about to humiliate my oldest and dearest friend in front of everyone at school.

'Is she in there?' he says, all trace of his earlier smile gone.

There's no point in pretending. 'Shall I go and get her?'

I don't wait for an answer, but start moving away from him, anxious to warn her, to protect her in the only way I know how. At least if I interrupt her dance with Kit, I can make sure there isn't an ugly scene. But his tone is hard and commanding, and it jerks me back like a lasso.

'No.'

I falter, not confident enough to challenge his unmistakeable authority. Then Dr Richard Carter pushes his way through the doors and strides into the disco.

# 34

The darkness was so dense it had texture.

Sara put her hands out in front of her and felt her way through the detritus of the garden shed – lawnmower, a set of ladders and a broom with rough bristles.

Fifteen minutes ago, the exterior lights of Hilltop House had spilled through the glass window and illuminated the guts of the squat wooden structure. The girl had used that shaft of deliverance to navigate her way to the centre of the shed, as far as possible from dusty corners filled with broken-up husks of earwigs and woodlice.

But then, without warning, the lights had gone out, plunging the shed into blackness.

Sara bit down on a scream, holding it inside her mouth like a secret. This was a road she had travelled before. As soon as her father had secured the padlock on the shed door, her mother must have walked down the garden and switched off the outside lights.

She pictured Dr Carter standing alone on the lawn, amongst the sleeping daffodils and tulips, a still, triumphant figure revelling in his acts of cruelty. She wondered what Mrs Carter was doing now. For the first time, she considered the possibility that her mother was as much in Dr Carter's thrall as his daughters were – and despised her for her weakness. The scraps of love she occasionally tossed them were no longer enough. Sara stuffed a hand into her mouth. However scared she felt, she would not give her father the satisfaction of articulating that fear.

She inhaled and exhaled until the impulse to cry out had passed.

When she had gathered herself, Sara's fingers closed around the metal frame of a garden chair. She worked at it, trying to open it, bent at the waist. As she straightened up, her head brushed something thick and matted. She touched her fingers to her crown, whimpering, and then her hands were batting at her face and hair and head. She pulled free a clump of web and dead insects, pawing at her blonde strands until she was certain there was nothing left, and flung it across the shed, tears spilling down her cheeks.

Sara fumbled her way into the chair and drew her knees up to her chin, trying to make herself as small as possible, using the heel of her hand to wipe away her sadness.

She closed her eyes.

The shed was not quite silent.

Through the darkness, she could hear the horses snickering in the stables that backed onto Hilltop House and the breath of the breeze through the trees. Beneath that, she could hear a faint scrabbling and caught the sense of movement. *Mice.*

She put her hands over her ears.

Sara started to count, the numbers appearing as bold outlines in her mind.

*One. Two. Three.*

She shut out the darkness of the shed and the bruise on her arm where her father had grabbed her, and the cold and wet pyjama bottoms clinging to her thighs.

*Four. Five. Six.*

She thought only of the numbers, precise and unshakeable, and found comfort in their familiarity.

*Seven. Eight. Nine.*

The last time her parents had locked her in the shed she had reached eleven thousand, nine hundred and forty-six.

The girl sat in the chair, counting, as the night deepened and clouds passed behind the moon. She could smell wood preservative, and manure from the stables, and the earthiness of her own urine.

*Eighty-five. Eighty-six. Eighty-seven.*

A feather-light sensation set off the nerve endings in her arm, all those tiny hairs standing on end. She jumped up, brushing at her skin, her heart knocking, panic spreading like fire, but there were no spiders, nothing there except the shadows of her imagination.

She slumped back down into the chair, worried about what was going to happen to Shannon when their parents found her. She strained to catch voices or the slamming of a door, but all she could hear was the night coming alive.

The air in the shed was so cold her breath was visible. She was shivering now, her thin pyjamas no protection against the dropping temperature. She wrapped her arms as tightly as she could around her body, trying to keep warm. The moon was rising, and through the slats, there was a glimmer of light. But for once, it didn't help.

It made the shadows bigger, and Sara couldn't help but wonder what was hiding in them. But there was nothing she could do, no place to put her fear. She stood up, deciding that moving around was the only way to keep warm.

But the darkness made her clumsy, and she tripped over the blade of her father's shovel and stumbled against the shed wall. Splinters buried their way into her upper arm through her sleeve, and the pain disoriented her. She knocked into an old picnic blanket that was hanging on a nail, dislodging the arthropod life that had made its home within it.

As the falling spiders cast out their draglines, their groping legs made contact with the skin at the neckline of Sara's pyjama top. They scuttered into the dark cavern, down her spine, towards the base of her vertebrae.

Sara screamed. An electric burst of fear. Her arms flailed, trying and failing to reach behind her. Urgent and afraid. *Get them off me.*

Spiders of all kinds lived in the shed. She had seen them last weekend when her father had sent her to fetch the weed killer. Black spiders with shiny backs imprinted with markings that looked like skulls. Pale spiders with jointed, oversized legs. Brown spiders, gorging on insects and covered in fine hairs.

She hated them all.

As quickly as she could, Sara whipped her top over her head and threw it on the floor, her senses aflame, imagining an army marching across her back, seeking out the crevices of her body.

In the secrecy of the night, she was plagued by what she couldn't see. She bent her arms behind her, trying to reach up between her shoulder blades, slapping at her skin in a frenzy.

She screamed again and again until her throat was swollen and she was reduced to nothing more than the sound of her fear.

Sara only stopped screaming when a spider crawled across her face, its legs exploring the dark opening of her mouth, and she collapsed to the floor in a dead faint.

# 35

Shannon didn't see him coming. She didn't stand a chance.

Her cheek was resting on Kit's shoulder, her eyes shut. She had never been so close to a boy before. The smell and feel of him made her feel dizzy, even though she'd consumed nothing more than a plastic cup of fruit punch. They shuffled together, still awkward with each other, finding their way.

She wondered what it would be like to kiss him, and whether it might happen that night and if it was true what the girls at school said, that boys used their tongues like a washing machine spin cycle instead of the chaste kisses she'd experienced from relatives.

'Shall we go outside in a bit?' His breath was warm against her ear, flipping her stomach.

She didn't want to betray her nervousness by looking at him, so she nodded, and he pulled her into him until the length of her body was pressed against his, no space between them.

The music changed to an up-tempo song, but neither of them moved, enjoying the sensation of teenage discovery.

The first indication that something was amiss was the

muttering that undulated across the dance floor like a murmuration of birds.

Shannon still had her eyes closed, inhaling Kit's cheap deodorant. She leaned into the solid shape of his chest, honed by years of swim training, a rare lightness inside her.

Beneath the music, she caught the rustle of many voices, handing observations to the next person and the next person and the next.

She opened her eyes.

The second indication was her awareness of space, that other students were backing away from them until Shannon and Kit were standing alone in the centre of the disco, lights playing across their faces.

Confused, Shannon half turned towards her classmates. They were lining the perimeter of the dance floor, watching them, an audience gathered for a public hanging. She glimpsed Brinley's agonized expression, and a wide smile of triumph from Danielle.

The third indication was the lifting of the needle from the record, and the violence of the silence that followed.

She turned her head, almost in slow motion, in the direction of that absence of sound.

Her father was standing at the DJ stand, the picture of benignity.

A wave of light-headedness threatened to take her legs from under her. If Kit hadn't been holding her, she might have collapsed to the floor. But he tightened his arm around her waist, keeping her upright.

In a failed attempt to gather herself, she hid her face in his chest, as if by looking away she could pretend Dr Carter was not there.

The awfulness of the situation made her nauseous. Not only had her father discovered her act of disobedience, he had marched across the village to find her. And now he was shaming her in front of *everyone*.

Her brain made connections at super-fast speed. Knowing him as she did, his need to maintain appearances would prevent him from making much more of a scene, but whatever happened here would pale in comparison to the punishment coming later, in the privacy of Hilltop House.

Her thoughts strayed to Sara, threaded by the bright heat of anger. Had her younger sister given her away? For God's sake, she had *told* her what to say. They had even rehearsed it.

In her mind's eye, she pictured Sara, lovingly eager and willing to please. Her sister was the most loyal person she knew. She would not have betrayed them – unless she was given no choice. Or perhaps her parents had worked it out by themselves. It was hardly rocket science.

The microphone crackled, a blur of feedback through the speakers.

*Oh no.*

'Apologies for interrupting your fun,' said Dr Carter, his voice tinny and amplified, filling every corner of the church hall. The DJ, no older than twenty, stood awkwardly behind him, no match for the force of the older man's personality. 'I'm looking for my daughter. Has anyone seen Shannon Carter?'

Shannon's skin grew hot.

Why was he doing this so publicly? Had her father not recognized her, standing in the centre of the dance floor?

Had he forgotten about her newly short hair? Perhaps he did not expect to see her in the arms of a boy. The thought of what he might do to Kit in a fit of temper dried her mouth.

She could not make her mind up. If she walked over to her father, she would have to deal with the stares and pointed fingers. If she ignored him, she would have to endure the excruciating prospect of him speaking into the microphone again.

The seconds stretched out, slowing down. She was aware of the pressure of Kit's hand on her back, and then a slight drawing away, as if he was embarrassed to be the centre of attention in this way.

Across the hall, the voices took up again, swelling in volume like the rush of a river in a storm.

Shannon's legs felt so heavy that lifting them seemed an impossible task. Pain sliced into her abdomen, high and sharp, just beneath her breastbone. Her face was coloured with shame.

She did not know what to do next, and that indecisiveness cost her.

Her father's voice echoed across the room again.

'Shannon Carter, please come to the DJ stand, where your father is waiting to take you home.'

Driven to end such public humiliation, to get as far away as possible, Shannon began to quietly explain to Kit her plan to slip from the church hall and make her own way across the village.

She was still standing on the dance floor when the first plastic cup hit her between the shoulder blades. She gasped as warm cider dripped down her back.

The whole room seemed to gasp too, a collective intake of breath. Kit backed away from her, inspecting his own clothes for splashes. Shannon pulled her soaking top away from her body, her cheeks burning. The hall was silent but the atmosphere was freighted with anticipation. Everyone was watching.

And then somebody laughed.

It was a girl's voice, just loud enough to be heard, and striated with cruelty. That was all it took.

Another girl joined in. And a third. A handful of boys were laughing too, nudging each other, embarrassed but hungry for a show, relieved it wasn't them. Within seconds, the place rang to a soundtrack of mockery.

The disco lights, flashing red and blue and green, lit up the expressions on the faces of the crowd. A boy in another class, teeth too big for his mouth, pointed at her and grinned. Shannon glimpsed a girl she played hockey with, eyes widened in faux shock, gossiping with her friend. Danielle whispered something to a tall boy standing next to her, and he slipped from view like smoke.

A second plastic cup struck her chest, spilling fruit punch across the front of her top.

Shannon barely had time to register the assault before another cup, thrown from the opposite side of the room, caught the edge of her jaw. Within seconds, she was under attack from all directions, plastic missiles spilling their contents over her, marking her with shame.

Kit, it turned out, was not the boy she thought he was. He had fled, and was now in the corner with his friends, his back to her, as if he couldn't bear to be associated with such indignity.

Shannon stood alone, unwilling or unable to move. Her clothes were clinging to her, the parquet floor slick with fruit punch and cider and lemonade, empty cups littered about her feet.

She wanted to die.

The adults seemed to have vanished. Even her father, who had been watching the scene unfold with a look of satisfaction, had slipped away, content with the havoc he'd wreaked.

Tears of mortification burned her eyes.

And then, from nowhere, a familiar figure was shielding her body from the plastic missiles and putting an arm around her shoulders, leading her away.

'Let's go,' said Brinley.

The crowd had turned uglier, if that was possible, a knot of students clustered around the doorway to the lobby, barring their exit.

With a courage that surprised Shannon, Brinley pushed her way through, shoving into the bodies that blocked them, words spilling from between gritted teeth. 'Get out of the way.'

Their escape was within touching distance. Shannon could see the lights of the village beyond the church hall exit sign, and the path that would take her home. She could not think beyond that. For now, all she wanted was the night air cooling her cheeks, and space to breathe and cry.

'Going so soon?' A voice drifted up from behind them. Danielle, arms folded across her chest, amusement in her voice.

'Ignore her,' said Brinley.

And Shannon intended to follow her friend's advice, but as she pushed against the double doors, humiliated but not beaten, she could not stop herself from throwing a final, scornful glance over her shoulder.

A plastic cup of something warm and foul-smelling hit her in the face.

Danielle and the tall boy shrieked with mirth, slapping each other on the back. Their friends joined in, whooping in delight. Feral and animalistic, a hunting pack.

Shannon stumbled outside. She heard one of the ladies from the church shout at the youngsters to go back inside the hall, heard the beat of the music restarting. She gagged and spat repeatedly on the grass. It was everywhere, in her hair and her eyes and mouth. The stink of it filled her nostrils.

Urine.

The lowest point of her life.

A longing for the comforting presence of her sister filled her up. She loved Brinley too, but Sara knew what it was to be the daughter of a man like Richard Carter. She would run her a bath and put her clothes in the washing machine. Poke fun at her tormentors and soothe her with the balm of her words. She would make her feel better. Loved. Her younger sister would do anything for her, and that was a powerful kind of knowledge. It made her feel safe. Mothered. She and Sara were a family. They didn't need anyone else.

Out of the corner of her eye, she saw her father emerge from the church hall. He hurried over to them, concern on his face.

'My poor girl. Let's get you home.' He put an arm around

her shoulder. She wanted to shake him off, but she knew there would be repercussions. Brinley caught her eye. It was clear from her expression that Dr Carter's act was not fooling her either.

Lies. All of it. He didn't care about her at all.

'You'd better get off, Brinley,' he said. 'Your father's expecting you.' He swept fingers through his hair, preening himself. 'I don't know. You girls will send us grey before our time.'

'Will you be OK?' said Brinley, in a low voice.

Shannon nodded. What other choice was there?

She watched her friend run off down the road towards the village, dreading what might happen now she was alone with her father.

His fingers gripped the top of her arm and they began to walk, their footsteps moving in unison.

Her wet clothing was making her shiver, and it reminded her of last week, in the park, when she saw a father take off his jumper and give it to his young son, who was complaining of being cold. The hem had hung well below his knees, the sleeves covering his hands, and the child had smiled up at his father, trusting and secure in his love. Richard Carter had never done anything like that for her; at least, not without an audience.

Only when they reached the footpath by the river did her father break his silence. The blue-black sky was vast. It promised a world beyond the barbarity of Hilltop House. The water pushed against pebbles again and again, like the sound of crying.

'Your mother,' he said, his tone light and conversational, 'should have aborted you.'

Shannon didn't reply. Long ago, she had learned there was no value in answering back. But one thought drummed its way through her head as they made their way back to the house.

*I hate you. I wish you were dead.*

# 36

'Your mother should have aborted you.'

I'm so shocked by Dr Carter's words I almost slide backwards into the river. I grab at the foliage of the bush I'm hiding behind and it's enough to steady me. My heart is playing drums against my ribs.

*Your mother should have aborted you.*

What an awful thing to say.

I should have been home by now, and I whisper an apology to my father, who is probably watching for me at the window, anxiety creasing his brow, but instead I've concealed myself behind a bank of shrubs that line the towpath because I'm scared for Shannon.

Despite his smiles and community spirit and generosity with money, I've always suspected Dr Carter is a wolf in sheep's clothing. Tonight has confirmed it.

I *saw* him. When he thought all eyes were on his daughter, I *saw* him. He watched them humiliate her – *instigated* it – and instead of stepping in, he left her to fend for herself, slipping away to join the supervising adults drinking tea in the kitchen, who were oblivious to the unfolding drama, distracted by village gossip and complaining about giving up their Saturday night.

For all his faults, I can't imagine my own father being so cruel.

*Hush now, Brinley.*

I hold my breath. Shannon and Dr Carter are so close I could reach out my hand and touch them as they pass.

A light drizzle has begun to fall. It's cold now, and the river is getting angrier. There are dirt and twigs on the ground, and a stone is digging into the sole of my boot. I shift, trying to keep quiet, peering through the bushes until I have a clearer view.

Shannon does not look like the girl I know. That girl is witty and warm, although her edges can cut occasionally. Her smile has gone, and the light in her eyes has flattened into darkness. I can see the sharp outline of her shoulder blades through her wet vest-top, and something about that makes me feel sad.

Dr Carter is holding her arm, but not in a supportive way. He says something else to her, but a sudden rush from the river drowns out the sound of his voice. Her face falls, and she starts to cry, gut-wrenching sobs that hurt my heart.

I should go. I've known Shannon since I was born, and she does not like anyone to see her upset. But if I slip away now, they'll notice me, and anyway, I can't leave her alone in the dark of the night because she's my friend, a sister to me in the absence of one of my own. I'm here for her, even when she doesn't know it.

She stumbles and lands on her knees. Instinctively, my hand jerks out to help her up, but I let it drop and watch instead.

Dr Carter grips her arm and drags her to her feet. She yelps in pain, his fingers pinching her skin, but he's impassive, nothing behind his eyes.

'Whore.'

The insult is precise and brutal, like a whip strike. She flinches. We've been doing *Much Ado About Nothing* at school. I know exactly what a whore is. We both do.

'I'm not.' But the defiance has leaked from her voice. She sounds frightened.

'What have you let him do to you?'

She is shaking her head, over and over again. 'Nothing, I promise. He's just a friend.'

He raises his hand, and for one terrible moment, I think he is going to hit her, and I want to run and fetch my father, because he has always abhorred violence against women and I know this would disgust him.

But there are voices coming along the footpath in the opposite direction, their merriment soaked in alcohol, and we are all saved by a couple on their way home from the pub.

Dr Carter takes off his jacket and is slipping it around Shannon's shoulders as they come into view.

'Evening, Doc,' says Mr Howarth, the village's butcher, raising an eyebrow. He nods his head in Shannon's direction. 'One shandy too many, eh?'

Dr Carter chuckles. 'Something like that.'

'Rain's setting in,' says his wife. 'Best get home. The forecast's for thunderstorms tomorrow.'

'Will do,' says Dr Carter. 'This one needs a warm bath . . .'

'And a cup of coffee, I'll bet.' Mr Howarth laughs loudly at his own joke.

Dr Carter smiles and nods at Mrs Howarth. 'Will I see you in the surgery next week? We'll have a chat about that knee op, shall we?'

She blushes. 'I'll make an appointment on Monday.' Lays a hand on his arm. 'You're a good 'un, you are, always busy, always thinking of others.'

He twinkles at her. 'No rest for the wicked, Mrs H.' She giggles. It is repulsive.

Then they are saying their goodbyes.

I watch Shannon and Dr Carter disappear into the night, his arm around her shoulder like a steel trap ready to tighten on its prey, and I wait for Mr and Mrs Howarth to get far enough away for me to creep out from behind the bush.

It's freezing now, but something burns bright inside me.

I make my way back along the river, the rain and dirt muddying the boots Shannon lent me. All at once, I feel homesick for the laboured breathing of my mother asleep in her bed. At least my father has come looking for me. At least he cares enough to wonder where I am.

The windows in my house are blank with darkness when I arrive except for one, which is lit by the glow of a lamp. The sight of it cheers me.

I find my key and unlock the front door. 'Daddy,' I say, a diminutive I haven't used for years. 'I'm home. I'm sorry I didn't tell you where I was.'

I kick off Shannon's boots and start looking for him, overwhelmed by a need to feel the comfort of his arms around me and reassure myself that not all fathers are like Dr Carter.

But he's not in the sitting room or the study. I pause by my mother's makeshift bedroom, a room that used to host noisy Sunday dinners before the long table was consigned to the garage. Now the only furniture is a single bed, a hard-backed chair, and a small free-standing cabinet covered in medication and a bowl of half-melted ice chips. Her breath is rattling like a penny in a charity box. I want to go to her, but I can't bear the idea of disturbing her, so I hover by the door until the sound hurts my ears and my heart.

The only room downstairs I haven't tried is the kitchen.

I push open the door. The surfaces are shining and clean, as if someone has scrubbed them. *Maureen Connolly*. It's certainly not my father. I assume that same someone has rescued the fish pie from the bin because there's a plate of it covered in clingfilm on the side and a note written in biro – *BRINLEY, MICROWAVE FOR FIVE MINS* – balanced on top of it.

The house feels too empty. My mother is here but she's not here. No radio playing, no television or music. But I still think my father is upstairs – he can't have left my mother alone – and any minute he's going to appear from the shower or his bedroom, and hug me, like he used to when I was five and had skinned my knees.

But then I notice another scrap of paper on the kitchen table, held in place by an upside-down glass, and it's another bruise to my heart.

*GONE TO PUB FOR A PINT. BACK SOON. DAD X*

# 37

The torchlight almost blinded her.

'Up you get,' said Mrs Carter.

Sara tried to stand, but her legs felt wobbly and there was a thickness in her head that clouded her ability to think of anything very much at all. Mrs Carter emptied a bottle of water in her face.

That shocked her into movement, and she forced herself upright, a painful feeling of fluid up her nose. The plunge into brightness after lying in the dark made her blink, lightning streaks flashing behind her eyes.

Mrs Carter caught her by the wrist and guided her out of the shed. The grass was wet against Sara's bare feet, drizzle filling the air, her lungs, coating her skin in a fine layer of moisture.

*One. Two. Three. Four. Five.*

Her mother's mouth was close to her ear. 'If you ever tell anyone about this, your father will lock you in the shed for a week without anything to eat or drink.'

*Six. Seven. Eight.*

'He can't help himself, you know. He wasn't always like this. He had a—'

*Nine. Ten.*

'—challenging childhood.'

*Eleven. Twelve. Thirteen.*

'He takes his duties as the head of our family very seriously.'

*Fourteen. Fifteen.*

'He doesn't enjoy uncertainties. He only wants the best for us all. He needs to feel like he's in control.'

*Sixteen. Seventeen. Eighteen.*

Mrs Carter's expression soured. 'Are you listening to me? Will you listen to your sister when she tells you how much she hates you for giving her secrets away?'

Even at the tender age of ten, Sara had learned to ignore her mother when she was in this kind of mood, but the barb about Shannon made her lose track of her counting. The idea that she might, somehow, be blamed by her sister made her stomach churn. Because if Shannon didn't love her, she had no family at all.

Her mother's parents did not like children and were not interested in Sara or her sister. They never sent birthday or Christmas gifts, and she could not recall the last time she had seen them. Dr Carter's mother and father had disinherited him years ago, although no one would tell her why. At the time, his anger had been a black, buzzing fly, crawling over everything, but now he did not mention them.

Her father's grandmother had always been kind – she remembered a warm, elegant woman with a sweep of silver hair folding a pound coin and her telephone number into her hand, a murmured question, asking if she was OK. But the passing of the years had lengthened the distance between them until they were no longer in touch with that side of the family, and the scrap of paper that might have been a lifeline had fallen to pieces.

Sara stumbled down the garden towards Hilltop House, Mrs Carter holding her by the arm. Light shone through the sash windows but it didn't look welcoming. It looked like the house was ready to swallow her up.

The bay trees threaded with tiny lights that bracketed the driveway; the vast and expensive crystal chandelier that dominated the hallway and was visible to passers-by; the wide front door painted a glossy black. These were the hallmarks of affluence, but to Sara they were nothing more than the trappings of a gilded cage.

She did not need to hear her father speak to know that Dr Richard Carter was home. The house trembled with it. The air was tinged with the aroma of his distinctive brand of aftershave and his jacket was hanging on the newel post at the bottom of the stairs. But even if these clues had not been evident, Sara would have known. His presence altered the fabric of the atmosphere, curdled it. He was the giant at the top of the beanstalk, the wolf in Grandma's cottage, the king who threatened to cut off the head of the miller's daughter unless she spun straw into gold.

The chandelier in the hallway made everything seem bright, almost white. Sara's teacher had said in an RE lesson that darkness cannot overcome the light. But Sara wished it would. The light meant there was nowhere to hide. It was clinical and harsh and unforgiving, exposing her weaknesses, the shaking of her hands, the fear she had not yet learned how to mask, as an adult might. The light was not a warm, friendly thing, but an enemy.

A scream, a rend in the thick curtain of silence of the house, erupted from upstairs.

Sara's head jerked upwards. Mrs Carter lifted her own chin and smiled. 'Let's go up and join them, shall we?'

Dr Carter was waiting in her bedroom, leaning against her chest of drawers, his arms crossed. There was no sign of her sister.

'Get in the shower. You stink. But cold water only.'

'Where's Shannon?' He might not answer her but she was compelled to ask. Her ears strained for the sound of movement from her sister's room, but it was quiet.

'That's for me to know and you to find out. Shower. Go to bed. And don't leave this room for the rest of the night.'

'Can I just see her? Please, Richard. Why was she screaming?' The words tumbled from her, fear for her sister emboldening her.

'Did you hear what I just said?'

She nodded miserably and did as she was told, supervised by Mrs Carter, who ensured the temperature dial did not rise beyond a certain point and who gazed at her body with such disdain that Sara crossed her arms over her chest. All the towels had been removed, so she was forced to run naked from the shower to her bedroom, wet hair dripping down her back.

Her parents did not allow her to dress but insisted that she climb into bed without drying herself, making the sheets damp and cold. She cuddled Raggedy Ann. A cousin in America had given her the rag doll when she was three and, even now, it remained a source of comfort.

'If we catch you out of your bedroom, there will be serious consequences for you both.' Dr Carter spoke in the same even tone that he always did.

Her father was almost at the door when he turned and walked back to the bed, yanking the rag doll from his daughter's hands. She resisted, holding on to it for as long as she could, but her father was much stronger.

'You're too old for this now,' he said. 'These are for babies.'

With that, Sara was left alone in the dark, tears soaking her pillow. But underneath the sorrow, she felt relief – an overwhelming surge of it – that her parents had left her alone for now.

And anger, as fierce and destructive as fire.

# 38

## Sunday, 20 April 1997

A thud and a muffled swear word.

I wake from a light sleep, cold and awkward, my neck stiff from dozing off in the chair by my mother's bed.

The moon is a perfect sphere, bright and watchful. It's moved around the sky and tells me it's late, gone midnight. I forgot to close the curtains and my mother is looking at me with dulled eyes, but there's love in the creak of her voice.

'He's lost his way. Don't hold it against him.'

So my stupid, drunken father has woken her up too. I reach for her hand across the covers. It's dry and weightless, sticks of bone covered in skin. 'But he's not here, is he? He should be with you.'

'He's doing his best, my love.' She's speaking so quietly I have to lean closer to hear her. 'It's a lot to take in. For all of us.'

'I hate him.' My whisper is full of resentment.

'Bitterness is a wasted emotion.' She gathers herself to say something more, but the effort is clear. Her words drift and fade, and I have to fill in the spaces, but I think I know what she's saying. 'Don't let it poison you.'

'He promised he wouldn't leave your side.'

The ghost of a smile and her hand twitches beneath mine. The silver chain she always wears catches in the warmth of the lamplight. The clock ticks on, counting out her minutes left in this world. And then, 'Lies are a necessary evil sometimes, sweet girl.'

She closes her eyes, and there's a rattle in her throat, and her breathing becomes even more laboured. I wait for her to speak again but she doesn't say anything, and I sing to her, softly, so only she can hear.

And for a brief and perfect time, it's just me and my mother, breathing and loving each other in the lonely heart of the night.

I smell him before I see him. Cigarettes and the damp outdoors. The sweet-sour breath of a drunk. Perfume. A beer can cracking open like the sound of a gunshot, and before I know it, he's leaning against the door frame, watching us.

'My two girls,' he says, his words slurring thickly together like water and earth to make mud. I want to snap at him, *What about Maureen Connolly?*, but I swallow it down for my mother's sake.

I stand up and go to him. 'The out-of-hours nurse came by. She's topped up her morphine but she says you're to do it later, if she needs it.'

'Yes, ma'am,' he says in a fake American accent, and nods in slow motion, his chin pressing against the top of his chest. 'You go to bed. I'll take it from here.'

He staggers across the room. I eye him doubtfully. 'Are you sure?'

## WHEN I WAS TEN

My father sits heavily in the chair and puts his beer can on my mother's medicine cabinet. He smiles and blinks at me, and through a haze of alcohol, I catch a glimpse of the man I love. 'I'm sure. Now go to sleep, it's late.'

I climb the stairs, brush my teeth and get into bed. I'm tired and I want to shut out the world, but as soon as I close my eyes, I can't stop thinking about my mother and Maureen Connolly, and the fate of the Carter sisters.

I can still see the expression of fear and capitulation on Shannon's face when, finally, sleep pulls me under.

# 39

Hilltop House is in silence but it is not asleep.

Rain is drumming on the roof and spilling over the gutters, thrown, like loose gravel, against the brickwork and windows. The rivulets running down the glass doors that open into the garden glint like eyes in the darkness.

The moon has moved again, but now she is behind the clouds. It is later. These are the hollow hours, when sleep makes vulnerable even the cruellest men and women.

The house is waiting for something to happen. Its walls are swollen with expectation. The clocks count down. The floors shift and settle, preparing themselves. Every house has a history that creeps into its cracks and contaminates the atmosphere, but this is different.

The house *knows*.

# 40

Sara opened her eyes.

She felt around for Raggedy Ann, but the sheet was cold and empty. A tear trickled out of one eye.

When they were younger, Dr Carter had taken Shannon's favourite teddy bear outside to the shed as punishment and cut off its arms and legs with a pair of shears. She hoped, with the fervent ardour of a ten-year-old, that Raggedy Ann would not meet the same fate.

She sat up in bed. Rain was pounding against her window. Sara leaned over to her bedside table and checked her wristwatch. 3.59 a.m.

She began to count, but not as a way of finding her safe place. This was for a different reason. When she reached sixty and the house was still quiet, she slipped out of bed.

She pulled on a clean pair of pyjamas, shivering in the dark eye of the night, but the monsters under her bed were less frightening than the ones asleep in the bedroom across the landing.

With light, careful steps, Sara crossed the carpet and turned her doorknob as quietly as she could manage.

The creak of the opening door sounded to her like a shriek in the darkness, and she paused, the blood pumping too loudly in her ears.

The landing was in the shape of a horseshoe, a balustraded gallery overlooking the hall below. Sara's bedroom was next to Shannon's, and Dr and Mrs Carter slept on the opposite side of the horseshoe, away from the girls.

Shannon's door was ajar.

She tiptoed along the landing and pushed against it. The room was in darkness but she could see enough to know that Shannon wasn't in there. She switched on the light.

The bed was empty but the floor was covered with scraps of paper. Sara crouched to retrieve one. It was covered in Shannon's handwriting: *The Habsburg dynasty was* . . . She grabbed another one: . . . *life cycle of a frog*. There were hundreds of them, all written in black ink on lined paper, all jagged around the edges, where they had been torn up. Her sister's homework – all of it – had been destroyed and scattered across the floor like twisted confetti.

Her sister's diaries – at least four of them – were strewn across the carpet too, but there were no words between the hard covers, just stumps of paper where the pages had been ripped out.

Their father's handiwork.

As she was deciding what to do next, she caught the groan of the staircase, and a few seconds later, sensed movement behind her.

Shannon was standing there, a glass of water in one hand, the other tucked behind her back.

'Did Richard . . . ?'

Sara indicated the mess on the floor but couldn't bring

herself to finish the question. The expression on her sister's face told her everything she needed to know.

Shannon still looked like her sister. She had a mole on her cheek and white-blonde hair and a mouth that was wide and full. But a blind had been lowered. Her eyes were dead, nothing behind them to power their winter-blue light. Her lips were set in a line, no smile twitching at their corners. No frown or anger. No sadness. An absence of emotion, of feeling. Of *anything*.

She was a husk, the life sucked from her.

A fury began to rise again in Sara, burning her up like a fever. 'Shannon.' She shook her shoulder, trying to provoke a response. 'Shannon.'

But her sister did not reply. She stood alone, fingers curled around her drink, other hand tucked away, and stared through Sara as if she were made of glass.

Sara took a step towards her, to try and coax her back to bed. But Shannon recoiled, widening the distance between them. The younger girl's hand brushed against her sister's arm. Her skin was cold and pale. The bloodless ghost of a twelve-year-old.

'Shannon, you're scaring me.'

She was pleading now, urging her sister to show herself, to make a joke or whisper a secret, or even gaze at Sara with disdain. But Shannon was lost in a distant land and Sara could not reach her.

A montage of her childhood flashed before her. The disgust etched on her mother's face when Sara had tried to hug her with dirty hands, one of her earliest and formative memories. The litany of insults and degrading punishments and lack of love. The humiliation and lies and manipulation of others. The occasional, confusing flashes of kindness. The benign tone of her father even as he uttered the most vicious of taunts. Richard Carter walked alongside the devil, and her mother followed them both.

Anger roared inside Sara, a blinding, terrible rage.

For their lost childhood.

For their powerlessness.

For their damaged hearts.

For a future that would always be tainted by the stain of their unhappy upbringing.

For the broken bits of her most beloved sister.

A bell rang with startling clarity in her young mind. For years and years, the sisters had blamed themselves for their treatment, believing they were unlovable, that their own greed or poor behaviour was somehow responsible for the living nightmare in which they were trapped. But all at once, Sara realized this was as far from the truth as their freedom.

Culpability was a big word. It had been one of their spellings at school and Mrs Jackson had explained what it meant. *Blame or fault. Accountability.*

Richard and Pamela Carter would be made to pay for what they had done.

# 41

Rain.

It wakes me up.

I was dreaming of my mother. The sense of loss is so acute it feels like I've been weeping and when I touch my fingers to my face, it's wet.

But then I realize I've forgotten to shut the window and the rain is coming in. A small puddle has collected on the sill. I stand on my bed and close it. My father says under the window is a stupid place for a bed, but my mother persuaded him to let me keep it there. She knows I like to look up and watch the stars as I fall asleep.

My throat closes up. It isn't fair. Why does *my* mother have to be ill? Why can't it be Maureen Connolly or Pamela Carter?

My mother would know what to do about Shannon and Sara. For so long, I've kept it a secret because I promised them I wouldn't tell, but the need to confide in my mother about what I witnessed last night – and all those other times – is overpowering. My mother would believe me. She would listen. Offer calm words and sensible advice. But she's too sick to do anything about it now, and I can't talk to my father like I can talk to her.

I want to see her.

The urge drives me out of bed, pulling a sweatshirt over my pyjamas and down the stairs.

My mother is asleep, the rattling penny back in her throat. Watching her soothes me. The lines of pain are smoothed into something approaching peace. She looks younger. More like my mother than she has done for weeks.

The same cannot be said of my father. He's supposed to be taking care of her, but he's asleep too, his snores drowning out the sound of the rain. Three beer cans sit on the cabinet-cum-table now, and the room smells of the pub and an underwash of something sickly sweet.

'Dad?' I say, but he doesn't stir.

A line of drool is escaping from his mouth and down his chin. Something red and smudged marks his cheek.

Maureen Connolly wears red lipstick.

The rain hammers down and I stand in my mother's room, and I remember what kind of woman she is. Her kindness. The way she listens. Her empathy. The importance she places on doing the right thing.

I think about Shannon, about that look on her face at the disco, all the broken parts of her. About comfort and friendship. About being there for someone when they need you, even when it's difficult. *Especially* when it's difficult.

And I make a choice.

I press my lips to my mother's cheek. 'I'll be back soon.'

*

The rain is cold and there's too much of it. It streams into my eyes and down the back of my coat, and there's a hole in my shoes, making my feet wet.

Hilltop House is in darkness, but I know where I'm going because I've been there so many times before.

I crawl through the hole in our fence and push through the shrubs and bushes until I find myself in next door's garden, but I keep to the dark edges to avoid the security lights.

There it is: the garage.

The trellis that clings to the side acts like a ladder, and I'm halfway up, feeling for footholds with my toes, before it occurs to me to that Shannon's window might be closed now. I glance upwards. It is.

I climb back down, cursing my stupidity, and grub in the dirt for a stone to throw at her window, but my aim is off, and it clatters against the guttering. The rain blinds me. *Go home, Brinley.*

The patio is wet and slippery, and I shelter under the lip of the conservatory while I decide what to do next, my trainers nosing against a metal foot scraper, pushed into the wall, close to the door.

The Carter family keep their spare key there. Shannon showed me last summer, when we'd come back here after school one day and she'd forgotten hers.

*Absolutely not.*

This is not my house. It would be wrong in a hundred different ways. Intrusive. Illicit. I can't just let myself in without permission.

*Can I?*

Bending down, I feel around in the darkness for the key,

half hoping it's not there. My fingers close around cold metal. It's a stupid idea. I'll get caught. The idea of running into Dr Carter and his false smile almost sends me back home.

*Home.*

I have a safe place to escape to, but Shannon has nowhere. A gust of wind threatens the trees and blows rain into my face, making my teeth chatter, and this decides me.

The lock is stiff but I jiggle the key for a few seconds and twist it, and the back door opens. It's not trespassing if my best friend lives here, is it? After all, I was supposed to be staying the night.

The kitchen hums with life. The expensive fridge that's twice the size of ours. The washing machine that's spinning in a slow circle like a bicycle wheel.

But there's no burglar alarm to worry about, no barking dog. I know Hilltop House almost as well as my own home. But I feel unsettled and out of place. A worm of doubt wriggles in my belly. I shouldn't be here.

It's late – the clock on the oven says 4.03 a.m. My fingers trail along the work surface. Now I'm inside, I want to leave, but I've come so far, and so I pretend to myself that I *am* staying the night. I hang my sodden coat on the back of a kitchen chair and run lightly up the stairs. I'll just open Shannon's door, check on my friend, and then I'll go home.

But in the black corridor of someone else's house, my bravado deflates. I stand at the top of the landing, heart running faster. What if Shannon screams when I go into her room? What if her parents wake up? What the effing blinders, as my father would say, am I doing here?

The boiler rumbles, making me jump, and I decide to

leave before I get caught. My foot is on the top step when I hear a grunt and a noise I can't place coming from her parents' room.

I hover, uncertain, and then tiptoe back across the landing and stand in the darkness, my eye to the crack of the door, a window into hell.

# 42

Pamela Carter could hear a wet sound, like the drip of a tap. Still sludgy with sleep, she listened to the darkness.

*raining a leak from the gutter fix it tomorrow*

She lay on her side, drowsy and warm under the goose-feather duvet, but the wind was playing a tune on the roof tiles and the percussion kept her awake. Her mind ambled down several pathways.

*roast lamb for Sunday lunch fresh rosemary from the garden girls can make do with cereal silly little disco liars finish knitting baby blankets more punishments tomorrow shed deserve it keep out of his way girls and me what's that what's that?*

A sense of displaced air.

Mrs Carter was not allowed to roll over or switch on the light in case it disturbed Richard, but she could see the digital clock, her cheek pressed against the pillow. *4.06 a.m.* She tensed, waiting to see if she had imagined it. Thirty seconds passed before she realized that something was very wrong – and by then, it was too late.

The scissor blades, pressed neatly together, struck her between the left and right scapula and missed her heart by a couple of centimetres. It didn't hurt, not at first, just a feeling of pressure. Before she had a chance to react, to turn over, to even cry out, the scissors were pulled free and driven down again with such force that the blades pierced one of her lungs, collapsing it.

Blood leaked from the wounds, soaking the expensive Egyptian cotton bed linen, dyeing it a darkly rich shade of suffering.

Mrs Carter heard a gasping and sucking sound like a fish out of water. She knew all about fish. Her father used to take her and her older brother down to the river, threading maggots onto the curved steel and casting the line into green murk, sun glinting on the water. It took her a moment to understand the sound was coming from her.

The scissor blades impaled her again and again, in a frenzy, a bloodlust. The hollow at the base of her throat. A patch of freckled skin above her pancreas. The force of one blow ruptured her spleen. She could not make herself move, the effort too great, save for the lifting of her head and thudding it back down on the pillow.

She heard her youngest daughter say something, urgent and high-pitched, and there was a relief from the pressure on her back for a few seconds as the bedroom light was switched on.

Mrs Carter's eyes hurt at the sudden assault of brightness and her manicured fingers twitched against her husband. She could not understand why he was not doing anything to halt this brutal attack on her, in the sanctity of their home, when she had given all of herself to him, although her thoughts were more muddied than that. With sheer force of will, she rotated the leaden weight of her head in his direction.

Dr Richard Carter was on the far side of the bed, throat

exposed, head lolling over the edge of the mattress, his eyes glassy with surprise. It was clear, even as his wife lay bleeding out, even as the edges of her vision blackened and blurred, that he was dead.

She tried to say something, to scream or beg for help, but blood bubbled in her windpipe, dribbling out of the corners of her mouth like juice from overripe fruit when the knife slides in.

*Whatshappeningwhatshappeninghurtsithurtssaraisherecall policephone*

The pain kicked up several notches.

Mrs Carter writhed, trying to escape herself and the burn of multiple stab wounds, but she was too badly injured for the movement to do much except accelerate the speed of her blood loss.

The life had leaked from Richard Carter in three minutes and fifty-six seconds. It took his wife longer to die.

# 43

Something wet touches my feet.

A dark and gleaming puddle is seeping under the bedroom door. It blooms across the landing carpet, a scarlet flower in the most unexpected of places.

The human instinct for self-preservation stops me from screaming, even though I want to. I stuff a hand into my mouth to stop it from spilling out, but I can feel it rising up from my stomach, through my chest and into my throat.

An eye to the crack of the door again.

Dr Carter is slumped over the edge of the mattress, a hole in the side of his neck. A *drip-drip* sound is coming from him. A word blazes in my mind. *Blood.* It hits the whitewashed floorboards with a delicate splash.

Mrs Carter is lying on the other side of the bed, a mess of subcutaneous fat, tissue and exposed bone, her fingers trailing against the floor.

The Carter sisters, white-haired and spattered with bodily matter, stand at the foot of the bed like avenging angels, a pair of bloodied kitchen scissors in Sara's hand.

Shannon, in her daisy-print pyjamas, is pale and silent, as still as a marble statue.

In shock, I stumble against the bedroom door, which widens and betrays me with a creak. Sara lowers the scissors and looks up. Across the broken bodies and the smell of rusty pipes, our eyes lock.

She takes a step towards me.

A moan slides from somewhere inside, and I back away, across the landing and into the main bathroom.

Slide the lock across the door.

Crawl across the tiles to the toilet.

Throw up until my stomach is an empty space.

Our sink is cemented with toothpaste but the Carters' is clean and as dry as bone. Crying and shaking, I splash my face and take long swallows from the tap.

Someone rattles the door handle. Says my name. It's Sara. Not shouting, but speaking, explaining, words tumbling from her like gifts. She asks me to unlock the door but I refuse. Her voice is soft and apologetic.

I fall backwards into the shower cubicle and slide the glass doors around me, as if that might afford me protection. Make myself as small as possible. Whisper the daily prayer we learned during the first term at school because there's comfort in the ebb and flow of the words.

I do not allow myself to think of Dr and Mrs Carter, no longer human but lumps of bleeding meat, or the skewering of the scissors into my own body because of what I've seen. I am now a witness. Bury my head in my knees and try to disappear. Box it up and push it as far away as possible.

I do not know how long it takes me to realize that the Carter sisters are not coming for me. But daylight is creeping over the windowsill and the birds have begun their merry calls when I dare to lift my head.

Even so, I cannot bring myself to move from the safety of the shower. Only the howl of a siren half an hour later jerks me from a dazed reverie into action.

Unfolding my body, I crawl across the tiles, across the stained landing carpet and, eyes screwed shut, into the bedroom, over the floorboards that hurt my knees, to where Mrs Carter is lying.

Morbid curiosity? Perhaps. But humanity, too, an urge to do what's right and check for signs of life.

Her fingers, hanging over the edge of the bed, graze my hair and I open my eyes. But when I touch her hand, tentative and repulsed, it is cold. One side of her head is matted with dark clots but her eyes are still blue and watchful. I press a fingertip to the sheets, the dampness reddening its whorls and grooves.

A pillow has fallen on the floor. I pick it up and hold it to my chest, a shield to ward off the evil that dwells here.

I make a decision.

I have never liked Mrs Carter, but I think again of my mother's counsel, of kindness, of giving of oneself for the sake of others. I could not bear my own mother to die alone, and because of that, I cannot bring myself to leave Mrs Carter by herself either, whatever her sins.

I sit next to her. Two or three minutes pass. I press my fingers against her eyelids until they close. And then I curl up and lie at the end of the bed, careful not to touch her again.

I do not look at Dr Carter at all.

By the time the police find me, Sara has dialled 999 and confessed to the murder of her parents, and I'm still lying next to her mother's body, my pyjamas so saturated with blood they think I'm dead too.

# 44

The next few hours pass in a blur.

I do not see the Carter sisters again, except the backs of their heads as they are guided from Hilltop House towards the waiting police cars.

The sky is grey with the promise of rain as we walk along the short stretch of pavement to my house, but the bluebells nod in the wind, their vibrant colouring a respite from the blood-drenched scene that plays in my memory in a never-ending loop. A swallow darts towards the river, riding low on the wing. The world has changed, but it looks the same.

The police lady wants to take a more detailed statement, but she escorts me next door to find my father because I ask her to, and because I want to see my mother.

When my father – unshaven and still wearing yesterday's T-shirt – opens the front door, he is crying.

The pain in my heart eases for a bit. He's crying because he's worried about me, what with my empty bed, and all the sirens and the police cars. But he barely registers the police lady, even though she is wearing a uniform and a sombre expression, or the stiffening pyjamas beneath my coat.

'Brinley . . .' he says. There's a crack in his voice.

'I'm sorry,' I say. And then my voice cracks too because his crumpled clothes and his baggy face bring home the horrors of the night, and it rushes up to me all at once, the scars these murders will leave on all of us, and the decisions I still have to make.

He shakes his head. 'Never mind about all that.'

And I think: *He doesn't know yet.*

And then he takes my hands.

And then he draws me inside.

And then he tells me my mother is dead.

I am twelve years old and I am running.

My feet pound the grass, powered by grief and fear. I do not stop until I reach the summit of Saltbox Hill, my breath coming harder and harder until I'm forced to bend and catch my breath.

The police are looking for me and so is my father, but I don't care. About them. About him. About anything at all.

My mother – my laughing, beautiful, funny mother – is dead.

The rain has started, fat drops that are cold and surprising against my face. I want to run. I want to keep on running until my lungs are empty and my heart gives up.

*Her silver chain coils in the palm of my father's hand. 'She wanted you to have this.'*

*I dry my eyes with a tissue and fasten it around my neck. 'Did she say anything about me before she died?'*

*A guilty look flashes across my father's face. He doesn't think to rose-tint the truth, to blur the lines. He blurts it out. 'I was asleep, love, when she passed. She was gone when I woke up.'*

My mother died alone and it's all his stupid, drunken fault.

At the top of Saltbox Hill, there's an oak tree. We used to have picnics there, my mother and me, fingers sticky with blackberries and iced buns, catching crickets in the sun. I run towards it, the only solid presence in a shifting world.

*The grown-ups are dead.*

*My mother is dead.*

*The Carter sisters are gone.*

Even at twelve, I know they won't be coming back. There'll be foster carers and social workers, a court case, probably. Prison.

The tears come then, hot and bitter. For everything I've lost. For my mother drawing her last, lonely breath while I watched over a woman who deserved to die and my father slept off the drink.

For the empty days ahead.

My head is a mumbled, jumbled-up mess.

I think about Sara and the words she spoke carefully through the bathroom door. She *wanted* to do it. For her sister, she said. But it's not right, is it? It's not.

*Lies are a necessary evil sometimes, sweet girl.* The last words my mother said to me.

I can only save one of them.

Shannon is my best friend. We're going to work in the same office and share a flat in London and live together until we're sixty. We can still do that. We can.

And Sara offered to do it. She *wanted* to.

I lean against the trunk of the old oak tree and slip my hands into my coat pocket. There's a small notebook inside that I didn't put there. It's covered in gold-coloured fabric and there's a strawberry sticker on the front. The smell is sweet and artificial.

The remnants of a bloodied handprint on the back of it, smudgy from the dampness.

Shannon must have slipped it into my coat pocket when I left it hanging over the kitchen chair at Hilltop House, after the murders and before the police came.

I open the notebook.

*Tonight I'm going to kill my mother and father.*

The letters are neat and sloping, and I recognize the handwriting. I should do. I sit next to its owner every day at school.

An electric flash of lightning opens up the sky, followed by an ominous rumble. The rain is coming down now, harder and faster, drumming against the earth, stirring it up. It reminds me of last night and the sound of the rain hitting Hilltop House as I stood in the dark hallway, watching the Carter sisters through the crack in the door.

*Sara is hovering over her parents' bed, a ghost in the moonlight. She opens the drawer of her father's bedside cabinet, plucks out her rag doll and tucks it under her arm.*

*Shannon presses a finger to her lips. Sara shakes her head. No. But Shannon stares down at her younger sister until she looks away.*

The rain is soaking my hair, my skin, running in rivulets down my back. I press closer to the tree, until I'm standing under a broad branch, a dense frill of leaves offering shelter.

I told the police everything I witnessed. I told them how I saw Sara pull a pair of scissors from behind her back and plunge them into her father's neck while he was sleeping. I told them how she did it again and again until he stopped moving and how the room was silent except for the sucking sound of blade into flesh.

I told them how Sara moved with purpose across the room, ignoring her sister, who was pulling on her arm, pleading at her to *stop, please, stop*, and how she stuck the scissors into her mother's back with a violence I'd never seen before until she was covered in blood and matter.

The sky lights up, electricity arcing across the horizon. The fields are covered in a mass of swarming flies, but when I look again, I realize it's not insects at all, but shifting shadows from the fast-moving clouds above.

I told them all that because Sara begged me to, through the bathroom door on a wet April night, the brutalized bodies of her parents a few feet away, insisting she was stronger than Shannon, and she would take the blame.

'*Say it was me. Promise, Brinley. Swear it.*'

I swore it.

I did not tell the officer who took my statement that when the Carter sisters walked down the garden path to the police cars, Sara was dressed in the blood-soaked daisy-print pyjamas Shannon had been wearing, or how they must have swapped nightclothes while I was hiding in the bathroom.

I did not tell them I saw Sara wipe clean the handles of the scissors on the edge of the duvet before closing her own fingers around them.

I did not tell them the statement I signed was the truth but not the whole truth, that everything I said *had* happened, except in the retelling, I had switched the sisters around.

That it had been Shannon with the scissors, not Sara.

Never Sara.

I did not tell them I found a notebook in my pocket

belonging to Shannon that proved her intent to kill that night. *Be careful, Brin,* I told myself. *Put it in a place no one will find it.*

I should have told them, but I did not.

As the lightning strikes and sends me sprawling across the grass, it occurs to me, in the break of time before I lose consciousness, that it's much too late to tell the police exactly what I saw.

How I witnessed my closest friend slaughter her parents, driving in the scissor blades as deeply as she could, an odd expression of enjoyment on her face.

# PART THREE

## WHEN?

# 45

## Thursday, 13 December 2018

Nobody spoke.

Catherine – the name Sara, although rightfully hers, belonged to another life now – folded her hands to stop them fluttering like distressed butterflies.

She waited for Honor and Edward to react, scanning her husband's face for signs he knew her secret, wondering how much of the truth Eliza had let slip. Anything – even accusation – would be better than the bruising silence that waited for her.

Concealing her past from the two people she loved most had been a lonely undertaking. For years, she'd imagined this scenario with a kind of excited dread, believing she would find relief in sloughing off her secrecy, but now her hand had been forced, she longed to reset the clock.

Tears were running down Honor's face.

Catherine put an arm around her daughter's shoulder, drawing her close. Honor didn't resist but she didn't reciprocate either. The baubles hanging from the miniature

Christmas tree on the girl's bedside table gleamed in the lamplight. They'd bought that tree in the January sales years ago and its familiarity made Catherine's insides ache. She could not allow Honor to believe she was a killer – and yet there was no disputing the black and white facts of her conviction.

As if he had read her mind, Edward stared down at Catherine. 'You're a convicted killer?' he said, enunciating each word as if he couldn't believe it. As if saying the words out loud would dispel them into dust. 'And you didn't think to tell me?' So Eliza *had* kept Catherine's secret to herself.

'I wanted to,' she said, rising from the edge of Honor's bed, reaching for him, her voice climbing too. 'I tried to.' He recoiled from her touch, one hand pushing through his hair. His laugh was hard and sarcastic. 'Of course you did. You tried *really* hard, didn't you?'

She spread her hands in a gesture of helplessness. 'How could I?' she said. 'Put yourself in my shoes for a minute.' A pleading note crept in. She waited for him to acknowledge the difficulty of her position, to paint his words with even the faintest shade of compassion, but he shook his head.

'I knew it. I bloody knew it.'

'Knew what?'

But he didn't answer her. He blew out the air from his lungs, making his cheeks inflate, and bent down to Honor, whispering something that Catherine couldn't hear. When he stood up, he wiped his eyes roughly with his shirtsleeve. His face was wan and belonged to someone else. With a flash of insight, she understood. It was not anger that prevented him from wrapping his wife in words of comfort, but distress. He was too stunned to speak.

Catherine considered telling the truth, could taste it rising from a place within. But she had kept it to herself for so long, parcelled up and put away, that she didn't know how to remove all the layers of deceit and painful history, suspecting that even if she did proffer up the gift of her innocence, it would be cast out.

She was ten when she confessed to killing her parents. A vulnerable and naive young girl. She had not understood the repercussions of the lie she had told. Only that, in the absence of loving role models, she had worshipped her sister with an intensity that meant she'd sacrificed herself at the altar of law to protect her. Put simply, it had felt like the right – the *only* – thing to do.

With the benefit of perspective – of adulthood and becoming a mother herself – she recognized that Shannon's failure to speak up had been selfish. Worse than selfish. Destructive.

Like Catherine, her sister had been a victim too. But if Shannon's conscience had not led her to confess, she should, at the very least, have tried to make reparation of some kind. Instead Shannon had stopped writing to her twenty years ago, eighteen months after Catherine had moved into the unit. When she was released and given a new identity, Catherine's last tie to her sister had been cut. The betrayal still stung, but she had learned to live with it.

Was that why Shannon was now seeking forgiveness in the most public of ways? Not for financial gain, but because she was genuinely sorry and wanted to be certain that her sister knew it all these years later. Perhaps she wanted to reconcile and make amends at last.

Even after everything, Catherine was still making excuses for her.

The doorbell rang, intrusive in the shock of the night. Edward glanced down the stairs, frowning. Honor stilled, eyes widening like a frightened rabbit.

Someone opened the letter box. 'Sara Carter?' A shout, tinged with antagonism. Killers didn't deserve sympathy, did they? 'Open the door. We know you're in there. Just give us a quote – something we can use – and we'll leave you alone.'

*Sara Carter.*

All at once, she couldn't breathe, her past polluting the air like a toxic gas. The telephone was ringing too, a shrill call to action from her bedroom. She hesitated, afraid it might be another journalist, before relenting and running along the landing to answer it, in case it was important. Edward had sprung to life and was helping Honor pull a jumper over her pyjamas.

'Hel-lo?' She despised herself for the way her greeting cracked apart in the middle.

'Catherine Allen?'

She didn't recognize his voice and so she didn't answer, her knuckles whitening as she gripped the receiver. It felt heavy in her hand, weighing her down. In the half-light of her bedroom she considered hanging up, but in the time it took for that thought to crystallize into a conscious act, the voice at the end of the line had spoken.

'Hi there, my name's Russell Parker and I'm calling from the *Sun*. I just wanted to ask you if—'

She pressed a finger to the hook switch and disconnected the call.

Her mobile, which was on the bedside table next to the landline telephone, vibrated. She stared at it, terrified, before glancing at the home screen with its half a dozen missed calls from a familiar number and snatching it up.

'Thank God,' she said, warmth from her mouth fogging the glass.

'I'm on my way,' said Eliza. 'Don't open the door. Don't move until I get there, OK?'

Tears threatened, but did not fall. She blinked them away.

'How long?'

'Half an hour, if that. Put some clothes in a bag. Be ready to leave.'

Her mouth dried. This was real. It was happening. 'Thank you.'

Back in Honor's room, her daughter was sitting on the edge of her bed, the life she had known for twelve years lying in broken pieces about her. Edward was nowhere to be seen.

'Honor . . .' Her daughter stared blankly at the carpet. Catherine crouched beside her. 'Nothing will ever change how much I love you,' she said. 'You understand that, sweetheart, don't you?'

Honor opened her mouth. Closed it again. Tears pooled in her eyes. 'I want my old mummy back,' she said.

A pain – sharp and bright – in her chest. Her daughter hadn't called her that for months.

'I'm still your mummy,' she said fiercely. 'I'll always be that.' But the words felt hollow, another lie.

The doorbell rang again, a rude and unrelenting assault, as if someone had glued their fingertip to the buzzer.

'Ignore it,' said Catherine, sounding calmer than she felt. Her hands were trembling, her stomach folding in on itself. She picked up Honor's school bag and handed it to her. 'Choose a couple of books, and Giraffe, and whatever else you want to take with you.'

Her daughter showed no signs of moving, but Catherine let it go for now. She had no energy for a fight. She needed to conserve everything she had for the long hours ahead.

Alone on the landing, she sagged against the wall, head bowed, her palms resting on the tops of her thighs. *One. Two. Three. Four. Five. Six. Seven. Eight.* Her breathing steadied.

She had always loved her home, but an urge to escape tugged at her with determined fingers: to a beach with a vast sky that swallowed her up or an isolated French farmhouse, hidden amongst lavender bushes and olive groves. The journalists outside were closing in on her, a rat in a trap.

But Catherine was a survivor. She could handle this, as she had handled her eight-year incarceration at Mayfields secure children's home, with its tall metal fences and the ladder of locked doors between her room and the outside world.

Her bed had been fixed to the floor so it couldn't be smashed apart. She'd had to sleep on a blue plastic gym mat, because it was easier than a mattress to remove if it was used to barricade a doorway. To prevent flooding as a gesture of protest, her shower's water flow was controlled. After every meal, the cutlery and plates were counted – and then locked away – so the residents could not use them as weapons on themselves or each other.

She had even survived the constant monitoring by unit staff, never allowed to have so much as a private conversation or switch on a light or climb the stairs alone, suffocated by life on the inside.

The summers she spent at Mayfields were the most difficult. She had longed to roam outside, to escape the simmering tensions that threatened to boil over in the heat. But Catherine was smart. She kept her head down, earning money by collecting merits for good behaviour or extra electricity for the television in her room.

She blinked away the memories of a time she had condemned to the dumping ground of the past, but a simple truth remained: even now, technically free, she was imprisoned by the choices she had made.

Edward was standing at their bedroom window, staring down at the journalists and photographers, camera crews, news vans and the lone police car, his handsome face serious, half in shadow.

'Shut the curtains,' she said, sounding sharper than she meant to. He ignored her.

'There's so many of them,' he said, with a kind of grudging awe. 'You're famous.'

Not famous.

*Infamous.*

Catherine dragged a suitcase from under their bed and began to throw in underwear and jumpers and jeans. It had become apparent that the small packed rucksack she had kept in her wardrobe in case she needed to make a swift escape, with one day's worth of clothes and a few essentials, would not be enough.

'They can't publish my name,' she said. 'It's protected.

By a court injunction.' She breathed deeply, as if she'd been starved of air for too long. 'Honor, too.'

Edward caught the fold of skin under his chin between his thumb and finger. 'But they know who you are now.'

'Yes.'

'You'll have to change your identity again—'

'Probably.'

'—and move away, start again.'

The prospect of upheaval upset her. 'Let's not think about that now.'

Even in her darkest imaginings, it had never occurred to her that Edward might not come with her, but he made no move to pack any of his clothes into the suitcase. Instead he stood there, observing the journalists below, his face unreadable.

He stayed like that, a watcher at the window, until Eliza Sheen, the supervising probation officer, fought her way through the crowd of journalists and he went downstairs to let her in.

I'm sorry I wasn't there to meet you on Monday. Something came up and I couldn't get away. The next few days might make it tricky for me to contact you. But I'll message you again as soon as I can.

I don't have much time – I need to leave in a couple of minutes – but I will tell you everything, I promise. Something tells me that we have more in common than we think. Hold tight, Hero – and a word of advice in these desperate times: the eye of the storm is the safest place to be.

# 46

'Who's that?' says the journalist from the *Daily Mail*.

The woman is slim, with dark hair in a ponytail, and has the type of face that suggests a fondness for cigarettes and holidays in the sun. She's wearing a thick coat to protect her from the cold. An on-the-ball photographer runs after her to get a shot, and the others follow suit, creating a domino effect of camera flashes, glinting in the frozen night. The woman turns up her collar and ignores them until she disappears through a crack in the Allens' front door.

I have no idea, but I hazard a guess. 'Probation? Social services?'

The *Daily Mail* journalist thumps his gloved hands together and stamps his feet. 'They've got a kid, haven't they?' When neither of us answers, he points to a worn rope swing suspended from a tree, dusted with snow.

'She's twelve,' I say. 'Honor Allen.'

The *Daily Mail* journalist fiddles with his mobile for a couple of minutes and holds it out. 'Look, she's on Facebook and Instagram.'

They roll their eyes with the cynicism of seasoned hacks. No privacy settings. If they had been allowed to publish her name, those images would be all over tomorrow's newspapers. As it was, some of the more ruthless news organizations had sought legal advice about pixelating her face.

Lawrie and the other guy are now discussing court injunctions and privacy and waiving anonymity, Scottish law and foreign jurisdictions, but I don't absorb what they're saying because one thought is burning in my brain, bright as fire.

Sara Carter's daughter is twelve. Too young for this intrusion. Too young to be stripped of her innocence in such a brutal way.

A rush of sympathy for them both fills me up because I'm one of only three people who know exactly what Sara sacrificed for Shannon, and what it must have cost her.

Is still costing her.

Fragments of memory tease me. The feel of the tiles against my back in the bathroom at Hilltop House. Sara's murmurings through the door. The catch-in-the-throat smell of congealing blood, ripening as the hours passed.

The truth has many faces and I wear them all.

I am a good person, but I was complicit, and the guilt of what I've done hems every aspect of my life.

The sky is pricked with stars that blur into flowers of light. With the end of my scarf, I dry my tears, a quick, rough gesture, and try to push down the rising well of heat and sadness that is threatening to overflow.

For years, the facts of that night have stayed buried in the ground, hidden amongst the bones of Dr and Mrs Carter and the dirt of our lies. But decay has a way of pushing to the surface, of spreading its spores until the rot has found a foothold and spoils everything from within.

Lawrie and the other journalist are still talking. Before I can think about what I'm doing, before I can examine the motives or the repercussions, the rights and wrongs, I walk swiftly to my car and let myself in.

Under the interior light, I scribble a note on lined paper from my pad. The handwriting is scruffy, the words hasty and uneven, but heartfelt. My breath lingers in the freezing air like a wraith.

I fold the scrap of paper in two and rummage in my work bag for an envelope. It's bent in the middle, a grubby mark on its white expanse, but it will do. I hesitate over the name, but in the end I print Sara on the outside, because that was her name and she'll always be Sara to me.

Then I'm walking right up to her front door, vaguely aware of Lawrie calling to me, the other journalists advancing behind me, convinced I know something they don't, but I don't acknowledge any of them. I don't even turn around. Instead I bend down and push it through the letter box before I have a chance to change my mind.

# 47

The Justice Secretary unlocked the cabinet and removed a bottle of eye-wateringly expensive Scotch whisky and a crystal cut-glass tumbler.

Heathcote sat at his desk, poured himself two fingers' worth and downed it in one swallow before measuring out another. The fumes on his breath leaked into his Commons office, a peaty scent of fire and earth. If his career was over, he'd damn well go down in style.

They had spent all evening discussing the Carter case, sliding into the early hours. Sara Carter, it turned out, owned a cottage in Coggsbridge, a stone's throw from Heathcote's constituency home. They'd probably drunk in the same pub.

The Official Solicitor had moved to close a loophole in the existing injunction that would allow Sara Carter and the village she lived in to be named in Scotland. None of them wanted a repeat of the fiasco when a now-retired Home Secretary was splashed all over the Scottish press as the minister whose son had been caught drug dealing while England and Wales were banned from reporting it. Now there was social media to contend with too, and the growing sense that the injunction was on the edge of collapse.

He would grab a few hours' rest on the sofa bed in his office. He had been asked to stay close by and, according to his wife, there were reporters crawling all over their London and Essex residences. While some MPs were cautious about funding second homes in the wake of the MPs expenses scandal and spent their Westminster working week in shared apartments or Airbnbs, the Heathcotes were independently wealthy. In the end, he had sent Barbara off to their Cotswolds farmhouse. A rural location and security gates would afford her some sort of privacy if matters got out of hand and the local freelance hack came sniffing at the door.

He sipped his second drink, aware that he needed to keep a clear head.

His problems were two-fold. Here were the facts:

Firstly, he was Secretary of State for Justice. His department was in charge of prisons. He had publicly urged for rehabilitation and support for all prisoners, especially young offenders. He had been caught, on a live mic, airing his personal views and calling for a return to capital punishment.

Lesser hypocrisy had seen off more high-profile careers than his.

Secondly, his assertion that Sara Carter should have been hanged for her crimes as a child had been spectacularly ill-timed. Ordinarily, his slip of the tongue might have blown over after a day or two, but the documentary featuring Shannon Carter had fuelled media interest – and so, inadvertently, had he. Once the press got the bit between their teeth, matters had a way of escalating.

He finished his glass of whisky and contemplated a third.

A soft knock at the office door stayed his hand.

'It's open,' he said, surprised by the late-night interruption.

Anna, his mistress, walked in and shut the door behind her. She placed her handbag on his desk and folded her designer coat carefully over her arm. He stared at the swell of her breasts beneath her silk shirt. The sight triggered the same physical reaction it always did, and he shifted in his chair.

'You're not supposed to be here.'

'I got bored waiting for you.'

Heathcote wondered who'd let her in. Some of the security guards could be trusted but not all, and he couldn't afford another scandal. But the smell of her perfume was more intoxicating than a bottle of his finest malt. Her lips were red and full. He knew exactly what she was able to do with her mouth. Christ, he wanted to fuck her.

She trailed a manicured finger around the rim of the crystal tumbler. 'How long are you going to be?'

He sighed, aroused by her presence but not quite able to disguise his impatience. 'I've got to work tonight, remember? Important government business. Why don't you go back to the hotel? I'll cover your expenses. We can talk tomorrow.'

She laughed at him, puncturing his pomposity. 'I don't need you to *cover my expenses*. I can pay for my own hotel rooms.' She poured herself a whisky and eyed him over the glass. 'I thought you might want some company, that's all, but if you're busy, I can always call someone else.'

Geoffrey Heathcote was a politician with a formidable career behind him, and a pin-sharp brain. But when it came to women, his ego was governed by a different part of his anatomy.

He was ageing well, a touch of grey at his temples, his weight controlled by running and a careful diet. But he wasn't naive. Women like Anna were seduced by power, not necessarily the men who wielded it. Perhaps she would move on if he lost his ministerial job. But he didn't think so. She might be thirty years younger than he was, but they shared a connection, didn't they?

He suspected he wasn't her only lover, but his most secret self hoped he was. In truth, Anna was the only woman he had ever considered leaving his wife for. Barbara was older now, and flabbier, dismissive and impatient much of the time. Their sex life had dwindled to twice a year.

'Like who?' He knew he sounded jealous but he didn't much care.

She raised her eyebrows and left him to fill in the blanks.

'Come here,' he said, his voice thickening.

Anna laid down her coat and made her way around the office towards him. A painting of Heathcote gazed down from the wall. Two silver-framed photographs of his wife and children sat on his desk. He pushed back his chair to make room for her, and she sat astride his lap, pressing herself against him.

He stared at her mouth, his hand slipping beneath her shirt, travelling over her stomach and towards her bra. She closed her eyes, lips parted, a hitch in her breath. Heathcote swallowed. If he was caught having sex with his mistress in his Commons office, he would almost certainly have to resign. But the place was almost deserted, his special advisers long gone.

She bent towards him, slid her tongue into his mouth.

The heat of her burned his resistance to ash.

# 48

The probation officer made mugs of tea, milky and sweet, and found some crumpets to toast. Then she sat the Allen family around the kitchen table and told them what would happen next.

'The police will take you into protective custody for the time being and move you to a secret location as soon as the press attention has calmed down,' she said. 'I'm afraid you won't be able to live here again if you wish to maintain anonymity.'

*You won't be able to live here again.*

Catherine glanced around the kitchen she loved so much. For twelve years, this had been the beating heart of their home. Curled-up paintings by five-year-old Honor pinned to the corkboard. An aloe vera plant on the window-sill, a gift from a friend on her twenty-eighth birthday. Laughter-filled meals and the smell of baking. Play-Doh and puzzles and games of Monopoly. Honor's homework spread messily across the table. The golden threads of the ordinary life she had promised herself as reward for protecting her sister.

Her eyes swam with unshed tears. Eliza reached across

the table and squeezed her fingers. Catherine replied with a not-quite-whole smile.

Eliza knew everything about Catherine's past. Except for the truth.

Although Catherine would always remain on licence, it was months since she had seen her probation officer, but when the older woman had stepped through the front door and held out her arms, she had fallen into them, clinging to her like a life raft, exactly as she had done on the day she left the secure unit as a frightened eighteen-year-old, feeling her way in a changing world.

In the early years, they had met with planned regularity. But once a week had become once a month and once every six months until the need for supervision had faded. Catherine had always known that any breach of her conditions or act of violence could see her back in prison, but Eliza had been so impressed with the way she had assimilated into society she had recently talked about writing to the Secretary of State to request a cancellation of her supervision conditions.

The publicity would put paid to that.

'What a fucking mess,' Eliza had said on arrival, blunt as usual, patting Catherine on the back and then lighting a cigarette. 'But we'll get it cleaned up. Try not to worry.'

'This is a no-smoking house.' It was clear Edward was unimpressed.

'We meet at last, Mr Allen. Glad I can put a face to the voice,' Eliza had said, taking a drag, unperturbed by his hostility. 'But I can hardly smoke out front with all them journalists.' She had followed him to the back door without further complaint, cupping her palm to collect falling ash.

That had been half an hour ago and now the four of them were sitting at the kitchen table, discussing the next move.

'We don't want a situation where you're hounded from town to town,' she said. 'Obviously, it takes a bit of time to organize the paperwork and practicalities that are part of a new identity. You will go into the care of a dedicated Identity Protection team. And social services will need some involvement too.'

'Honor isn't a ward of court,' said Catherine, a heat rising in her cheeks.

'I know that,' said Eliza. 'But this affects her, and you must understand that social services have to be informed of any changes in circumstances and the potential impact they will have on her.'

'What if Honor and I want to stay here?' Edward didn't look at Catherine when he said this. He put his mug on the table and rubbed a whorl in the wood with his thumb. 'Will she be protected?'

Catherine's world tipped off its axis. 'What do you mean?' She pushed back her chair, half rising. 'You have to come with me. You're my family.'

He turned on her, his tone curt. 'We don't *have* to do anything. You lied to us.'

'I didn't want to—'

'But you did—'

'Stop it!' Honor's distress was palpable. Catherine moved to comfort her, but she jerked out of reach, leaning into her father. He put an arm around her shoulder.

'This isn't helping anyone,' said Eliza, no-nonsense and firm. Her hair had come loose and she pulled out the elastic and redid her ponytail. Then she put both her elbows on the table and rested her chin on her hands.

'You're under no obligation to come with us, Mr Allen, but it makes sense for us to keep the three of you together for now. These kind of important decisions don't need to be made tonight. The priority is to get you away from the press.' She touched Edward's arm. 'And Honor needs to get some sleep.'

The probation officer did not mention the budget constraints of protecting the family at separate addresses, but Catherine suspected that was what she'd meant.

Edward sat very still and then gave a sharp nod, his face folded in on itself. He didn't look at his wife once.

*Are you there? I need to talk to you.*

. . .

*Hero?*

. . .

*Hero?*

# 49

The darkest hour of the night.

The Allen family stood at the bottom of the stairs with their suitcases and bags, trussed up in gloves and hats. A female police officer who'd arrived twenty minutes ago, slipping past the couple of journalists stationed by the back gate, was about the same height and colouring as Catherine. She buttoned up her coat and wrapped a scarf around her face. A male officer – drafted in to act as her escort – lingered nearby, checking his watch.

Eliza handed the female constable a pair of sunglasses and ran through the plan they had concocted together. 'Keep your head down and don't engage. Take the main road to the motorway and pull in at the first service station. Call me then. If any of the journalists decide to follow you, it will be a good diversionary tactic and buy us some time.'

'You're using a decoy?' Edward was incredulous, as if he couldn't believe what was happening.

The probation officer laughed. 'How else do you think we're going to get you out of here?'

At Eliza's insistence, the family gathered by the back door

until the signal was given. Then they hurried across the dark garden, fresh snow crunching underfoot.

Honor started to say something. Eliza pressed a finger to her lips. Across the still of the night, they heard shouts and the rapid-fire click of camera shutters as the disguised female police officer and her colleague exited the front door and ran the gauntlet of photographers on their way to the decoy vehicle.

At the top of the lane that ran behind their cottage, an unmarked car was waiting for the Allens. The two journalists covering the back entrance, distracted by the hullabaloo at the front, had wandered down the lane to see what was going on and missed the family by seconds. As they drove away, Catherine strained to catch a glimpse of her home for the last time, a sickness in the pit of her stomach.

A photographer, who suspected something was afoot when 'Catherine' emerged without her family, slid down the icy lane after them, camera high above his head, hiccoughing flashes. But he was too late to get a decent frame, and by the time he'd jogged back to tell his colleagues they'd been played, the Allens were long gone.

Honor was asleep within minutes, her head resting on her father's shoulder. Edward shut his eyes too, lulled into a doze by the blast of the heater and the rumble of tyres as they ate up the miles.

Eliza, who was sitting in the front passenger seat, handed Catherine a bundle of letters and business cards she'd collected from her doormat.

'They'll be offering you loads of money,' she said. 'Before you get any ideas, any interviews will have to be approved by the Official Solicitor. I wouldn't advise accepting any payments. You'll be torn apart for profiting from your crime.'

'I'm not planning on giving any interviews.' She leaned back against her seat and closed her eyes. The first streaks of dawn were breaking open the sky, the stars luminous against the pale wash of blue. The driver – a police officer, she guessed, or someone who worked with Eliza – was focused on the road and did not look at her at all.

'I thought you were going to tell Edward about your past,' said Eliza softly. 'He rang me last night, asking all sorts of questions.'

'How much did he know?' Catherine thought she might cry at the thought of Edward carrying this burden alone.

'He had an inkling that something was up. Apparently, he overheard a conversation between us a couple of weeks ago when he came home early from work. Did a bit of digging of his own.' Eliza withdrew a cigarette from the packet and put it behind her ear. 'With all the coverage the documentary's been getting, he was struck by the resemblance between you and Shannon as young women, but he didn't suspect the truth, at least, not at first. He thought you were cousins.' She paused for breath. 'You said you were going to tell him.'

She *had* always planned to. On her release, the probation team had warned her about a similar scenario. They had encouraged her to think carefully about whom she told and when, suggesting Catherine wait until she was confident of their feelings for her, and of a mutual trust.

She had thought about confessing in those glowing hours and weeks after Honor was born, the words bubbling up inside, a hectic, heat-filled disclosure. But it was always easier not to. She had boxed up that part of her life, all the photographs and the hundreds of press cuttings, the death threats from her father's patients that had started to arrive while she was on remand, the vitriolic letters and the cards, the mourning song of the village community, and left it behind in the unit.

On the day she had walked out of Mayfields and entered Identity Protection, a fresh page had turned and her life had begun again.

Often, she wondered if it had been easier for her because she hadn't killed them. That although she carried the scars of an eight-year sentence, she was not freighted down with guilt. For all her freedom, Shannon would always drag behind her the heavy chains of what she had done.

Several times, during those terrible years in Mayfields, she had almost confessed the truth to her barrister. But she had witnessed the shock and confusion of fellow residents when they discovered, too late, that denial of guilt could adversely influence the decision of the Parole Board.

'It's considered an indicator of continuing risk,' her barrister had explained.

She had not been prepared to take that chance.

The car settled into silence. Catherine had no idea where they were going and did not ask. Above them, the sky was lightening at pace. The driver stopped at a service station and Eliza, leaning against the door, smoked her cigarette in quick drags. Catherine rubbed her eyes, gritty with lack of sleep, but she wasn't tired. Every nerve ending was jangling with adrenalin and what the day might bring.

The driver set off again, exited the motorway, negotiated several roundabouts and drove them down a long, narrow road flanked with bare trees and snow-covered fields. A rabbit, startled by the noise of the car, streaked across the road. There were few cars and fewer houses.

Honor mumbled in her sleep, beginning to stir. The sound woke Edward.

'Where are we?' he said, stifling a yawn.

They were pulling into the car park of a hotel, neither too big nor too small. It was part of a chain with clean, impersonal rooms, a quick turnover of guests, both business and leisure, and a degree of anonymity. Nobody would ask too many questions. This was a place for itinerants. A place to get lost.

'Just for tonight,' said Eliza, 'until we find you somewhere more permanent. It's paid for. Don't volunteer information, but if you're put on the spot, explain you're changing jobs and you've come to look at some houses with your family and explore the area.'

The probation officer handed Catherine an envelope. 'There's some cash in here, not much, but enough for a couple of days. No social media. Don't use your credit or debit cards, or your mobile phones. The press has ways of tracing them.'

Edward and Honor, blinking in the cold air, walked through the glass doors into the hotel lobby.

Eliza hugged Catherine. She smelled of cigarette smoke and kinship. 'Try not to worry.'

Catherine held on to her, tearful. Eliza was the closest thing she had to a mother. With so much at stake, the idea of losing her husband and daughter was enough to break her.

'Come now,' said Eliza, gruff-voiced, patting her on the

back. The older woman tucked a strand of Catherine's hair behind her ear. 'You'll be all right.' Catherine nodded, unable to speak.

Catherine watched the car until its tail lights disappeared into the bleached winter landscape. She was still standing on the tarmac when Honor, sulky-faced and reluctant, came to tell her that breakfast was now being served.

# 50

The newspapers are spread across the table, their pages marked with grease, egg yolk and scattered granules of sugar.

A sausage sandwich arrives, butter oozing from thick slices of bread, and I take a large bite, ketchup at the corners of my mouth. After a freezing all-nighter on Sara Carter's doorstep, my stomach was rumbling when we walked, en masse, into this cafe. The food is warm and delicious, but Lawrie is poring over today's papers, and I put the sandwich back on my plate, hunger suddenly gone.

My byline is printed on the front page of the newspaper alongside the headline:

## MY FRIEND, THE ANGEL OF DEATH

The story carries an 'exclusive' tag and there's a photograph of me, Shannon and Sara when we were about nine and she was seven. My mother must have taken it, although the memories are fuzzy now, like the dust has collected in them.

Sara is wearing a pair of brightly coloured shorts and she's laughing, her halo of hair bleached a dazzling white by the sun. I'm freckled and, for once, unselfconscious, waving a garden hose with glorious abandon, the water arcing and catching the light. Shannon is crouched in the grass, inspecting something.

We look happy.

The opening paragraph is a classic drop intro:

Our summers were filled with sunshine, but something very dark was happening at Hilltop House.

Wincing at the melodramatic scene-setting – the sub-editor must have got his hands on that – I scan the feature, seeking out a particular paragraph, heart running faster.

As soon as I confirm it hasn't been edited out, I stop reading, unable to stomach the sight of my half-truths printed in the national press, wishing I hadn't caved in to pressure from Lawrie and Colin, seduced by the prospect of a splash.

'Looks great,' says Lawrie, stirring a spoonful of sugar into his coffee, flashing me a grin. 'Well done.' Some of the other reporters sit at tables around us, going through the morning's papers, sussing out the stories their rivals have filed, looking for an angle. Even though most media outlets have an online presence, nothing can replicate the feel of a real newspaper.

'Dark horse, aren't you?' says Russell, the *Sun* reporter, pulling out a chair and sitting at our table. 'Any more surprises tomorrow?'

Lawrie raises an eyebrow. 'If we tell you, we'd have to kill you.'

'Don't be a dick,' says Russell. 'Obviously, you've got *something.*' He flicks the newspaper sharply between his hands, clears his throat and reads aloud. *'Buy tomorrow's newspaper for more exclusive revelations.'*

'It's just more of the same,' I say quickly. 'A couple of extra photographs, that's all.'

'Got any spares you're not planning to use?' says Russell.

'No, mate,' says Lawrie, and I can tell by the way he says *mate* that Russell isn't one at all. Russell's mobile phone rings and he wanders out of the cafe, a secretive hand covering his mouth. He's playing the game, being friendly with the opposition but keeping his exclusives to himself. The unspoken rules of Fleet Street engagement.

A couple of other journalists offer their congratulations, but it's grudging. All of us know that for today, at least, my story is the one to beat. In newsrooms across the capital, editors will be laying on the pressure, urging reporters to up their game. But even though it's barely 8 a.m., today's papers are now out of date. Already, the hunger for a fresh exclusive is biting. By tomorrow, I'll be old news.

The cafe is emptying, the pack spreading out in search of stories. We pay for our breakfast and head into the cold.

'We need to find her,' says Lawrie. He doesn't say her name, but I know who he means. Sara Carter. *'You* need to find her.'

But nobody knows where she is.

*Where are you? How are you? It feels too long since I've heard from you. I'm worried. Please let me know that you're OK.*

# 51

Room 22 was suffocating.

Because of the snow outside, the hotel had cranked up the heat, but Catherine could barely breathe. She took off her jumper and sat on the small hard-backed chair in front of the mirror, fanning her face with a room service menu. The place was soulless. A pad of paper and a Gideon bible in the drawer. A cheap hairdryer. Identikit artwork on the walls.

Edward lay on the double bed, his eyes closed, pretending to sleep. Honor was sprawled on the single bed under the window, scrolling through her mobile phone.

'I should be having double PE right now,' she said suddenly, not quite able to conceal her glee.

'You need to come off your phone,' said Catherine. 'Eliza said not to use it.'

She didn't elaborate, frightened of rupturing a peace that was becoming more and more fragile, but Eliza had explained in a low, serious voice how many people in Identity Protection were traced because of their children.

'It's so difficult for them,' she'd said in the hotel car park, a couple of minutes before she'd driven off. 'They don't understand why they have to stop using Instagram or Snapchat, posting pictures, that sort of thing, and the temptation is huge.

'We give them back-stories, like "Dad has been relocated because of work", but the problem is, a couple of weeks later, when the child has made a new best friend, they tell them everything.'

Catherine understood. But would her daughter?

Honor's phone pinged with a notification, and she read it, her cheeks pinking, a secret smile on her face. 'So what shall I tell my friends when I go back to Sweetwood?'

Catherine's mouth was dry. She ran her fingers across the surface of the cheap hotel drawers. The wood was sticky where it hadn't been wiped properly.

'You won't be going back to Sweetwood, love.'

Honor sat up, her mouth a circle of shock. 'What do you mean? Of course I'll be going back. I have to go to school, you know.' Disdainful now. 'It's the law.'

'We'll find you a new school.'

'I don't want to go to a new school.'

'If we go back home, the press will hound us. All of us. We'll never get a moment's peace.'

Honor's eyes were flashing in anger, her voice getting louder. 'But that's not my fault, is it? None of this is my fault.'

'Keep your voice down, please.' Catherine's neck was red and blotchy. 'Let's not give ourselves away on the first day.'

'I don't want to be here. Don't you understand that?' Honor was shouting now. 'This is nothing to do with me and everything to do with you. Why do Dad and I have to suffer for what you've done?'

Honor was standing on the bed, her colour hectic, hair falling in strands around her face. The anger thrummed from her, a physical thing. She spat out the words, as if the taste of truth was unpalatable. Catherine didn't have an answer because there wasn't one.

*Because you love me* was the only reply she could think of. But the needlessness of it, the guilt of putting her family through this ordeal – and an urge to cleanse herself with the truth – threatened to consume her.

'What's going on?' Edward was sitting up on the double bed, rubbing his eyes, his hair sticking up, shirt crumpled. He looked exhausted.

'Her,' said Honor, jerking her head in the direction of her mother.

Edward sighed, but did not chastise his daughter for her rudeness. Instead, he looked his wife in the eye for the first time in hours. 'What I don't understand,' he said, 'is why you killed them.'

Their cruelty, she wanted to say. The taking apart of a childhood, layer by painful layer. The threat of violence, and the scars it left. But if the court hadn't accepted this in mitigation, why would he? In any case, she *hadn't* killed them and could not bring herself to find excuses for so savage an act to the man she loved most in the world.

'Let's go and get some fresh air,' he said, disappointed by her silence. From the tone of his voice, it was clear Catherine wasn't invited.

As soon as they were gone, Catherine opened a window, the crisp air cooling the rush of blood in her veins.

Perhaps it would be better for them all if she walked out

of this hotel and disappeared from their lives. It wouldn't be the first time she had cut all ties, hauled up the anchor and moved on.

But a fury of a different kind burned within her, drawing its heat from the injustices she had suffered. This was her family. She loved them, and she would fight for them, even if it meant throwing herself to the lions.

She uncapped a bottle of water and switched on her laptop. No social media, but that didn't mean she couldn't look at the newspapers.

The headlines shocked her, a wash of black and white in both the red tops and the so-called quality press. She had been here before, but, at ten, she'd been too young to pay much attention, too sheltered from the news reports to care what they said about her.

But now, even though she wasn't publicly identified, reading about herself, her crime distilled into a tempting soundbite for a hungry public, and knowing these newspapers would be on sale in supermarkets and garage forecourts and newsagents across the country, made bile rise in her throat. She ran to the toilet, her body expelling its meagre breakfast.

When she had stopped trembling, she rinsed her mouth and returned to the computer, scrolling through each newspaper in turn.

Most of the stories were a rehash of the previous day's events: the closing of the loophole in the injunction to prevent the Scottish press from identifying her and Honor; a weak statement from the Justice Secretary; an aerial photograph of the media scrum outside her house, the street sign pixelated, although still recognizable to those who lived or worked in Coggsbridge; some quotes from the mother of a boy at Honor's school who she'd met once, although Sweetwood hadn't been named; and an interview with their old nemesis Danielle, who had crawled out of the woodwork to cash in on their tragedy.

A headline and photograph in one of the tabloids caught her eye – **MY FRIEND, THE ANGEL OF DEATH** – but it was the byline that made her sit up and breathe out her shock into the empty hotel room.

EXCLUSIVE by Brinley Booth.

*Brinley Booth.*
A memory of childhood rose lightly inside her. A warm day – the summers had seemed so impossibly long – and their skirts tucked into their knickers, paddling in the river. Brinley's mother had packed them a picnic of cheese sandwiches, ripe peaches, slabs of bittersweet lemon cake and cartons of juice. Shannon, Brinley and her. The Three Musketeers.

Because so much time had lapsed since the murders with no word of her former playmate, she'd always assumed that Brinley had kicked over the traces of the past and moved on, as she had tried to do. Unlike Catherine, Brinley *had* been protected by the courts, the judge imposing reporting restrictions that meant her evidence, as a witness for the prosecution, could be printed in the newspapers, but her name could not. But this. This was too much. What kind of a perverse game was her old friend playing?

In spite of herself, Catherine devoured every paragraph of the feature, the knocking of her heart echoing in all her empty spaces. Then she read it again, more slowly this time, savouring its lack of sensationalism, lingering over the final lines.

> Sara Carter might be a convicted killer. She might have stabbed her abusive parents with a pair of scissors fourteen times when she was ten years old. But there are two sides to the story, two faces of the same coin. She was my childhood friend, my playmate. Even after all these years, I'd still trust her with my life. She spared mine, after all.

A heat burned behind Catherine's eyes. She pressed the tip of her finger to the screen, touched Brinley's face. Sadness engulfed her, for everything that was lost, for everything still to be lost: the home she loved so much; her sense of security and her family unit.

Honor's innocence.

The new life she had so carefully constructed had been blown apart and would need to be remade, brick by painstaking brick. Who was she anyway? Catherine Allen? Sara Carter? A sister? Wife? Mother? *A killer?* She didn't know anymore.

She was a lost cause, drifting further from land, caught in the riptide of an inhospitable sea. When she was a child, she had made a willing sacrifice, but she was still paying for it, her lies weakening the foundations of everything she held dear.

Catherine placed her head on the desk and wept for her ten-year-old self and the woman she had become, a ghost of a presence in her own dead life.

*Please, don't apologize – I'm so happy that you're back. What an awful shock it must have been. I saw the newspapers today and everything fell into place. All those lonely years waiting and you were right here, if only I'd known where to look.*

*The time has come for me to tell you my story, Hero. I think it might surprise you.*

*Once upon a time there were two sisters who loved each other very much. They did everything together because it was safer than being alone with parents who did not want them. They had plans to escape as soon as they were old enough, but it all went wrong and one day, the younger of those sisters killed their mother and father. She went to prison and now she has a daughter of her own.*

*Have you worked it out yet? It seems my instincts were correct – we are bound, you and me, by the thickness of blood. Family, Hero. At last.*

# 52

It was fitting that the Right Honourable Geoffrey Heathcote – a hypocrite and morally bankrupt cheat – having enjoyed the best night of his fifty-six years on this earth, was about to endure his worst day.

His mouth was bruised and tender, his back a criss-cross of painful welts. He had no idea how he was going to explain away the scratches to Barbara, but when Anna had raked her nails down his skin, he had lacked the impulse to stop her. In fact, he had begged her to continue.

They had hardly slept, and now his tongue was thick with stale whisky and the taste of his mistress, but he was smiling to himself as he splashed his face in the toilets, shaved with his electric razor and brushed his teeth, his monogrammed wash bag balanced on the enamel sink.

With a generous spray of aftershave, clean underwear and a freshly laundered white shirt, he looked and felt almost as good as new.

He wandered along the corridors to the Members' Tea Room in search of breakfast. An inner sanctum, the room had the feel of a gentlemen's club, a holy place reserved for trusted confidences and whispered plots. A knot of Labour

MPs were gossiping around their usual table. 'Not planning any more fuck-ups today, Geoffrey?' one of them called out, and they all laughed.

'Very funny,' said Geoffrey good-naturedly, always keen to show he could take a joke with the best of them. He walked towards the bank of pink armchairs reserved for the Conservatives, a tradition scrupulously observed by all shades of the political spectrum. 'Lefty cunts,' he said to a junior Tory minister sipping his tea. The minister mimed shooting himself in the head and went back to his newspaper. Geoffrey chuckled to himself. If only they knew what he'd been up to a few hours ago.

He helped himself to a bowl of prunes and sat down alone, checking his mobile phone.

A missed call from Barbara. An email from one of his daughters. Still no text from Anna.

Almost as soon as she'd left that morning, slipping out of his Commons office at around five to six, he'd sent her a message, asking if he could see her again that night.

Barbara would be down at the farmhouse for the next few days. He would have to put in an appearance in his Essex constituency at some point, but with no wife wondering about his absences, he could come and go as he pleased – and sweet Jesus, he pleased.

Anna was like no woman he had met before. She *bewitched* him. He couldn't think of a better word to describe the effect she had on him.

It wasn't a purely physical connection, although that was part of it. Her intellect aroused him, and her ruthless streak. She demanded things of him. Not a passive observer, like Barbara had become over the years, but a worthy adversary.

Anna challenged him to exercise his own brain. Made him work for the privilege of enjoying her company. Perhaps it was his ego, but he *wanted* her to want him too.

Although he should have been dealing with paperwork last night, her arrival had excited him, especially the prospect of getting caught in the act by a parliamentary colleague. If Barbara was a dumpy Shetland pony, Anna was a thoroughbred.

A new email pinged on his phone. Subject line: SARA CARTER.

He groaned so loudly the junior minister looked up from his newspaper. But Geoffrey couldn't help himself. This story was like a fucking zombie. He'd thought they'd killed it off, and here it was, rearing its ugly head again. He read on.

> Dear Geoff,
>
> Just a note to keep you in the loop. Sara Carter has now been referred by Essex Police back to the UK Protected Persons Service (UKPPS) who will work closely with her to find her a new identity and rehome both her and her family in an undisclosed location (no longer in your constituency). Keep a low profile for a while, old chap. With a bit of luck, it's a storm in a teacup and it will blow over in no time.
>
> Supper soon?
>
> Stanley

Geoffrey sat up straighter. This was good news. Great news, actually. Sara Carter and her family had gone to ground and were now out of the media spotlight for the foreseeable future.

He wasn't terribly familiar with UKPPS, but he understood enough to know she wouldn't be found by the press unless she wanted to be found. The police and National Crime Agency officers who worked inside the witness protection scheme went to great lengths to maintain the secrecy of their charges' new homes. No one outside the scheme knew where they had moved to, and to prevent corrupt police officers from getting hold of this highly sensitive information and selling it on, separate computer systems were used.

As for the documentary, they would have released all their best material to the newspapers. Once it had been broadcast tonight, the story would die. He was almost home and dry.

He pushed aside his bowl of prunes. Diet be damned. Geoffrey Heathcote was going to celebrate with a Danish pastry.

*I loved her so much. I still do. And she loved me. I forgave her a long time ago – I don't think I ever blamed her – but now it is me who seeks absolution, for not being there when she needed me most.*

*For years and years, I've been looking for her, but with no success. When the documentary makers invited me to make a television programme, I only agreed because I hoped the publicity might lead us back to each other. But fate intervened. Now I have found you. We have found each other. Surely a gift from above.*

*Please don't tell your mother and father yet. What a wonderful surprise it will be.*

# 53

A gunshot rang out.

Catherine tried to run, her feet thundering against the pavement, but she was too slow. Her body became its own ballet, a staccato choreography of jerks and shudders as bullets tore through her chest cavity and spine and abdomen.

She collapsed to the concrete, her blood a running river, and she couldn't breathe, she was drowning in it, and she swum up and up through layers of consciousness until she broke the surface, still thick with sleep.

She opened her eyes to see identikit art and inoffensive décor. A familiar face. She blinked twice, her vision adjusting, her brain catching up. Not a gunshot after all, but the slam of a hotel room door and her daughter shaking her awake from the darkest of nightmares.

'Some people are here to see you.'

There were two of them, a man and a woman. They looked like hotel guests. She was wearing a pair of jeans and a mustard-coloured shirt. Diamond studs in her ears and white trainers that had never been on a run. He was tall but slouched. A threat of stubble. A decent haircut. He was wearing jeans too.

But they weren't hotel guests. They were plain-clothes police officers.

The woman smiled and held out her hand. 'I'm Detective Sergeant Carla Stroud and this is Detective Constable James Hart.' The man gave a half-wave while Carla explained who they were. 'We're from ERPPU, part of the UKPPS. You've been fully briefed on what that is?'

Edward, back from his walk, answered with an air of bewilderment. 'We're normal folk. We don't understand complicated police acronyms.'

Catherine flushed. The room felt unbearably crowded. 'My probation officer told me you were coming but I can't remember . . .' She tailed off, the enormity of their situation striking her with the blunted savagery of a cricket bat.

'It's the Eastern Region Protected Persons Unit,' said Hart. 'We're here to make this transition as smooth as possible.'

Catherine and Edward sat side by side on the double bed. The gap between their bodies spoke volumes about the state of their marriage. Two weeks ago, she would have leaned into him, thighs pressed together, fingers entwined, never giving their physical proximity a second thought. Now there was a wall. Invisible but unbreachable.

Honor lay on her pull-out bed, tapping the touchscreen of her mobile phone. When she caught the police officers looking at her, she dropped it guiltily.

'I know it's difficult,' said Stroud, crouching by the girl's bed. She didn't lecture or chastise or remonstrate and for that Catherine was grateful. 'But it's something we'll have to talk about soon, OK?'

'We know you're familiar with our protection schemes, but things have changed a bit since you left Mayfields,' said Hart. 'We still do the same job, though. We'll give you a new identity, a place to live and some money until you're back on your feet.'

Catherine stared at them, a million questions in her head, but unable to articulate any of them.

'Do we get any say in this?' Edward was sitting ramrod straight, as if altering his posture would signify a weakening of his position, but his face was crumpled from the strain. 'What about my job? I can't phone in sick forever.'

'You get to choose your own name and where you'd like to live, location-wise,' said Stroud.

Hart was more matter-of-fact. 'We'll help you find a new job, come up with an authentic back-story and sort you out with a car, that kind of thing.'

'But it does involve cutting yourself off completely from friends and family,' said Stroud, her voice gentle. 'No contact by phone, no interaction on social media and no emails or texts. It's a clean slate, you'll be starting over, and we will facilitate that, but you – all of you – must be completely on board, otherwise you'll be found.'

The police officers were quiet then, a respectful pause to allow the Allen family to process the weight of their words. Few made the transition without difficulties. Many struggled for years, their old lives dead – a butchered, bloody mess of abandoned relationships and unanswered questions – while their hearts were still beating. Still loving. Grieving for all that was. It was a lonely journey.

'We've found you a place to stay for a month or so,' said Stroud. 'It's a three-bedroomed holiday let in a rural location. It will buy us some time, and allow you some privacy to come to terms with what's happening and make some important decisions.'

By the time Stroud and Hart left, arranging to pick them up early next morning, the shadows had lengthened and the walls were dappled with glowing pockets of wintry late-afternoon sun.

Catherine gathered up their possessions, thinking about the friendships she had made – and would now lose – in the village. An instinct for self-preservation meant she had always kept others at arm's length but she would miss the companionship, the lunches and coffees. Honor lay on her bed, watching YouTube videos on her phone. Once or twice, Catherine watched her tap out a message and the answering flash of blue light, but she lacked the stomach to challenge her. Edward was listening to podcasts, earphones plugged in, but emotionally checked out. His sister had rung him a couple of times, but he hadn't picked up, unsure if any journalists had tracked her down yet and unable to cope if they had.

The hours crawled by in hell's waiting room, each of them lost in their own way. At seven o'clock, the family ate overcooked steak and lukewarm chips in the hotel restaurant. They went to bed early because there was nothing to say.

*Did you see me on the television tonight? Every word of it was true. I wrote to your mother every week, on a Wednesday, so she would have my letter in time for the weekend. But it's not like today, when contact is encouraged between separated families. My foster carers didn't like it. They were decent people who opened their home to a damaged soul, but they'd been given a sanitized version of my case history and had young children of their own.*

*They didn't want her letters arriving through the letter box of their suburban semi, stained by the sins of what she had done, and I suppose I wasn't confident enough to challenge them. A small part of me almost didn't mind. Every letter was an elegy to the past, a painful reminder of all that had happened. Every page rang with her distress, it made me feel guilty for being free when she was locked into her bedroom each night.*

*I skipped a week here and there – blaming homework and trips to the cinema with my friends – until I stopped writing altogether and, eventually, she did too. It was easier not to think about it. Easier to forget about everyone from that time and look to the future instead of behind me. Weeks turned into months and years until writing a letter became harder than not writing one.*

*By the time I'd grown up and realized what I had lost, she had been released from the unit and I had no idea where she was.*

# 54

Coggsbridge's only pub may be a cut-price version of the Hope and Anchor but the beer's still cold. The handful of journalists left on the job have gathered here, their news desks clinging to a story not related to Brexit, refusing to let it die.

Lawrie and I make our way to a table where Garth, the photographer, is already nursing a pint. He salutes when he sees us.

'Fucking waste of a day,' he says.

We murmur in sympathy. Sara Carter has gone to ground and although we're ever hopeful, none of us expects to see her back at the cottage.

When Sara was first charged with her parents' murders, she received hundreds of death threats in the post. In an early letter to me, she'd explained, matter-of-factly, how one of her father's patients had written to her at the unit, suggesting she should be put down like a dog. He had enclosed a choke chain to do the job.

The staff at Mayfields had intercepted the parcel, but one of the other residents – they call them that, not inmates – overheard them talking about it and word had spread.

These threats – which continued throughout her incarceration – were one of the reasons Sara was given a new identity. The prosecution had done an excellent job of undermining the sisters' account of the suffering they had endured at the hands of their parents. That, and the relentless press coverage, had vilified her until she became a caricature of evil, as far as the national consciousness was concerned.

Plunging a pair of scissors fourteen times into the bodies of her sleeping parents was an act of terrible savagery. But it went beyond that. This ten-year-old girl, who looked like an angel, had been demonized by a public hungry – no, ravenous – for all the blood-soaked thrills of her parricide.

Now the only thing we're certain of is that she is in hiding. Sara Carter and Catherine Allen may be dead but the woman who lived those names is not. Her life has detonated and we pressed the red button. It feels wrong. All of it.

'Thank God for Brinley,' Lawrie says. 'At least we've got the second part of her exclusive running tomorrow. Otherwise, we'd be fucked.' He gifts me a smile so dazzling I want to kiss him, but I can't because he's Lawrie and I'm Brinley, and we don't think about each other in that way, do we?

Russell from the *Sun* saunters over. There's an energy about him. It's in his walk and the restless drumming of his fingers against his thigh and the swing of his packed leather holdall. Garth has gone to the bar.

'Leaving so soon?' says Lawrie, eyeing our rival over the rim of his beer bottle.

'Something like that.' And it's the evasive way he doesn't quite meet our eyes that gives him away. Russell has got a story. A bloody good one, by the looks of it.

'So what's your angle tomorrow?' says Lawrie. His tone is casual, as if it doesn't matter, but we all know it does. We all know it makes the difference between a good night's sleep and a bollocking from the editor.

Russell glances at his watch. I know what he's thinking. *Is it late enough to tell them? Will it give them a chance to catch us up?*

'We have got something, yes,' he says, relenting. 'But I can't tell you what it is. If it's any consolation, I doubt you'll get a hard time from your desk, OK?'

Before we can question him further, he's gone, slipping through the pub doors and into the night.

'Great,' sighs Lawrie. We talk shop for a while. Listen to the pub quiz. But he's distracted and it's clear he's worried about Russell's story. His hand is resting on the scarred wooden table and, without thinking, I lay my palm across it. He looks up at me and there's a question mark in his expression. My heart runs faster.

He puts down his beer bottle, a smile playing around his lips. Not arrogant or self-satisfied. Not a smirk. But a secret kind of joy, that's the only way I can think to describe it, and it floors me, that smile. Because it's a long time since anyone has smiled at me like that.

'Brinley . . .' he says.

The laughter lines around his eyes deepen. He moves his chair closer until our legs are touching and passes his thumb across the back of my hand. The feel of him loosens something inside me.

His phone sits on the table next to mine. A journalist's anti-social habit, that impulse to be contactable, day or night. He opens his mouth to say something more, but in perfect synchronicity, they begin to ring.

Our eyes meet. We both understand.

'Hello?' he says.

'Hello?' I say.

I'm vaguely aware of Lawrie's voice and his exclamation of surprise, but then the pub and the bright lights and the smell of spilled beer recede until I'm only aware of the roar in my ears and the sting behind my eyelids, the opening up of a dark place inside.

It's Pearline on the phone, my aunt's neighbour, and I remember, too late, that I was supposed to ring Peg this morning, but I was busy with work, and forgot.

She's talking to me, but I'm not listening anymore, I can't hear anything beyond the very first sentence and her words spray over me like warm blood.

Aunt Peg is dead.

# 55

Geoffrey Heathcote was thinking about a glass of Argentinian Malbec, full-bodied and reassuringly expensive. A fillet steak or roasted haunch of venison, or perhaps, if he was feeling particularly in need of comfort, steamed steak and kidney suet pudding. He was starving, the end of another long day making decisions on behalf of the proletariat. Rules, a restaurant older than time itself, would be just the ticket.

John, his driver, took nine minutes to get him from the Ministry of Justice in Petty France to Covent Garden's Maiden Lane. A white van followed them through the streets of central London but neither man noticed. During the journey, Heathcote barely uttered a word because he was preoccupied not with business, but the pursuit of pleasure.

Anna had not answered his texts or his telephone calls. He had found himself checking her social media feeds, a foreign country to him, and had even tried the hotel in case she'd gone there to sleep off their late night. He would be charged the full price, the receptionist had informed him sniffily, even though no one had checked in. At lunchtime, he had broken one of his own strict rules and left her a voicemail.

As day turned into night, he felt the first stirrings of concern for her welfare.

The restaurant, housed in a tall Victorian house, was still busy, even at this late hour, but he had called ahead to reserve a table. They always found him one. Heathcote never minded dining alone. He rather relished the luxury of it.

He liked to froth out his napkin and tuck it in the front of his shirt. Savour his wine. Eat his meal in peace. Brandy, an after-dinner cigar. Privileges oiled by power, prestige and money.

John pulled into the kerbside, the tick of the indicator breaking the library-silence of the car.

'Here we are, sir. Enjoy your evening.'

'Thanks, old chap. What time shall we say? Eleven thirty pick-up?'

Neither man noticed the white van that had pulled in a few metres behind them. The Right Honourable Geoffrey Heathcote stepped out of the ministerial car and into the eye of a photographer's lens.

He staggered backwards, blindsided by the rapid fire of the flash against the dark of the evening, and then a reporter was in front of him, a dictaphone hovering in front of his face.

'Russell Parker, from the *Sun*. Do you know an Anna Hadley, Mr Heathcote?'

An ambush.

The minister faltered, his stomach plunging at the mention of her name, but then he remembered his media training. Bridging, they called it, the art of digression and evasion.

'I'm not sure, young man. I know lots of people.'

'Let me refresh your memory,' said the journalist. He reached inside his jacket and pulled out a sheaf of images that had been copied and colour-printed onto A5 paper.

Heathcote glanced down at them, but he would not take them from the journalist's hand. The Westminster corridors and gentlemen's clubs had always been a safe harbour in an aggressive world, but now the floors were shaking and the walls were crumbling to dust.

It was unmistakeably him. Shirt unbuttoned and trousers around his ankles, sitting in his chair in his office at the House of Commons, Anna Hadley straddled across his lap, an expression of pleasure on his face.

The fucking bitch.

He knew now why she wasn't answering her mobile phone. She wasn't in trouble. She was ignoring him. The cold-hearted slag had stitched him up.

*Think, Geoffrey. Think.*

He turned away from the journalist without speaking and crossed the pavement in contained, angry strides. John, his driver, had witnessed the exchange in the rear-view mirror after he'd pulled away, and now reversed up the one-way street at speed, tyres shrieking against the asphalt. He nipped sharply into the kerb, about twenty metres from the MP. Heathcote picked up his pace.

'This is going to appear on the front page of tomorrow's newspaper,' the journalist said, running alongside him. 'How long have you been together? Is there anything you'd like to say?'

He paused, giving Heathcote an opportunity to answer. A right to reply, it was called. In the interests of fairness.

But Heathcote didn't have anything to say. This was a disaster. A shitstorm. A fucktonne of a catastrophe, bearing down on him like a truck.

Had Anna been wearing a hidden camera? No, it wasn't possible. She had removed all her clothes except her skirt and her bra. He would have seen it. And the angle was wrong. Too much distance between him and Anna in the photographs for the camera to have been on her person.

He wracked his brains, his ego unwilling to let him believe his lover could have humiliated him in so public a way. Perhaps one of his political enemies had bugged his office. Now that made sense. This was the handiwork of a devious mind.

But Anna had a devious mind. A scene, as piercing as betrayal, replayed in his memory. Anna walking into his office and putting her handbag on his desk. A handbag large enough to discreetly house a camera placed opposite his chair. A classic sting.

It was over.

His affair. His marriage. His political career.

He was almost at the car, desperate to sink into the leather seats and put some distance between himself and the press. *Not far to go. Keep looking forward and don't react.*

The journalist was matching him stride for stride. 'One of my newspaper colleagues is at your Cotswolds farmhouse with a copy of these photographs. He's knocking on the door right now.'

*A pincer movement. Hit us both at the same time. Poor Barbara.*

'Do you have a message for your wife? An apology, perhaps?' The journalist, coated in that greasy sheen of youth and arrogance, smirked. 'Thirty years married. How do you think she'll react to your affair with Anna Hadley?'

Heathcote stopped walking. Another car drove up the narrow street. The lights of the restaurants were beacons in the darkness. A couple, arm in arm, were lost in conversation. In each other. He envied the simplicity of their lives.

The media interest in him had been dying, but the revelation of his affair would be like pouring petrol on its embers.

The coldness inside him hardened until every sensation was lost and all that remained was a flat, numb feeling. The world about him slowed. He turned, lifted his arm and pulled it back. He heard John call his name. He saw the mouth of the journalist open and widen. He was conscious of the photographer raising his camera and the repeating fire of the flash. But he didn't care.

His fist connected with the journalist's nose and broke it.

The world sped up again. John was tugging at his jacket, pulling him away, the photographer was still taking pictures, and Russell Parker from the *Sun* was covering the lower half of his face, swearing and making threats about police and assault charges.

Heathcote, in a daze, allowed John to steer him back to the car and the journalist disappeared into the van, talking to someone on his mobile phone in a thickened voice, his nose at an odd angle.

Russell Parker had a bright stain on the front of his shirt. Geoffrey Heathcote's cuffs and trousers were spattered with dozens of carmine specks.

Both of them had blood on their hands.

*Where are you? Are you safe, dear Hero? No one would blame you if you needed some breathing space. It's a lot to take in. If you'd like, I could come and get you.*

# 56

The country roads at night are as quiet as death itself.

We don't talk much, but Lawrie drives my car through the ice with care, not too fast, but with enough determined concentration to deliver me home to Aunt Peg as quickly as possible.

Heat pricks the back of my eyes. In the last twenty-one years, my great-aunt has been my mother and father, my sister and brother. My home and family. She's been Sunday dinners and supermarket shopping trips, Scrabble and Gene Kelly musicals, home-made knitted gloves for Christmas and a safe harbour in life's choppy seas.

My throat feels like it's got something stuck in it that can't be cleared. The road hums beneath us. Lawrie has turned on the radio, the music filling up the space between us. Words rise inside me but get caught in the net of my grief, unable to free themselves. I bite down on my lip and watch the snow flurries, torn paper scraps trapped in the glare of the headlamps.

I was the first to hang up.

Pearline hadn't shared more than a few scant details. Only that Aunt Peg's body had been found in our flat, and I must come quickly.

'How did it happen?' My voice had sounded surprisingly calm. Aunt Peg was eighty-four, after all. I'd expected her to say a heart attack or stroke, or a nasty fall.

But she didn't. A hesitation, a stumble over words. 'It's complicated,' she'd said in the familiar rhythms of her Jamaican patois. 'Get here first. The police will talk to you then.'

The pub had been full of noise and colour. Lawrie was still talking to Colin, our news editor. I'd stood there, a crack in my heart, thinking about *Before* and *After*. How life can turn on a moment. That death visits us all. A few minutes earlier, I'd been laughing and drinking, the world as it should be. Now everything was shaded by loss.

Lawrie had ended his call, and turned to me, his eyes bright with gossip straight from the newsroom. 'Heathcote's been shagging his mistress for a year. Classic kiss-and-tell.'

He'd swallowed a mouthful of his lager. 'First edition of the *Sun*'s dropped. They've got pictures, an interview, the full works. This will keep the story running for a couple more days.' He'd grinned, delighted by the turn of events. 'And keep us out of the office a bit longer.'

But then he'd caught sight of my expression. 'Christ, it's not that bad, is it? I thought we'd been having a laugh. No one's died, you know.' When I hadn't answered, he'd said, 'Oh shit. Oh, Brinley, my stupid mouth. I'm sorry.'

He'd offered to drive me back, downed a coffee and a sandwich from the bar menu, and now here we were, heading to east London along the dark vein of the A13, choked with high-rises and cranes that rise out of the ground like ghostly arms.

Pearline's light is on, a bright spot in the run-down block

of flats that was Aunt Peg's home for almost all her life. My great-aunt had wanted to raise her family here, but after five stillbirths had given up hope. She'd lived here with her husband Alfred, squeezed into three rooms and a tiny bathroom. A make-do-and-mend life, but a happy one, until he'd been taken from her by mesothelioma. When my mother had died, and I couldn't stand to be near my father, she had opened her home to me.

The lift isn't working and someone has tried – unsuccessfully – to clean up the vomit in the corner of the stairwell, that curious stink of parmesan and disinfectant. God knows what Lawrie thinks, but whatever it is, he doesn't say it.

Pearline has invited me to knock on her door as soon we arrive, however late it is, but I want to go straight to Aunt Peg's flat, and the keys are already in my hand when we reach the fourth floor.

The security light at the top of the stairwell comes on automatically, spotlighting a row of identical front doors. Many years of my life have been spent here, but as I've grown older, my job opening up new places and experiences, I've come to understand that Aunt Peg and the other inhabitants of this estate have always existed on the fringes of poverty, and it hurts my heart.

We walk in silence down the narrow corridor, graffitied notes of despair on the walls, a concrete balcony overlooking the floor below. Aunt Peg's flat is number twenty-three and we're almost there, almost home, when I stop so sharply that Lawrie, who is a couple of footsteps behind, knocks into me.

A metal padlock – new and shiny – hangs against the

chipped red paint of the front door. A desolate bunting of blue and white police tape announces her death.

The words rise again but they cannot fight their way out, and I make a sound, a low grunt of pain. Lawrie slips his hand into mine and squeezes it, but I can't think of anything beyond what that loop of tape means and how my great-aunt has died.

The key is in the lock before I consider the repercussions, and I turn it, tugging hard, but the padlock stops the front door from opening fully. Through the crack, I can smell memories of home, stale food and washing powder and love, but there's something else, an edge of darkness that I can taste at the back of my mouth until it's washed away by the bitter salt of my tears.

Pearline is in her dressing gown. She's a few years younger than Aunt Peg but I've known her for almost two decades. She's square and comfortable, and she pulls me into an embrace.

'Let me look at you,' she says. 'I haven't seen you for a long time. I miss you.' She casts an appraising eye over Lawrie. 'This your boyfriend?'

We're both quick to deny it, and she raises her eyebrows, but doesn't say anything more. Instead she guides us into her immaculate sitting room and brings us steaming cups of Rooibos tea.

'What happened?'

Pearline doesn't answer my question straight away. She pours herself a cup and adds a heaped teaspoon of sugar. She stirs it slowly, taking her time. Her eyes, when they meet mine, are liquid with sorrow.

'I didn't see Peg,' she says, shaking her head. 'I didn't hear her. No radio. No singing.' She chuckles at the memory of my aunt's love of musicals before growing serious again. 'There was nothing.'

Her face crumples. She tells us she waited a whole day before knocking on Aunt Peg's door – even though she knew something wasn't right – and when Peg didn't answer, she let herself in with the spare key she keeps in a broken teapot for emergencies.

Pearline thumps her ringed hand against her sofa cushion and adjusts the plate of grater cakes she has laid out. She presses a finger to a stray crumb of sweetened coconut, and then to her mouth. Fury at her delaying tactics whitens my vision – why can't she just come out and say it? – but then the crashing cymbals of clarity strike. She's composing herself.

The front door wouldn't open, she says, as if something was blocking it. 'I called for Peg,' she says, 'I called and called.' But my aunt didn't answer.

Pearline rallied a few of the neighbours and they managed to force their way in. She takes a sip of her tea, and a tear snakes its way down her cheek.

'Peg was lying in the hallway.' She draws us a picture with words. My aunt was wearing her nightie, a spilled mug of Ovaltine on the carpet, this morning's post scattered about her. Face down, her skin as cold as the snow on the ground outside.

'It sounds like a heart attack,' I say, reaching out to squeeze her warm hand. 'Or a stroke. Just one of those awful things.'

But Pearline is shaking her head back and forth, a violent

denial. She pulls herself from the sofa, slowly but with purpose, drawing her floral dressing gown more tightly around her wide hips, humming an old gospel spiritual. A bureau is pressed against the wall, the wood gleaming, the brass handles polished. She rummages in a drawer, old bits of paper and letters flying about. She retrieves a small business card and hands it to me.

DETECTIVE CONSTABLE MARVIN LYLE.

His name is printed in the centre, sandwiched between the Metropolitan Police insignia and a telephone number.

Between them, they'd decided the news of Aunt Peg's death was better coming from Pearline, she explains. But the police officer has asked me to call him in the morning.

Pearline reads the question mark in my expression and her face, the one I have known for so long, seems to reduce and age in front of me, the parentheses around her mouth deepening, her dark curls turning to dust, living time-lapse photography. But tiredness has me in its vice and when I rub my eyes and look again, she's back to how she was.

'Hold her hand,' she says to Lawrie in her forthright way, and he does as she asks, but I pull away from him, eschewing all distractions in pursuit of the truth. My eyes meet Pearline's and the broken bits of my heart are reflected in hers.

'She was killed,' she says, a sorrowful shake of her head. 'Murdered.'

'How?'

The question rots a hole through the coconut-sweetness of her sitting room. Pearline seems to shrink into herself, glancing out of the window at the blot of the night, shying from the spectre of death that fills the shadows of her flat.

This movement alerts me, triggering a preternatural instinct for what she's about to say next, and those four words become the last turn of the key, opening up the box of secrets kept locked for so long.

'Scissors in her neck.'

*It's natural to want to defend her. I feel exactly the same way as you do. But caution should be applied here. For all her remorse, your mother is a killer, convicted by the courts. Of course you love her. I love her too. But she's never been above a little manipulation. Whatever she says, your mother isn't who you think she is. Don't forget that.*

*There was blood on her doll, I remember that. A fleck of it on your mother's cheek. Blood under her nails and collected in the dry-skin grooves of her knees. She was a good sister but not a good daughter. She had evil in her then. Ask yourself this: where does that evil go?*

# 57

## Friday, 14 December 2018

Honor's screams sliced open the night-time stillness of the hotel.

In the room above, someone banged on the floor, and Catherine, crouched by her daughter's bed, muttering words of comfort, thought how easily a murder might be ignored.

Honor's face was wet with tears, the back of her pyjama top soaked with sweat. Catherine used childhood endearments – 'pumpkin' and 'pickle' and 'sweetheart' – to soothe her, but the girl resisted her mother's touch. After a few minutes, Honor settled back into sleep. Catherine lay on her own bed, not touching Edward, watching the darkness thin into dawn.

At ten to five, she woke up her husband and daughter, and they dressed in bleary-eyed silence. Most of their belongings had been packed away the night before and they were passing through the hotel lobby when the hour struck.

'Up bright and early,' said the receptionist, all service-industry smiles. 'Off anywhere nice?'

Honor rolled her eyes and flinched at her mother's touch. Catherine managed a weak smile. 'Magical mystery tour.'

The receptionist laughed and wagged her finger at them. 'Don't get lost.'

*Lost.*

Catherine had been lost for years, but this time there was no breadcrumb trail, no rope to guide her home.

The police officers were waiting for them in the car park, blurred shapes wreathed in freezing fog. They loaded the bags into a nondescript black estate car. No one spoke, the bitter wind sharpening the sense of despair, the hotel's lights illuminating their heartbreak.

The holiday let was hidden down a pot-holed lane bracketed by trees and bushes. The fog had lifted and a frosted farmer's field ran as far as the eye could see. Branches were silhouetted against the grey skies of Norfolk, yearning towards the horizon. It was the only house for miles.

Detective Sergeant Carla Stroud pressed some numbers into a keypad on the small black safe on the side of the property and withdrew a set of keys.

'Let's get you settled, shall we?'

They trudged in behind her, but with none of the giddy excitement that comes from arriving at a strange place on holiday. The owners had left a welcome basket filled with marmalade and crusty bread, fruit and biscuits and wine. A fresh Christmas tree in a pot was decorated with tinsel. A tray with pretty cups and a sugar bowl and cafetière was waiting on the table. But the jauntiness felt off-kilter.

If any of the neighbours happened to ask, their own house had been flooded.

Honor, headphones plugged in, opened the biscuits without asking and slumped down at the table, tear tracks still visible on her face.

As they had driven across the Suffolk border, halfway through their two-hour journey, she had screamed without warning. DC James Hart, who was driving, had jumped and swerved, cursing under his breath. He had pulled into the nearest services, a ramshackle cafe on the A12.

In broken, sobbing sentences, Honor had told them what she had just seen on Instagram. Photographs of her old home, her school, her picture splashed across social media. Even though it was breaking the injunction. Even though it was against the law. According to a news report she'd read on Twitter, the police had arrested three people for naming the family and publishing their address. The original posts had been removed, but the roots had spread and it was impossible to contain their insidious growth.

Worse still were the messages of abuse from school friends, who now knew whose daughter she was.

In the tiny shop which sold postcards and out-of-date crisps, Honor had thrust her phone at her mother. 'This is all your fault,' she had said. 'I hate you and everything you've done.' A dead-eyed stare. '*Sa-ra.*' Each syllable resonated with a sing-song sarcasm.

Catherine had looked at her sharply. 'Don't call me that. My name's Catherine now, and I'm still your mother.'

A mumble of words.

'What did you say?'

'I *said*, "Some mother you turned out to be."'

'Honor!'

She had taken a step towards her daughter, her tone streaked with hurt, but empathy too. The girl flinched, pressing herself into the racks of postcards. 'What are you going to do, *Sa-ra*? *Kill* me?'

Catherine quelled an instinct to shake some humanity into her daughter. Her mockery stung but she understood it. Honor was behaving like a cornered animal, lashing out, and who could blame her?

'Of course not,' she had said.

'Liar.'

Catherine, exhausted with being her daughter's punch bag, had shot back, 'You're a liar too.'

'No, I'm not,' said Honor, with the outraged hauteur of a pubescent girl.

'Are you sure about that?' Catherine had met her daughter's gaze, a defiance in her own. 'Why did you get a bus to Halstead on Monday morning and miss school?'

Honor had opened her mouth and shut it again, but she hadn't denied it.

Much later, when the police officers had deposited bags of shopping and left with promises to return tomorrow, Catherine found herself staring out of the bedroom window.

Why shouldn't she tell the truth? She had sacrificed everything for Shannon, but her sister had claimed Catherine's freedom for herself, the memories of her childish heroism slipping through her fingers like sand. Catherine owed her sister nothing.

But who would believe her after all these years?

Catherine hung their clothes in the wardrobe and put

her book on the bedside table. She watched a partridge make steady progress across the field, its plumage brown and unremarkable, like her.

She touched her hair, the dye she had used for years masking its natural blonde brightness. Would the world still turn if she stopped colouring it? Of course it would. The secret was out now.

A thin flame of optimism flared inside her. They *could* do it. Start again. It would just take time. She sensed a presence in the doorway. Edward was watching her. She held out her hand in welcome.

He took a step towards her but he didn't touch her. His expression was agonized. 'I can't do this.'

The words hung between them, a demarcation line.

'This' – he gestured around him – 'is fucked up. This place, this situation. My job.' He shook his head, as if he couldn't believe what was happening. 'I don't want to give up everything.'

'You're not giving up *me*,' she said. 'Or Honor. We're still here.'

'Honor wants to come too.'

He stated it so matter-of-factly that she didn't understand what he meant until he retrieved his jeans from the wardrobe and his toothbrush from the en suite.

'We're checking into a hotel.'

In the brutal light of the bathroom, his skin was a patchwork of lines, a sprinkling of grey at his temples. The events of the last few days were written in the stoop of his shoulders and the too-loose shirt that had always fitted him so well. His eyes were flat and unforgiving. No sign of his wedding ring. A stranger.

'Our whole marriage has been a sham,' he said. 'You're not the woman I thought you were. You deceived me. I would never have married you if I'd known the truth.'

'I'm still me,' she said, but the words were thick in the back of her throat.

'But you're not though, are you? You were never the you I thought you were.'

And what could she say to that?

She trailed him around the house like a lamb, bleating out entreaties, begging him to stay and despising herself for it.

At one point, she tugged on his arm, desperate for any scraps of his attention. 'I didn't do it,' she blurted out, and his look of contempt skewered any hope she had of convincing him of the truth.

By dusk, it was clear he had made up his mind.

The ERPPU had lent them a car – a grey Fiesta, a couple of scratches on the door, about five years old, easily forgettable – and Catherine pressed the key into Edward's hand.

'You can't call a taxi,' she had said after finding him rummaging through takeaway menus and business cards in the drawer. The incredulous laugh that had slipped from her broke up into a sob she couldn't contain.

Edward patted her awkwardly on the shoulder. Honor was on her phone, leaning against the wall of the hallway, waiting to leave. She didn't look at her mother once.

'We'll call you tomorrow,' he said. 'A bit of space will do us all good.'

And then they were gone.

\*

As night closed in, the room darkened. The silence became a physical pain. Catherine sat on the edge of someone else's sofa and shivered until it consumed her. But there was no one to make her a cup of tea or fetch a blanket, and eventually she levered herself up, hands like ice. She warmed herself a tin of soup in someone else's kitchen and climbed into someone else's bed, palms cupped around someone else's mug. She closed her eyes, caught the screech of an owl at hunt. She was alone again. But she had been here before. She would survive, because what other choice was there?

A headache was needling the bridge of her nose and she reached across the bedside table for her handbag, in search of paracetamol.

Throat sweets and loose coins and plasters and a packet of tissues. A biro and Tampax, an old shopping list. Painkillers. A forgotten bundle of letters and business cards, their edges torn from being in her bag since yesterday, held together by an elastic band.

Letters from the *Daily Telegraph*, the *Sun*, *Daily Mirror*, *The Times*, *Daily Mail*, *Sunday Times*, Press Association, Sky News, BBC, ITN, Channel 4.

They were all clamouring to speak to her, an exclusive with the Angel of Death who stabbed her parents to death in a frenzy of bloodlust. None of them would want to hear the inconvenient truth, much less publish it. Who would believe *her*, Sara Carter, convicted killer, with all the evidence to the contrary?

She scanned the letters, all variations on the same theme. *Your side of the story. Reunited with your sister. Donation to a charity of your choice.*

She had almost given up hope, resigned to the collapse of her family, until she saw, on the bottom of one of the last letters, as if the hand of fate itself was guiding her, a name she knew as well as her own.

# 58

'There's nothing more I can do. You can try and persuade Barbara to pose for a photograph outside your house. It's a big ask, I suppose, but it's worked in the past.'

The senior communications officer, Romily Dawson, was all clipped efficiency. There was none of the previous warmth or affectionate exasperation of the last few days.

'I've always thought there's a dignity in resigning quickly, though, don't you? Party before political career, and all that,' she said.

Geoffrey Heathcote gripped the telephone receiver more tightly. He knew whose voice was behind that sentiment and it wasn't Romily Dawson's. The Prime Minister liked neat and tidy. He was a loose end.

'Barbara will do it,' he said, even though he wasn't certain. Even though she hadn't answered the landline since last night when she'd called him a 'lying, cheating bastard pig'. Barbara never swore, so he knew she was upset, but he'd just have to persuade the old girl. He'd always managed to talk her round in the past.

Romily sighed. He could hear her tapping her pen against

her front tooth, mulling it over. 'It would have been more useful today, Geoffrey.'

He knew that, of course he did. Breach of fucking privacy, this was. But Romily said the paper was arguing it was in the public interest, and anyway, the damage had been done. The tabloids had been full of his indiscretion and the press had been camped outside his Mayfair home since first light. If he and Barbara had put on a united front today, the picture would have been used in all tomorrow's newspapers. Now there would likely be another run of salacious stories.

'Tomorrow,' he promised. 'First thing. Here or at the farmhouse?'

'Hmmm.' He could almost hear the cogs of Romily's brain whirring. 'I think it will sit better with your constituents if you bring Barbara back to Essex. You're fighting to save your marriage and your political career. You need to appear contrite. Go and pick her up, don't make her come running to you. Make your constituents feel like they matter.'

Four hours later, and now Geoffrey was knee-deep in a bottle of Irish malt. That bitch Anna had fucked him over.

He tried to ring the farmhouse again, but there was no reply. He imagined Barbara, sitting in the darkness, sipping her gin and tonic and ignoring him. Her refusal to engage enraged him, the impotent fury he felt at Anna finding its target in his wife. Stupid cow. She liked her expensive lifestyle, didn't she? Her Marc Jacobs handbags and holidays at the Sandy Lane hotel. His job as an MP opened doors for them both. It won him seats in company boardrooms and consultancies and fat pay cheques. She hadn't worked a day since they married, the lazy cunt.

He pressed redial again and the long, unanswered rings wound him tighter still.

How dare she ignore him? He was fighting for his political life. His wife should be supporting him. *That* was her fucking job. Not sitting on her arse, drinking her sorrows away.

Geoffrey Heathcote stumbled from his study and grabbed his overcoat. No ministerial car for him this evening. That privilege had been withdrawn pretty sharpish. His car keys were hanging on their hook and he reached for them, throwing and catching them in one hand. Tossing it up. Making a choice.

The street was empty, the journalists and photographers long gone, a tinge of ice in the midnight air. Even in the midst of personal crisis, he took a moment to admire his Mayfair townhouse, with its painted black railings and chequer-board pathway. It was mortgage-free, the reward for a life in the City before politics consumed him.

The roll-top shutter that led to his underground garage was open and he climbed into his bottle green F-Type Jaguar. The cold air had sobered him up and the masochist in him wanted to know exactly what tomorrow would bring. He withdrew his mobile phone and looked at the *Sun*'s Twitter feed, to see if tomorrow's front page had gone live yet. The headline blared at him.

**EXCLUSIVE: 'SECRETS FOR SEX' SCANDAL**

The bottom of his stomach dropped out.

He clicked on the link to the story.

Another photograph of the interior of his Westminster

office, but this time a close-up of the paperwork relating to the Sara Carter case – the green light for her new identity – which he'd left on his desk. Strictly speaking, he ought to have filed it away when Anna showed up, but he'd been . . . distracted. He scanned the opening paragraph of the story.

Pervy prisons boss Geoffrey Heathcote let his mistress read confidential files during their steamy sex sessions.

Oh fuck, the bitch had really done a number on him. He read down. *The Right Dishonourable Heathcote* . . . He slammed the flat of his hand against the steering wheel and reversed out of the garage at speed.

He tried to call Anna on hands-free as he drove west across London to the M40 but it rang once and diverted to voicemail. The cunt had blocked him. He tried Barbara again. And again. And again. After seven rings, she picked up, her tone threaded with weariness.

'What do you want?'

He'd bloody well known she was at home. A Bruce Springsteen song came on the radio. He turned it down. A flurry of snow hit the windscreen and the wipers automatically sprang into action, dragging across the glass. His mouth tasted of whisky and regret.

'I'm on my way to see you,' he said, forcing a bright note of conciliation into his tone. Even he wasn't stupid enough to say why. He would talk her round when he got home. In the morning, she could put on a nice dress and some make-up, and they would drive back to Essex and pose by the gate by the holly bush, a picture of cosy domesticity. The snow was falling faster now, and he squinted into the darkness, an ache in his temples.

'Don't bother,' she said. 'I won't be here.'

'What do you mean?' he said, his eyes glancing into the rear-view mirror and back at the road. And then again, more sharply. 'What do you mean?'

'I'm going to stay with my sister for a bit.'

'You're going to Australia?' he said stupidly.

'Yes, Geoffrey, I am.'

'When?'

'In about an hour's time, not that it's any business of yours.'

'You can't.'

'I can do exactly as I please.'

The snow was coming down faster now, the cars on the M40 slowing to a crawl. Traffic, even at this time of night. Geoffrey leaned forward in the driver's seat, trying to get a clearer look through the glass. His vision swam. Perhaps he wasn't as sober as he'd thought.

'I forbid it,' he said.

She laughed. The bitch actually laughed. 'You can't forbid me. I'm not your property.'

Clutching at straws now, seeing his career disappear down the plughole, he went for the jugular. 'I'll put a stop on the credit card. Cancel your plane ticket.'

To his surprise, she laughed again. 'You must think I'm stupid,' she said. 'I've been saving up for years. My rainy day fund. And it's raining now. Very heavily.'

He switched tack. 'Please don't go, darling. Or put it off for a couple of days, at least.' He lowered his voice, grovelling. 'I need you.'

The red lights of the car in front of him flared and his foot pumped the brake, narrowly avoiding a collision. He swore into the quiet of the car. That was a close call.

'Barbara?' he said, mentally crossing his fingers his entreaty had worked. 'Barbara?'

But she had hung up on him.

He hit redial but the landline was engaged. She must have taken the phone off the hook.

His mind sparked into life. Where would she fly from? Heathrow, most likely. The traffic was starting to move again. He would make his way to the airport, meet her there. She hated public scenes. If he was quick, he could cut across to the M4 and catch her before she went through security. Make her change her mind.

He turned up the radio, glanced into his rear-view mirror and pulled into the middle lane.

A long, low sound filled the air, like the groan of a wounded animal.

Too late, Geoffrey saw the twin headlights of a petrol tanker bearing down on him, its horn blaring into the frozen night. Too late, he realized he'd misjudged its distance, its travelling speed.

He grasped the steering wheel, making hard, frantic turns, but the tyres wouldn't bite, spinning on the icy road. He veered into the slow lane, but a minibus, too close now to brake, hit the flank of his car and pushed it back into the path of the tanker.

The petrol tanker's driver, David Mason, a father of five and keen gambler, tried to avoid the car just ahead as it spun in circles like a roulette wheel, but there were vehicles in both lanes either side of him and there was nowhere for him to go. The odds were not in his favour.

Mr Mason closed his eyes, muttered a prayer and braced for impact, not yet knowing that the next twenty seconds would confine him to a wheelchair for the rest of his life.

The Right Honourable Geoffrey Heathcote, Justice Secretary and Member of Parliament, was still conscious when the petrol tanker ploughed into the side of his Jaguar, rupturing his spleen, breaking his right arm and both legs, collapsing his lung, splintering five ribs and caving in the side of his skull.

He was barely conscious when another vehicle – a second-hand Mini driven by an eighteen-year-old girl on her way home from university for the holidays – struck the opposite side of his car, the force of the impact killing her instantly and shattering his windscreen, flakes of snow drifting through the jagged edges of the glass to land on his face like tears.

By the time fire licked its flaming tongue against the dashboard, melting the radio into silence and guaranteeing him a final front page, Geoffrey Heathcote, whose self-inflicted downfall had been forensically documented by an unforgiving press, was dead.

# 59

Pearline's sofa is battered but squashy, and the lace-edged back covers scratching my face offer a strange kind of comfort. I doze in front of the electric fire, my feet tucked beneath a blanket.

It's late, touching midnight. Time has taken on an elastic quality, stretching and retracting, and it's twenty-four hours since I heard about Aunt Peg, and it feels like forever and no time at all.

Lawrie is gone, back on the job. He'd explained to Colin what had happened – not the details, just the fact that Peg was dead – and the news editor had told him to tell me to take some time off, although I bet he's complaining behind my back. Lawrie had splashed his face in Pearline's sink and downed a cup of her strong coffee before heading down to Kent to collect his car and get back out on the story.

'Take care of yourself,' he'd said, and his eyes had added something more, although I couldn't read what it was. 'Will you stay here for a while?'

I'd shrugged, uncertain. For obvious reasons, I can't go back to the flat I shared with my aunt, and I like it at

Pearline's. It makes me feel close to Peg, and our neighbour has a warmth about her that soothes me, cooking nutritious meals and enfolding me in sudden hugs.

As soon as Lawrie had closed the door behind him, I'd called the police officer who'd left his card for me. He arrives an hour later, bringing in the cold day on his fiery hair and the heightened patches of colour on his cheeks.

'Did your aunt have any enemies?' He sniffs Pearline's Rooibos tea dubiously and puts it back on the table without taking a sip.

I'm so shocked by this line of questioning I laugh. 'Everyone loved her.'

'Did she owe money?'

'Not that I know of.'

He frowns then, tapping his pen against his notebook, his freckles standing out against his skin. 'But you say nothing was taken.'

'Not that I could see.'

'And there were no signs of forced entry.' He scribbles something down. 'She must have opened the door to her attacker at some point on Thursday morning.'

I think of Aunt Peg, shuffling along the hallway in her worn slippers, her face wreathed in a welcome smile, expecting the meter man or Pearline, or another friend from the estate, and bow my head. Suspicion whispers in my ear.

The detective – Marvin Lyle – shifts about on the edge of Pearline's best armchair. He mutters something about family liaison officers – I tell him I don't want a fuss, strangers at my side – and formal identification.

'We – uh – how would you feel about this? You won't

have to move from the sofa, we can show you a photograph of your aunt, or perhaps via a video link, if that makes you feel more comfortable.'

'I *want* to see her,' I say. 'I want to say goodbye.'

He stops what he's doing then, glances up at me. 'I'm not sure that's a good idea. Her injuries were – um – extensive.'

But I've made up my mind.

Later, we're standing outside the hospital mortuary in Whitechapel. Pearline offered to come with me but she's already had so much to deal with and it's been Peg and I for so long, this feels like the right thing to do.

They've moved her body to the Chapel of Rest, a small brick room next to the morgue. I've been here before, to interview a family whose son was killed in a train crash caused by a signal error. They'd insisted on coming here but they weren't allowed to see him because there was nothing much of his remains left to see.

His parents were angry, vocal, desperate to keep his memory alive. A knot of relatives had gathered outside, crying and shouting. A need to be heard. Some families are like that. Driven to vocalize their hurt, advocate for their dead, not wanting to let them down, or for their passing to be nothing more than a footnote in history. Others withdraw into silence, the glare of the public gaze like a scald on exposed skin.

That boy was identified by his teeth. We're all flesh and bone in the end.

The Chapel of Rest smells of nothing except the faintest scent of cleaning fluid. A display of dusty silk flowers sits on the windowsill. No religious iconography. No music. The temperature is cool, to preserve the body.

'I'm afraid you can't touch her,' says DC Lyle, his apology in the shape of his shoulders, the clasping together of his hands. 'Forensics haven't finished yet.'

Lyle warns me what to expect. Peg was stabbed in the neck with a pair of scissors, and in the back, chest and the insides of her thighs. He doesn't need to tell me how brutal it was.

'Just take a quick look at her face,' he says, 'and then we're done here.'

Aunt Peg is lying on a gurney with wheels. A white sheet is covering her body, all the way up to her chin to obscure the injuries to her neck. Her hair, which she always wore in a bun, has been arranged around her face, grey and wispy like fescue grass. But mostly, she's hidden from me, her body barely indenting the sheet. Her skin is the colour of sour milk. It doesn't look like her.

'It's her,' I say, even though by the time formal identification takes place, the police are almost always certain, and it's just that – a formality.

Eighty-four years on this earth and all that's left behind is an empty sack of flesh. I don't cry.

Back on the estate, Pearline places a bowl of brown stew chicken in front of me and waits for every bit to be gone. 'Eat,' she says. 'Strong girl.' But I'm not a strong girl. I am weak.

The rest of the day passes. I telephone a couple of Peg's friends from the church and ask them to pass on the news of her murder. I think about the coroner and the death certificate and a funeral, but I can't get beyond thinking and into doing. Lying on Pearline's sofa is all I can manage.

Mulling over, too, what DC Marvin Lyle told me as we were driving back from the Chapel of Rest.

Aunt Peg was killed on the same morning my story about Sara Carter appeared in the newspaper. Her attacker inflicted fourteen separate wounds with a pair of kitchen scissors, which had been wiped clean.

*Fourteen.*

I feel it, deep inside my gut. Not a coincidence, but a warning.

I'm still mulling it over at gone midnight, feet under the blanket, cheek resting against Pearline's scratchy sofa back covers, wondering how I'll explain it all to DC Lyle, to *convince* him, when my mobile rings and a voice says, 'Hello, Brinley. My name is Catherine Allen, but you might remember me as Sara Carter.'

# 60

## Saturday, 15 December 2018

The snow had stopped, but the leaves and bushes were already silvered with frost, even though the hollow hour was still to come.

Catherine pulled on her winter coat and boots, switched on the torch she had found in one of the kitchen cupboards and walked up the narrow lane, her lungs filled with ice.

The night sky was so dark she was lost in it, but the hard, bright eyes of the stars followed her as she turned the corner and waited at the junction of the empty road, where a four-way wooden sign told her which direction and how many miles it was to Norwich and London.

Across the still of the nightscape, she caught the rumble of tyres and, after a few minutes, the sweep of headlights.

*One. Two. Three. Four. Five. Six.*

She only stopped counting when the car drew alongside her, the window rolled down and a familiar face – much older now, but eyes don't change – spoke her name.

Three hours had passed since their telephone call. Brinley had driven straight to her.

The air between them was freighted with tension, these two women who had once meant something to each other. The one who was baptized Sara Carter leaned down to the window and Brinley touched her fingertips to her old friend's face.

'It *is* you. I used to think you were a ghost, you know.'

'I suppose I was.' Catherine gestured in the direction of the house down the lane. 'Still am, if I'm honest. That's why I'm hiding here.' Her voice softened. 'I don't know who I'm supposed to be.'

Brinley stared down at her hands and said the words that had haunted the past two decades of her own life. 'This is my fault too.'

Catherine walked around the car and climbed into the passenger seat. Twenty-one years of history lay between them. Of silence and regret and ruin. Of lies and half-truths, futility and waste.

Neither woman spoke, afraid of what the other might say.

'I'm sorry,' said Brinley eventually, breaking the stillness that had settled across them. 'I should have done something to help you. Lying about what happened is the stupidest thing I've ever done.' The air lightened, a lessening of pressure. The journalist lifted her foot from the brake and began to ease forwards, towards the cottage. 'Is that why you called me?'

Catherine's eyes were bright with tears. 'I didn't know what else to do. Even my family has left me.' She stared out of the window as the night-time fields rolled by. 'You're the only one who knows the truth. I don't want to be *that* Sara Carter anymore. I want to be me.'

Although they shared a brutal history, Catherine was not naive. She understood she was talking to a tabloid journalist who might be recording their conversation, a dictaphone hidden in her pocket, an eye on the prize. But on the simplest of levels, she trusted her. Brinley had guarded their secret for all these years. Perhaps now it was time to let that secret go.

Catherine knew she risked alienating Eliza and the officers from the Protected Persons Unit if she was photographed and interviewed in a newspaper, but with Edward and Honor gone, she had nothing left to lose. Everyone she loved had abandoned her. The only route open to her now was the truth.

Brinley parked the car in front of the house in the middle of nowhere. They sat in silence, the protection of the night a salve to them both. Catherine glanced at Brinley. Her head was bowed, her knuckles whitened against the steering wheel. She mistook it for refusal.

'I'll make a statement to the police. I'll do everything I can to make it as official as possible.' The words fell from her, garbled and desperate. 'I won't change my mind, I promise. I know it's a lot to ask, but please say you'll help me. You're the only one who can corroborate my story.'

Brinley didn't move, her head still bowed. Catherine stopped talking, despair tightening her throat, closing it up.

The night was as bright and sharp as a pin. Frost scattered the road with tiny diamonds. The undergrowth rustled with unseen life, shying away from the moon. Catherine had been hiding herself for so long now, but it was time to step into the light. She would just have to do it on her own.

She was halfway out of the car when Brinley spoke again, her voice varnished with sorrow.

'I've brought something – a notebook. It might help you,' she said.

Catherine turned to her, a smile of relief breaking across her face, a hand reaching out to her. But her stomach dropped away at the expression on Brinley's face.

'What is it?' she said. 'What's wrong?'

Brinley drew in a lungful of cold air. Her hands were trembling when she spoke. 'The body of my great-aunt was found in our flat yesterday. She'd been stabbed fourteen times. A pair of kitchen scissors was recovered at the scene.' She looked up at Catherine, her eyes burning with grief and shock. 'I think your sister killed her.'

*I didn't mean to do it. Sometimes things happen and I don't know why. A screen comes down until I'm blinded by it, grasping in the darkness with no sense of what I'm doing. Does that ever happen to you?*

*I only wanted to talk to her. It's important to me that you know that. Even after all these years, her address hadn't changed. I could hardly believe my luck. But the old woman wouldn't let me in and so I had to persuade her, and then matters got out of hand. The past belongs in the past. I trust your mother understands that too.*

*Look at me, droning on. Ignore me. I'd like to hear all about you instead. Tell me again about your lovely new home.*

# 61

We talk until night fades into morning.

The spectrum of colour moves from the lushness of navy into streaks of the palest pearl. When the sun finally rises, the flames of dawn play across our faces as we lie on our stomachs on the rug in the sitting room, not having been to bed.

My notepad is filled with dozens of shorthand pages of testimony, and I've had to use my dictaphone's spare memory card. For once, I remember Colin's instructions, and I film Sara – I can't bring myself to call her Catherine – on my mobile phone. My hand shakes and the footage is grainy, the sound quality poor, and I'll know he'll complain, but she does not want a videographer or a photographer here, or any money for this interview.

All she wants is to tell the truth.

It's explosive.

There's a convincing clarity to her story, an honesty about the way she stumbles through this tale of broken families and murder and sibling love. She refuses to condemn her sister. Or the police. Or the legal system. Or me.

She just wants to be free again.

Part of me wants to applaud her courage. But the other

part – the self-interested part – knows that she will make headlines around the world with this extraordinary story of personal sacrifice. That now, even more than before, she will not be able to escape the truth of who she is and the lies she told. That although I lied too, she is the one who will be hounded and questioned, and face potential charges of perjury, of wasting police time. Her choices will be examined and discussed, turned over and criticized. She will be mocked, deified, ridiculed and lauded.

But then I think, *She knows this, the risk of it*, and her need to confess – to cleanse herself for the love of her daughter – outweighs even that.

I dare not think what Lawrie will say when he realizes I've cut him out of the story of a lifetime and come here alone, or what the commentators and the police will make of my part in it all. But it will be worth it – whatever the cost – to be free of the guilt I have borne for so long.

Sara gives a crooked grin for the camera, as if asking not to be judged too harshly. 'So that's my story. I've carried it for years, and whatever happens now, I'm lighter for it.' And her smile is one of such heartbreaking relief that tears prick my eyes.

We look at each other – properly look – and then, impossibly, we laugh.

The hug she gives me feels like coming home.

The day is awake now, the birds in full song, the fields still covered in their coat of frost. We drink tea and eat boiled eggs and toast with marmalade, and she yawns.

'Go to bed,' I say. 'Get some sleep.'

\*

I write. I write for most of the day. I write while Sara sleeps and when she wakes. I write while she calls the ERPPU officers and tells them not to come because she is sick, and when she prepares us a late lunch of sandwiches and soup. I'm still writing when she speaks to her husband and daughter, a stilted, difficult conversation, but she tells no one of what she's done.

Because we're waiting for me to finish what we've started.

By the time I type the last sentence, the moon is a smile in the night sky. It's the best thing I've ever written.

While I shower and change out of yesterday's clothes, I leave Sara downstairs to read it.

Her face is wet when I come back. She wipes at her eyes with a torn piece of kitchen towel and squeezes my hand until it hurts.

'What now?' she says.

'We unleash this bombshell on my newspaper.'

*I admire your loyalty, your defence of her actions, but don't squander your love on her. Your mother is not deserving of it when she has no loyalty to me.*

*It's cold tonight, the moon bright against the sky – and so quiet here. The roofs are covered in a layer of frost, the air sharp with it. The fields stretch out for miles and miles.*

*All I wanted was for us to be a family again but I know what she's up to, trying to claim my life for herself. I won't let her. I won't let either of them.*

*Sorry. Have I spoken out of turn? I can be too frank at times. I'm hurt, I suppose. About her and the journalist. Did you know we all used to be friends? The two of them should know better by now. Let sleeping dogs lie. Otherwise, they might bite you on the hand.*

*Deep breath. It's OK. I'm OK. Nervous, I think. A little overwhelmed. But please don't tell her about me yet. I so want our reunion to be a surprise.*

# 62

Catherine sat at the kitchen table, her stomach a mess of knots. It was too late to change her mind, even if she wanted to.

Brinley's eyes might carry those same flecks of hazel, the same almond shape of their childhood, but she was not the girl she was. Neither was Catherine. The burden of the past had damaged them both.

'They'll probably ask me to rewrite it,' said Brinley, words tumbling from her, jittery with adrenalin and nerves. 'And spread the coverage over a few days. But you'll be safe here, at least for a while. Lay low until the furore blows over.'

'I'll have to tell my probation officer. There are procedures—'

'Not yet,' said Brinley, a knife-edge to her voice, but Catherine didn't take it personally. Brinley wanted to protect her exclusive. The situation needed handling with care.

A whole day had passed. A day in which Catherine had felt more herself than she had done in years. A day of firsts. Of letting go and putting things right.

What would happen to Shannon now? Would her older sister be arrested? Charged? Would she go into hiding? Or fight dirty, claws out, teeth bared?

And what about the murder of her old friend's great-aunt? Was it really possible that her sister had killed again, warning Brinley off? Catherine gave an internal head-shake. No, Brinley must be mistaken, grief, in all its confusing guises, sending her groping for blame down a blind alley.

But, like a plip of rain breaking the surface of a stagnant pond, a memory stirred. Twelve-year-old Shannon, pyjamas soaked with the blood of their parents, scissors raised high above her head. Teeth gleaming against the rust spots that spattered her skin. A halo of joy crowning the dark reaches of her soul. And doubt gripped Catherine with its cold fingers.

'Colin, it's me.' Brinley had put the news editor on speakerphone, expecting him to be at home. But in the background was the noise and hubbub of the newsroom. Work-aholic tendencies meant he was married to the job, not his girlfriend. 'You're in the office on your day off?'

'Don't you listen to the news?' he said, with a hint of irritation. Then contrition. 'Sorry about your aunt. How *are* you?'

She ignored his question. 'What's happened?'

He sighed down the phone. 'Geoffrey Heathcote died in a car crash last night. Press hounded him to death, appar-ently. Even though he was the one shagging his mistress. We're doing a fucking mop-up job here. What can I do for you?'

Catherine held her breath. One last chance to change

her mind. But the moment passed and Brinley told him everything.

Colin listened, uncharacteristically quiet, until she had finished.

'Massive dangling bollocks, slapping against the arse of implausibility,' he said.

'Every word of it is true.'

He let out a low whistle. 'That's one hell of a story.'

'I know.'

'And you have Sara Carter with you right now?'

'Yes, I have hours of recordings, everything. I've written up the whole thing. It's dynamite.'

A sense of movement, of Colin Baxter, fifty-five-year-old news editor of a national newspaper, experienced but set in his ways, shifting behind his desk and weighing things up.

'If it is true, it's a bloody fantastic exclusive, but we can't just accuse Shannon Carter of murder. That's libel. Surely you understand that.'

'I know, but—'

'Send it to me. I'll read through it tonight when things have calmed down a bit. I'm assuming it will hold until Monday's paper.' For all their parent company's PR fluff about running a seven-day operation, there was still a rivalry between the daily and its Sunday stablemate. Although the editors sometimes shared stories that would otherwise leak, both were keen to preserve their own exclusives. He broke off to shout at the unfortunate duty reporter, who'd been hoping for a quiet shift, before turning his attention back to them. 'In the eyes of the law, Sara Carter is a convicted killer. If she wants her story to be heard, she needs to make a formal statement to the police. At least then, we'll have a way in, something to hang it on.'

'Colin, this is a huge story—'

'Look, get her under contract, don't let her out of your sight and we'll talk in the morning. We'll find a way to run something, but I need to think about it. Well done, love. Good job. But I've got to go now. Call me tomorrow.'

With that, he was gone.

'He's right,' said Catherine softly. 'We can't just expect the public to believe us. I'll go to the police station in the morning and make a statement. That's the new angle, right?'

Disappointment was coming off Brinley in waves. She nodded, furious tears in her eyes. She typed out an email to Colin, attached several word documents, two photographs and pressed send. 'Sorry. I've let you down again.'

'I've waited twenty-one years for justice,' said Catherine. 'I can wait another night.'

The women lit the fire. They drank red wine and ate blue-veined cheese and salted crackers, olives stuffed with garlic and chilli. They talked of the years since the killings at Hilltop House, their lives and loves, their families and heartbreaks. The loneliness of carrying a secret that could not be shared. Of wasted chances and guilt and fear.

When they had finished talking, they sat in the kind of quiet contemplation that comes from relief and understanding, a remaking of friendship, the tender shoots of hope.

The night drew its cloak around them, trying to shield them. But even in its dark grasp, they were not protected, the uncurtained window of light drawing the gaze of the unwelcome.

At five to midnight, they hugged each other goodnight.

At twenty-seven minutes past twelve, both women were asleep.

At half past one, a small panel of glass in the back door was broken and the breaker in the fuse-box was tripped, killing all power to the house.

*I cannot tell how this will end, only that it will. It is late. You are sleeping. By the time you read this, our future will be set. Thank you for burning bright during the darkness of these days. I have been lost for a long time, but you have steered me down the righteous path. There is joy in my heart to know that I have found my family again. Sleep tight.*

# 63

My dreams are full of blood and darkness, and the sharpened edge of a scissor blade.

Heart running, I open my eyes. My first thought is this: *Aunt Peg is dead.* Tears are waiting for me, hot and immediate. When I've put myself back together again, I wipe my face with the sheet.

The bedroom is unfamiliar, much bigger than the flat and much blacker, thick with it. It wants to suffocate me, this night, so I struggle upwards, kicking off the duvet.

From the heaviness in my head, I can tell I haven't slept for long. Interviewing Sara might have opened up the dark flower of memory, but something else has disturbed me and it stirs an unease.

I stretch out a hand for my mobile phone, but it's not on the bedside table. Frowning, I scour the floorboards and under the bed, but there's no sign of it. I don't recall leaving it downstairs, but I must have done. Things don't just disappear.

My bare feet press against the rug. It's cold, winter cold, and the gooseflesh rises on me. Through a break in the curtains, the fields unfurl before me in frosty swathes. The moon, with her smile, is a witness.

A stab of impatience. Where did I leave my phone? I need it to check my emails, to find out if Colin has done as he promised and read my stories, and whether the paper can use them. But it's nowhere, and there's a warning in this, except I don't see it yet.

Tea, I think. And my laptop.

I'm halfway down the stairs when a sound fills up the quiet corners of the house. It's an odd sort of noise, a sharp cry cut off before it reaches its climax. I stop and listen but all I can hear is the ring of silence and, for a glorious moment of not-knowing, I dismiss it as the yelp of an animal.

Somewhere above, a floorboard creaks.

I tell myself I'm being ridiculous, that reliving those memories has revived old ghosts. I tell myself I double-locked the front door and nobody except the authorities knows we're here.

Sara Carter screams.

My heart throws itself against the walls of my chest. Adrenalin sings in my blood. Driven not by bravery but by instinct, I run back up the stairs, along the narrow landing and into her bedroom. The curtains are open and the moon is watching with her dispassionate eye.

The present throws me back to the past. I've been here before. The slippery smell of blood. A rawness in the air. Butchered meat and old keys. Except this time it's not a twelve-year-old girl in daisy-print pyjamas, but a woman with grey streaks in her hair and eyes the colour of dust.

The steel blades of the scissors in her hand are dulled by a slick of blood.

Shannon Carter smiles at me, and mumbles something about a hero.

Sara is lying on the bed. Blood soaks the sheet. Her face is pale, her eyes lock mine.

As I stand there, hesitating, Shannon lifts the scissors, high above her head, and Sara screams again, a long, high note striated with fear. The memory of her mother's screams echo down the years until all I can hear is the song of their suffering, and I want to run from the Carter sisters, who bring death with them.

But Sara is bleeding, and if I run, she will die, so I grab Shannon's hair and pull sharply.

Her head jerks backwards but she does not let go of the scissors, and instead turns and slashes at me, half blinded by night.

But the pale blur of my skin gives me away and the point of the blade catches my arm, and there's a fire, white-hot, above the inside of my wrist, and a wetness that stipples the carpet with dozens of dark spots.

I stare, disbelieving, at the mess of my arm and she stabs me in the shoulder.

'Stop it, Shannon,' I say, in painful understatement. But she shakes her head and laughs.

When I look down, the loops of the scissor handles are sticking out of my body. The burn of pain is deadened by adrenalin and a surge of fury that this woman – this *stranger* who once meant everything to me – has killed someone I love and lived the life that should have been Sara's.

And then I realize she's gifted me a weapon.

The scissors are slippery between my fingers, warm with blood. Pulling them out has opened up the wound. Shannon is watching me and watching Sara, her eyes flicking between us both. She doesn't speak, but carries an aura of righteousness, a belief that she is following the path of her destiny.

'Please,' I say. 'Let us go.'

'No,' she says. Cocks her head in consideration. 'If I did that, what would happen to me?'

I see at once, with pin-sharp clarity, that she will not relinquish the freedom she has, even though it is not rightfully hers. That she will never accept responsibility for what she started when she was twelve years old, and what Sara and I finished on her behalf because we loved her then, more than ourselves. That she has always been content to let others step up for her and shoulder the responsibility.

As true today as it was when we were children.

There's another truth, too, evidenced in the flatness of her expression and the cook's knife she is withdrawing from the bag on the floor.

To keep her secret, she will kill us both.

# 64

'It's too late,' said Brinley, but Catherine heard the break in the journalist's s voice which betrayed her fear. 'Your sister has given a full account of who killed your parents. I've documented and corroborated it.'

Shannon shrugged, as if to say it won't much matter when you're dead.

*Your sister . . .*

Sara Carter. Catherine Allen. Which one was she? Catherine no longer knew. She'd waited so long to see her older sister again. To hear her voice and fall into her arms, to weep together for all they had lost. But this was not her sister. This was a stranger who wore her sister's face. The sister she had loved with every part of herself had died in their childhood. This woman was monstrous.

Catherine – her middle name, pretty yet ordinary, had become her first name when she was eighteen, to help her weave the threads of her old self into her new identity – lay on her side on someone else's bed, life leaking from her.

The clock moved on a minute. The hands blurred. Came into sharp focus. Blurred again. Her heartbeat slowed. No significance to the hour except, if she didn't stop bleeding, it would mark her time of death, recorded on a certificate, filed in a register on a computer somewhere.

Honor's face filled her heart. The corners of Catherine's mouth twitched upwards. Such love, in spite of everything. A fierce, protective, motherly love. She might not live long enough to untangle the knot in the weft of their relationship, but it didn't matter. All she had left was love. A sense she had, at last, done right by her daughter, whatever happened next.

'Mummy,' her little girl said, and her heart listened. 'Mummy.' She was holding Honor in her arms, the weight of her memory a ballast in this listing, unstable world.

A wave of pain threw her overboard.

Catherine opened her mouth to speak, but a bubble of spittle and blood burst against her lips. She tried to count. *One. Two.* But she couldn't remember what came next. She was aware of a commotion between Brinley and her older sister, but in the detached manner of a distant observer with no hope of intervening.

*I'm dying.*

The thought drifted from her – a balloon flying skywards on an untethered string – and, with it, came that ever-present sense of melancholy, a longing to remake the tattered shape of her past. For the world to know the truth.

She moved her lips again but no one bore witness to her testimony this time. No newspaper journalist or court-room attendant, no police or probation officer, no judge or jury, except perhaps the one in the sky, but she wasn't sure she believed in Him.

*Honor.*

And then Sara Carter, who was Catherine Allen, who was a wife and mother, sister, friend, tabloid sensation, figure of hate, innocent child and convicted killer, let go of the pain and closed her eyes.

# 65

Sara isn't moving.

I don't know if she's unconscious or dead, but there's blood on my hands, and no strength in my legs, and it's over, isn't it?

Shannon nudges Sara with the tip of the knife, and there's the tiniest sound, an exhalation of breath, and I will her to live for her daughter and her husband. For herself.

The moon rides higher, throwing its light across the landscape, the fields and the streams and the houses hidden under the cover of night, and the leather bag slumped like a carcass in the corner of the bedroom.

Shannon has our mobile phones, I can see them in the bag. A torch. The silver rectangle of my laptop, and my dictaphone and the memory cards that tell Sara's story.

When I'd emailed Colin, I'd sent thousands of written words, and photographs of Sara and the notebook, but not the recordings. They could wait until morning, I'd thought. But we're not going to see the morning again, Sara and I.

I'm crying now, but the fear leaves me and is replaced by a preternatural calm.

*Is this what it is to face death?*

'Shannon . . .'

The ends of her hair look like they've been sucked damp by a child, but the truth is much darker than that.

'Shannon . . .'

I'm trying to reach her, to find the humanity inside the abyss, and there are so many questions I want to ask her, so many whys, but her expression is blank and she's raising the knife, and the reach of her blade goes further than the scissors, and—

*Run, Brinley.*

And I do.

Out of the bedroom, away from the knife and the unmoving body of Sara, stumbling down the stairs. I need to move faster, but I can't seem to do it, I'm falling over myself, slowing, and I'm so tired and all I want to do is sleep, but the front door's ahead, and I'll make it, I know it, and I'll find another house, and I can taste the sweet air and the bite of the wind, and a new beginning, and the longing is so intense and—

I trip.

On the edge of a rug. The scissors fly out of my hand. It's laughable that something so mundane, so ordinary as a threadbare rug could bring me to my knees.

Stupid, clumsy Brinley.

Then she's on me, knife in her hand.

# 66

How long does it take to die?

When I draw in my last breath, will I know it's the end? Will angels sing and trumpets play? Or will the clock simply stop, mid-tick? Aunt Peg had faith in a merciful God. I don't have faith in anything except the belief that our bodies become earth and air. But if death means I'll see my mother again, I will throw myself onto the blade.

A torch flicks on, throwing shadows down in challenge.

My cheek is pressed against the tiles of the hallway floor, my head turned to the wall. The fall has accelerated the bleeding in my shoulder and the warmth spreads beneath me, but it's so cold my body is shaking. I'm lying on my stomach. From here, I can see our shoes and coats and scarves. A pair of wellies. An umbrella and a couple of walking sticks in a stand. My eyes close and open.

I have nothing left to give.

The shadows move, making me flinch. Head twist. Knees pulled into stomach. Turn on my side, to see what's coming next.

Shannon is standing above me. The knife is in her hand. All she has to do is bring it down. But she doesn't. She cocks her head again, as if she's listening to something. A noise from upstairs, a thud of something heavy falling to the floor.

She steps over me and walks to the bottom of the stairs to listen again.

From a place inside the locked corners of my heart, my mother's voice urges me on. Familiar and forgotten, loving and firm, impatient even. She sings to me, and I drag myself to my hands and knees, head swimming, walls rippling, and crawl through the pain to where the coats are hanging.

I try to hold it in, but it slides from me, the sound of dying, and Shannon turns and walks back, knife extended, arm raised, as if she's a revolutionary, as if she is killing for the cause she believes in.

I suppose she is.

My hands grasp blindly, catch the edge of the umbrella stand and knock it over. They close around wire and nylon, and she's there with her blade, pressing it into my neck.

Our eyes meet and I fall into them.

She is dust and darkness, scarred by the loneliness of the years, tormented by her past. I try to speak, but my mouth is sand, and the words are stuck somewhere inside.

But she reads me and leans in, until her mouth is close to my ear, and her breath is warm and smells of oranges, and she says, 'You, of all people, should know about keeping secrets, Brinley Booth.'

She puts pressure on the knife and it begins to bite, and she's looking at the blood beading along its blade, and when, finally, she lifts her eyes back to mine, I am ready.

The stainless steel tip at the end of the umbrella penetrates the inner corner of her left eye, pushes into the dark spaces beyond, the mass of cells and matter and neurons that control her impulse to kill. I push harder, with everything I have and everything I don't have.

She lets out a high, tight scream. Her hands flutter around the umbrella, pulling at the black nylon canopy and its wire ribs, but they lack commitment, and in half a minute, they still.

Slumped against the wall, blood trickling like the truth from my own wounds, I pay my debt and watch Shannon Carter die.

# 67

## Three weeks later

The walls of the private hospital were obscured by cards sent by well-wishers from as far afield as Australia, the United States and Japan.

Catherine Allen – after much consideration, she had decided to keep that name – pushed herself up against the pillows and sipped tea from a china cup and saucer, her stay at this exclusive clinic paid for by an anonymous benefactor, a gift to make up for the years she had spent at Mayfields.

Her story had been syndicated in newspapers and magazines around the world. It had been the subject of countless television news specials and several documentaries were in the pipeline. The lengths one might go to to protect those we love. How the system lets down our youngest offenders. The abuse the Carter sisters suffered at the hands of their parents. The fiery crash that claimed the life of MP Geoffrey Heathcote. The murder of eighty-four-year-old Margaret 'Peg' Ablethorpe, and the attempted murders of Catherine Allen and Brinley Booth. Shannon Carter's own desperate end. Of friendship lost and found. The story had it all. It ran and ran and ran.

When she was discharged and well enough to travel, Catherine had been invited to appear on *The Ellen DeGeneres Show, Yang Lan One-on-One* and *The Morning Show*. She was collaborating on a book with the journalist who had broken her story and there was talk of a film, a Hollywood studio optioning the rights before the first words were on the page.

But most importantly, she had survived.

Catherine had no recollection of the hours and days after her sister had tried to kill her. But Edward, rushed to hospital by police escort, had, when she'd finally regained consciousness, filled in the gaps, his grief and bewilderment palpable.

'The doctors didn't expect you to live,' he'd explained, his face crumpling. 'We kissed you goodbye.' He swallowed a couple of times to compose himself, but the tears came anyway. 'You'd lost so much blood, your bladder had been punctured, one of your veins had been nicked . . .' He'd grinned at her, a flash of sun in the rain. 'They think you tried to get up and help Brinley, and you fell off the bed.' He'd squeezed her hand. 'That probably saved her life.'

And her heart had lifted at that.

She had fiddled with the cannula in her hand, eyes on the plastic tubing. 'Do the police know how Shannon found us?'

Edward's expression darkened and he'd dropped his head. The whole sorry saga had come tumbling out.

Honor's football team had been trying to raise money for one of their midfielders, a girl diagnosed with a rare pancreatic tumour that had metastasized. Their photograph had been plastered over social media sites and in the local newspaper. When the dying girl's favourite pop star, moved by her plight, had surprised her and her teammates at their football club's end-of-season disco, the story had been picked up by the national press.

Having breakfast in a cafe one morning, Shannon Carter had seen a short piece about it in a magazine. She'd been struck by the picture of Honor, the likeness to her sister and her unusual name, which had belonged to their father's grandmother.

'Eventually, she found Honor on social media,' he'd explained. 'But she didn't say who she was, not at first, just someone who had lived through a family tragedy.

'They talked online most days. She wanted to know all about you. As Honor shared bits and pieces of your past, Shannon worked out who you were. She hinted to Honor that she thought she was related to you.' His fingers had tugged at the lambswool blanket. 'You know how desperate Honor was to get to know your family. Shannon played on that. She persuaded Honor to catch the bus and meet her when she should have been at school, but your sister got cold feet and didn't show up.'

Catherine let herself breathe again. Honor's incessant questions about her family. The spate of night terrors triggered by Shannon Carter's messages. The girl's obsession with her mobile phone. All of it made sense now. Her heart had filled with empathy for her daughter.

'It was impossible for Honor to unpick the truth from the lies. It confused her, the things Shannon was saying about you. But Shannon had an agenda. The police believe she'd been searching for you for years, concerned the truth would emerge, and had agreed to the television interview in an attempt to flush you out.' He held out his phone to show her a picture. 'She manipulated Honor into sending her this photograph of the holiday let in Norfolk. Honor didn't say where it was, she wasn't that daft.' A hollow laugh. 'But it was a stupid thing to do. Shannon did a reverse image search. She found you without even trying.'

Catherine remembered the warning from her probation officer, how so many people in Identity Protection were given away by their children.

Edward kissed her cheek, offered a rueful smile. 'I'm so sorry,' he said. 'I let you down very badly. I should have believed you.' He rubbed his beard. 'We'll be all right, though, won't we?' But he could not conceal the doubt in his voice.

Her anger had faded now, washed away to nothing, but her sorrow had not. Honor was easy to forgive. She was still a child, prone to poor judgement. During that first visit to her mother, she had wept through her apology, dampening the sheet with tears. 'This is all my fault.' Catherine had stroked her bent head, full of comfort and love.

But Edward was different. He should have known better. Trusted her. Or at least given her an opportunity to explain. Instead, he had run at the first sign of trouble. She didn't know yet if their marriage was worth salvaging. She still loved him but the shine had dulled. She was making no promises.

Brinley had been to visit too.

She'd walked in with a stick – she'd damaged the nerve endings in her leg when she'd tripped over the rug – but she'd waved her injuries away with an airy hand. 'I'm fine, but how are you?'

Catherine had answered, quite truthfully, that, despite her sister's death, she felt lighter than she had done in years.

Brinley had squeezed her friend's arm, and told her about her pay rise, and the job offer at a prestigious newspaper abroad, and how she had found it within herself to crawl up the stairs, retrieve a phone from Shannon's bag and call for an ambulance, but had almost died from blood loss herself.

'What about your aunt?'

A shadow had passed over the journalist's face. A speck of Shannon Carter's DNA had been found on Peg's night-dress, she'd explained. Careful – but not careful enough. The messages to Honor proved Carter had been intent on confronting Brinley to stop her exposing the truth. Her elderly great-aunt had been collateral damage.

This early forensic confirmation had lent the stamp of authenticity to their sensational allegations.

With exclusive photographs, recordings and interviews – and safe in the knowledge it was impossible to libel the dead – Brinley's newspaper devoted several pages to the story, creating a special souvenir edition. The rest of the press pack followed. The story dominated the headlines for days.

Legal moves had begun to quash Catherine's conviction, the rightful killer now exposed. A neat ending to the Hilltop House murders, tidied up between the pages of a tabloid by the only journalist with a ringside seat.

'Thank you for everything you've done for me,' said Catherine, her smiling face resting against the hospital pillows. 'For giving me back my life.'

Brinley had smiled back.

# 68

When I was twelve, I was struck by lightning. It left a scar on my back in the shape of a tree.

Now I have other scars. An indentation on my shoulder, a hollow in my leg, a long, thin smile running down the length of my neck.

A scar on my conscience, too.

The flat is filled with flowers. From the newspaper – *Congratulations Brinley, and get well soon!* – and the publisher – *We're so excited to have you on board* – and the Allen family – *Thank you for all you have done for us, love Catherine, Edward and Honor x*

A new beginning for everyone, including me.

My father visits. He sits in Aunt Peg's favourite armchair and tells me he has carried the weight of my mother's death for years.

'I loved her,' he says. 'But even when she was alive, she'd already left me. She knew she was dying. She *wanted* me to find a mother for you.' His eyes fill with unshed tears. 'Afterwards, you were so angry all the time. The lightning strike, the murders, I couldn't seem to reach you. With the Carter girls gone, Peg offered to try.' He smiles. 'And she did a fine job. You do understand that, don't you? It wasn't Maureen's fault.'

I tell him I know that now. I tell him I understand.

My father is the only family I have left. We may drift together or apart, it's too early to tell. All those years of hurt to be undone. But it's a start – and that is better than nothing.

Lawrie arrives one evening with an oversized bag of crisps, a six-pack of beer and a pile of books.

I'm surprised to see him. He didn't come to visit me in hospital.

His hair's a bit longer and curls around the nape of his neck. Is he a friend? A colleague? For so long, I've lived a solitary life with no one but Peg to rely on. I've forgotten how friendship works.

'Are you angry?' I say. 'That I went to Norfolk by myself?'

He uncaps two bottles. Beer froths up and out. He passes one to me and drinks from the other, wiping his mouth with the back of his hand.

'I was, at first. I mean, we'd been on the story together. We were on the same team. I didn't expect you to have such a ruthless streak.' He looks away, the betrayal still tender. 'But then I stopped caring about that and started caring that you'd been hurt.'

'Why didn't you get in touch sooner?'

He shifts in the armchair, awkward at the question. 'I wasn't sure you'd want to see me. I was worried I'd said something to upset you and that's why you went off on the story by yourself.' His eyes meet mine. 'But I couldn't stay away.'

He's broken up with his girlfriend, he says. He's heard

the new Italian around the corner from me is good. We smile at each other, hope softening our edges.

So that's it, I guess. Brinley Booth is typing *ends* on her story.

Sara Carter has been released from the prison of her past. My father and I are talking again. Shannon Carter is dead.

And buried with her, in the silt and dirt, is the last secret of Hilltop House.

A lightning strike can rewire the brain. Trigger severe bouts of depression. Personality changes. The kind of pressure that can break a grieving family – a daughter and her father – apart.

The strike on Saltbox Hill – coupled with the emotional strain of my mother's death and the brutality I'd witnessed from my oldest friend – was the reason I struggled so much in the months that followed that devastating April weekend. Fired my need to run from the village, to move to London to be with Aunt Peg, to create a distance between myself and my past.

At least, that's what everyone believed.

And it was true – part of it, anyway. Part, but not all. Because there was another reason. A darker reason.

Shannon didn't kill her mother.

I did.

The rain-dirty pavement shines in the glow of the street lamps. Empty streets and empty pockets, the post-December blues. The last train grinds through the darkness and the Canary Wharf lights blink on and off. Lawrie left hours ago, and I'm alone again. In this, I will always be alone.

When I stumbled into their bedroom on that wet spring

night, Mrs Carter was still alive. Bleeding heavily, yes, but she was breathing. I could have helped her. I should have done. Called an ambulance. The police. Tried to staunch the flow of blood.

Instead I picked up a pillow and pressed it over her face until she was completely still.

In my bleakest moments of regret, I tell myself she would not have survived. Blood loss would have killed her in the end. But I don't know that. I will never know.

Pearline and the women from church scrubbed Aunt Peg's blood from the hallway carpet while I cried out my grief in a hospital bed. They filled my fridge with spicy stews and clingfilmed bowls of coconut rice and beans. Told me stories of Nine Night, the Jamaican tradition of celebrating the dead with rum and food on the ninth night of their passing. But their love and warmth only reminds me I have lost both my mothers now.

Pamela Carter had *seen* me. She had known what Shannon had done to her, what Sara hadn't. Like me, Mrs Carter was a witness. Her survival was to risk her telling the police everything. I had to choose a sister to save.

When she was dead, I turned round and Shannon was standing there, framed in the bedroom door. A look of complicity arced between us. If I told the police what Shannon had done, she would tell on me. Tit for tat. A deal with the devil's daughter.

Both of us allowed Sara to shoulder the blame to save ourselves.

That guilt has soaked into every minute of my life. Not for killing Mrs Carter – she reaped what she had sown – but for what it did to the youngest Carter sister.

And now, to me. My act of murder has, finally, exacted its terrible price.

For every action, there is an equal and opposite reaction.

I chose to save Shannon. Because of that, Aunt Peg is dead.

This knowledge stains every breath, every pump and beat of my heart, every sunrise and sunset, every human touch. It pollutes my dreams, smears itself across my future, and the weight of my sorrow drives me into the dirt. There are no winners here. For all the malignancies that tainted her, Shannon was a victim too.

Rain streaks the window. I stand alone in the midnight stillness of my aunt's flat, overlooking this city of mine. Across the blackened smudge of the horizon, a vast spark of lightning illuminates the sky.

*One-one-thousand.*

*Two-one-thousand.*

*Three-one-thousand.*

A groan of thunder. The lights go out. I fumble in the drawer for a candle and matches. Power outages are not uncommon on this estate, but it's the first time in years the weather's been to blame. In a minute, I will check on Pearline.

Somewhere, in the quiet places of my memory, I can smell my aunt's cooking and her voice fills me up. *Courage and caution, Brinley Ada Booth.* My face is wet with tears.

I strike the match and press its burning tip to the candle wick. A tiny flame burns bright in the darkness. Pearline bangs on the sitting room wall to tell me she's OK and I bang back.

Ten miles south of here, a woman called Catherine Allen

is asleep in her room in a private hospital. Despite years of humiliation and mental suffering at the hands of her parents, imprisoned for a double murder she did not commit, she has survived her own tragedy. At 11 a.m. tomorrow, she will be discharged. Her daughter has made her a 'Welcome Home' banner. Their second-chance future is as bright as the candle flame.

When I was twelve, I was struck by lightning. Aunt Peg insists it was God's doing, that he fired a thunderbolt at me for telling a lie.

*Lies are a necessary evil sometimes, sweet girl.*

At the memory of my mother's voice down the sweep of years, a smile breaks through my tears, a redemptive shaft of hope.

After all this time, I have atoned for the sins of my childhood. Like the lightning tree on my back, the scars can, at last, begin to heal.

# ACKNOWLEDGEMENTS

Sometimes I think writing acknowledgements is harder than the book itself. It's taken me weeks to finish these. I'm not sure why. Perhaps it's because there's still a part of me that finds it difficult to believe this is my fourth novel and one day the joyous privilege of writing for a living will disappear in a puff of smoke.

Despite many hours working alone on a book, publication is never a solitary endeavour and there are so many excellent people to thank: my editor and champion Trisha Jackson, who never stops banging the drum on my behalf, and the fantastic team at Pan Macmillan, including Jayne Osborne, Rosie Wilson, Stuart Dwyer, Lucy Hine, Rebecca Kellaway, James Annal, Samantha Fletcher and Fraser Crichton. Huge thanks must also go to my ever-brilliant agents Sophie Lambert at C&W and Kari Stuart at ICM, Nish Panchal, Meredith Ford (never has the phrase 'the dog ate my homework' been more apt), Kate Burton and the rest of the C&W crew.

Writing a novel that deals with the act of murder by a child (and the media's reaction to it) is a complex issue which I have tried to handle with sensitivity, compassion and as much truth as the story allows. Thank you to Imran Mahmood, who was so generous with his time and patience in answering my questions about the legal framework in cases such as these. Any mistakes are my own.

Grateful thanks must also go to Michael Greenwood for refreshing my memory about newspaper practice, James Brabazon for advice about cameras and for supplying one of my favourite lines in the book, Laura Shepherd-Robinson for her insights into the messy world of politics, Linda Dove at Marie Curie for answering my questions in such a helpful and thoughtful way, and Patricia Nkere-Uwem for her fabulousness regarding all things Jamaican.

Thank you, as always, to the brilliant booksellers, librarians, reviewers, bloggers, readers and all my crime-writing compadres who ride this rollercoaster with me. A special shout-out to Jake Kerridge, Jon Coates, Nina Pottell and Deirdre O'Brien, four members of the press who are nothing like some of the characters in *When I Was Ten* and who have been so supportive from the very start.

This book was inspired by the dark deeds of child killer Mary Bell, who had been living under an assumed name for some years when the press tracked her down, preparing to unmask her. She was forced to wake up her young daughter in the dead of night and reveal her true identity. I wondered what that might feel like. I'm indebted to Gitta Sereny and her book, *Cries Unheard*.

While taking a life can never be excused, there are many children living in homes where they are humiliated and abused by those who are supposed to love them most. The damage that causes is immeasurable. As a society, we owe it to those children to protect them.

# WHEN I WAS TEN

Seven years ago, when my own children were small, I took a leap of faith and gave myself permission to write. No safety net. No guarantees. As my writing career has flourished, I've been privileged to watch them grow into the very best kind of humans. Like everything in my life, this book is for them.